PRAISE FOR THE FIRST
which was nominated

"Oh, I love Rhetta McCarter! She's hilarious, smart, savvy, tenacious, loving--and just the teensiest bit stubborn. (Good thing, or her hometown would be in serious trouble.) "Killerwatt" is a high-voltage, high-speed adventure--with humor, heart, and a frighteningly realistic story!"
Hank Phillippi Ryan, Anthony, Macavity and Agatha-winning author

"Feisty amateur sleuth Rhetta McCarter takes us along on a thrilling ride in her '79 Camaro as she tries to stop a terrorist plot that could mean lights out for the country...and for Rhetta! An exciting, fast-paced thriller from a promising debut author."
Sharon Potts, award-winning author of IN THEIR BLOOD and SOMEONE'S WATCHING

"Killerwatt is as fun and fast-paced as riding around in McCarter's '79 Camaro with the top down. Well-rounded characters and great writing make the frighteningly real terrorist scenario come to life."
D. Alan Lewis, author of THE BLOOD IN SNOWFLAKE GARDEN

From *"Top Book Reviewers"* http://www.topbookreviewers.com

"Hopkins has written a solid mystery thriller that will appeal to a wide audience. Her style takes a fun, light-hearted approach to a serious subject which kept me reading it in one go. Even when my eyes were trying to close, I had to read the next chapter to see what would happen next to Rhetta. Hopkins has created a likable heroine that I could see become a series of books quickly. KILLERWATT is an entertaining read that shows how vulnerable we are. I hope it never really happens in my lifetime."

From Readers:

"I really enjoyed KILLERWATT and being introduced to protagonist Rhetta McCarter. She's spunky, smart, determined and opinionated— everything a reader wants in a leading lady and amateur sleuth. The book is set in Missouri and painted with such care you'll feel like you're zooming along the back roads, riding shotgun in Rhetta's prize Camaro."

"Sharon Woods Hopkins knocked this out of the park. She creates a suspenseful tale with well-drawn, believable characters."

Acknowledgements

I HAVE SO MANY people to thank!
At the top of my list is my wonderful husband and best friend, Bill, who is always there for me. I couldn't do this without his love and support.

Thanks to my wonderful readers who showed such love and enthusiasm for Rhetta McCarter. A great big *thank you* to my early manuscript readers: Paula Mayfield, Ruthie Burkman and Lyndie Kempfer. Your input helped me so much!

To Malcom Griffith and Mylene Allard, who kindly loaned me their names to use for two unusual characters in the story.

Thanks to my friend Charlie Hutchings, the Bollinger County Coroner, who patiently answered all my questions, and didn't report me for asking about dead bodies in barns.

Thanks, Chief Paul White Eagle, for allowing me to enjoy your peaceful farm and to paint your picturesque barn.

Thanks to my chief mechanic and business partner, my wonderful son Jeff Snowden, and to my delightful daughter in law, Wendy and my very tall and terrific grandson, Dylan. Love you guys!

A giant THANK YOU to Sue Ann Jaffarian, Deborah Sharp and Joanna Campbell Slan, who took time out of their busy writing schedules to read KILLERFIND.

To my mother, Agnes Vienneau Woods (1920-1973) who raised me with Agatha Christie mysteries. Thank you, Mom for buying me books. I miss you.

To my father, John (Harry) Woods (1915-1984) who taught me to read before I started school. He also taught me to read upside down and backwards. Actually, Dad, I never made a cent from that.

Barn: noun, a large outbuilding on a farm used to store grain or shelter livestock

Find: noun, a discovery

Barnfind: noun, *"In the auto realm, it is the near mythical, all original, parked-for decades and all but forgotten, much prized and potentially very valuable, collector car." Malcom Griffith*

KILLERFIND: noun, a barnfind turned deadly

Chapter 1

Rhetta McCarter swiveled her office chair and stared at the "before" picture of a bedraggled-looking 1981 Z28 that occupied the left side of a double frame on her desktop. The blank right side waited for the "after" picture. Her grasp on the phone tightened.

She stood, her voice rising. "Did I hear you right? You found a wallet belonging to Malcom Griffith in the frame of my Z28?"

James Woodhouse "Woody" Zelinski, one of her employees, stopped on his way to the copier. "Malcom Griffith disappeared fifteen years ago," he said, stopping at her desk, making no effort to hide his eavesdropping.

Rhetta glowered at him, and went on speaking to Ricky. "How can that be? That car was in that barn for twenty-five years."

Rhetta, the branch manager of Missouri Community Bank Mortgage and Insurance, paced the small square of carpeting in the cube that was her office. She waited for some kind of reasonable explanation from her best friend and mechanic, Ricky Lane of Fast Lane Muscle Cars. Ricky, short for Victoria, was working her magic on a 1981 Camaro Z28, a replacement for Cami, Rhetta's beloved '79 Camaro that was destroyed in a fire several months earlier.

When LuEllen, office secretary-cum-receptionist informed her that Ricky was on the line, Rhetta assumed Ricky was going to catch her up on the car's progress, and ask for a payment for parts. Rhetta had already pulled out her checkbook and clutched her pen, ready to write. At last estimate, Ricky thought it would take about three more weeks to complete the restoration.

"Not really," Ricky said.

"Thank goodness. That's not funny. You had me going there for a minute." Rhetta let out a sigh of relief. If it had been true, it could mean at least a six months' delay if the police had to impound her car.

"It was more behind a front inner fender well."

"Crap." Rhetta ran her hands through her mass of spiky brown hair, tinged in blonde this week. She glanced at the calendar to see when six months would be. At that rate, she doubted if she would even have the car for next summer. She groaned.

Ricky continued, "When I loosened the fender well, it fell out, along with an old pair of sunglasses, and a wrench."

"Tell me about it." Rhetta said, snapping her checkbook shut, and sticking the end of the pen in her mouth, chewing rapidly.

"The sunglasses were pretty old and beat up. One arm was bent. The wrench is good, though."

"Ricky, I don't care about the sunglasses or the wrench." Rhetta threw the pen down on the desk, snatched a tissue, and wiped her mouth, hoping that no ink had streaked her face.

"Right. Naturally, I looked at the wallet, too." Ricky chuckled. "How else would I know who it belonged to? Malcom Griffith's driver's license picture stared at me as soon as I flipped it open. I glanced through it, and discovered quite a bit of money and some credit cards, too."

"Great. Now that you've fondled the thing, you've probably messed up any DNA or fingerprints."

"No, I didn't. For your information, I was wearing vinyl gloves, like I always do when I use rust dissolver. As soon as I saw whose wallet it was, I called you."

"Did you call the police and report it?" Rhetta backed into her chair and sat heavily. The defective hydraulic lifter caused the chair to sink all the way to the lowest point and she nearly grazed her chin on the desk top.

Ricky hesitated. "No, I called you first."

Rhetta reached down, grabbed the chair handle and tugged. The chair popped upward. "I know you have a reason, so tell me when I get there. I'm coming right over." Rhetta disconnected, pushed the chair back and snatched her purse off her desk.

"I'm coming with you," Woody said. He beat his boss to the door.

* * *

Woody folded his tall frame into the front seat of Rhetta's silver Trailblazer. Being nearly a foot taller than Rhetta required that he slide the seat all the way back before he could fit. He barely had the door shut before Rhetta slammed into reverse and backed out of the parking slot. She spun the SUV around and headed south on Kingshighway, bound for Ricky's shop in Gordonville, about ten minutes away from their office in Cape Girardeau, Missouri, when the traffic was light or when she exceeded the speed limit. The trip today might take longer, since traffic was crawling along William Street.

Rhetta usually drove her SUV only in the winter, or when grocery shopping. She'd preferred enjoying the exhilaration of driving Cami during spring, fall and summer. Southeast Missouri rarely had winter weather, and that was only for a couple of months after Christmas. Since Cami was gone, she was making the effort to convince herself she was looking forward to Cami's replacement. Knowing there was still plenty of nice weather left to enjoy it had kept her spirits buoyed. When the car was destroyed, Rhetta was devastated. Eventually, between her husband, Randolph, and her friend Ricky's enthusiasm for the replacement, she was slowly coming round. She hadn't, however, come up with a name for the Z28 yet. She named all their vehicles, as well as their farm and even the garage. She christened the Trailblazer Streak, short for Silver Streak. Although it didn't streak anywhere. It was no speed machine, like Cami, but it was practical. She longed for her old Camaro.

"Can you believe the bad luck? Ricky finds Malcom Griffith's wallet in the Z28. Wonder how long that will hold up the restoration? Crap. The cops will probably impound the car." She tapped impatiently on the steering wheel as they stopped for a red light. Woody further maneuvered the seat to his comfort. Or, at least to where his knees weren't up around his chin.

"Wasn't Malcom Griffith that high-rolling real estate developer who disappeared without a trace?" Woody asked. Once the seat was in place, he finished snapping the seatbelt buckle, and wriggled to get comfortable.

"Sure was. His wife appeared on television several times in the first few weeks after his disappearance, pleading for whoever had him to return him. You know how it is, the media interest soon died down." Rhetta swerved to avoid a bicyclist pedaling furiously alongside her. "Rumor had it that Griffith made off to a foreign country with his money and then-current extra marital affair, an exotic pole dancer, who coincidentally vanished about the same time. In fact, Randolph was the judge who declared him dead several years later. His wife never remarried."

She wove through traffic lined up to turn into the shopping mall where Jenn, Woody's wife worked, then sped along Route K and through Gordonville. She breezed past the fire station where a constable car usually parked. She glanced at her speedometer, slowing reflexively when she saw the needle pointing at fifty. On the highway on either side of town, the speed limit was fifty miles per hour, but in town, the posted speed limit was twenty-five. Luckily, no constable occupied the decades-old cruiser today. When the old white sedan parked there, constable or no, it served as a great speed deterrent. Except for Rhetta.

Past the edge of town, Rhetta turned left onto the county road leading to Fast Lane. Streak stirred up billowy grey dust as they rolled along the chat-covered road. Although the limestone-derived gravel made a firm road base, the dust covered all the foliage and everything else that grew along the sides of the road, from weeds to trees. A good rain would wash it off. Without the rain, growth would shrivel and die from being smothered. Everything, that is, except kudzu, which was nearly impossible to kill.

"Did you call Randolph and tell him what's going on?" Woody asked, glancing sideways at her.

Rhetta peered over her reading glasses at Woody. He'd been at her side since she got the phone call, so he knew full well she hadn't called her husband. Woody stared straight ahead. Did she detect a smile tweaking the corner of his mouth? Hard to tell under the grey whiskers that made him appear older than forty-two. Two tours as a Marine contributed to the grey. Hard to know about any grey in the hair on his head since Woody kept his head shaved smooth. In fact, it was hard to tell if Woody even had any hair on his head.

"I will. I want to see it first before he makes us call the police," Rhetta said. Woody's right eyebrow shot up. He had a way of making her feel like his younger, capricious sister, even though she had a full year on him. Fourteen months, to be exact.

Her husband, a retired judge, would insist she call the cops. He was anal about law and order details like that. "Besides, he's probably in his studio, painting. He went there straight after our run this morning." Rhetta rose early to run almost daily, in an effort to discourage any middle-aged relocation of body mass. Randolph joined her most mornings. On the days when she craved extra sleep, she thought about throwing in the towel and letting Nature take its course. Then she'd look in the mirror and go running again.

"His cell phone doesn't work in the studio?" Woody studied the gravel road ahead of them.

"You know as well as I do, he'd probably call the cops right away. They'd beat me to Ricky's and I wouldn't get a chance to inspect the wallet."

"You shouldn't be inspecting it anyway. Leave that to the cops."

"Is that why you came along, to make sure I call the cops?"

"Heck, no. I came along because I'm as nosy as you are."

* * *

Fifteen minutes later, Rhetta emerged from a maelstrom of dust and swung a left into Fast Lane's paved driveway. Ricky's shop was located in a converted wooden barn that sat about fifty feet from an old farmhouse that Ricky had inherited and painstakingly restored. She'd installed a green, metal-roofed breezeway that connected the house and shop; the breezeway matched both for one continuous roof.

Ricky stood in the open roll-up doorway to the shop and waved them in. Her long red hair was pulled back into a ponytail that dangled through the back of a ball cap emblazoned with her garage logo. She was outfitted in full mechanic garb—a pair of pale green mechanic's coveralls that camouflaged her petite frame. When she worked at her day job as a real estate agent, she looked so different that most folks who knew her as a Realtor never recognized her alter ego. Her true passion was restoring muscle cars, and she'd recently told Rhetta that she would soon be doing that full time and putting her real estate license on inactive.

Ricky was an inch taller than Rhetta's five feet two. Due to Rhetta's passion for wearing high-heeled sandals or shoes, Rhetta always appeared taller than Ricky. Rhetta dressed up every day—the fashionista to Ricky's garage-ista.

"Let's see what you have, girlfriend," Rhetta said as she followed Ricky through the shop, carefully dodging the assorted parts and tools spread out near her car, and stopping in front of the workbench. She glanced at her buff-colored sandals to see if she'd attracted any grease along the way. *Not a spot, thank goodness!* She really should've changed into the tennis shoes she carried in the back of her vehicle.

A worn leather tri-fold wallet lay atop a clean paper towel on the workbench. Next to it sat a forlorn-looking pair of sunglasses, one metal arm badly distorted. A narrow wrench, which appeared to be stained with dried grease or oil, lay on a separate towel alongside the first two items.

"So, tell me, how did all this just happen to fall out of my Camaro?" Rhetta cocked her thumb toward the car.

"Come here, I'll show you," Ricky said, leading Rhetta around to the front of what remained of it. The hood was off, the engine was out and both doors sat propped against the wall. The nose, which included the bumper, or front clip, as Ricky called it, was also missing. The body was an empty metal hulk, stripped bare of the old interior. The new custom upholstered seats sat covered by a tarp under the workbench. Ricky had started sanding the body, readying it for painting.

Woody trailed after them, peering over the two women's shoulders into the Camaro's empty engine compartment. It awaited the LS1 Corvette powerhouse that was still on a truck inbound from Ohio. The inside fender covering the passenger side front wheel was still in place.

"This fender well is still on, so I can show you how that might have happened," Ricky said and pointed to the bulbous-shaped inside fender. "See how it's rounded on top?" She slid her hand over the crest. "These cars are notorious for suckering a mechanic into setting a tool there, just for a second. It slides down, and nine times out of ten, if the tool is narrow enough, it falls through this slot." She pointed to an opening that measured about one inch by three inches, midway down the fender well. "Whatever slid down wound up staying inside on an inner ledge, with nowhere to go. There are weep holes in that ledge bottom, but they're only large enough to let water out. Tools stayed trapped. Almost every second generation Camaro mechanic has experienced finding a tool or something in there when they remove the inner fender wells." Ricky pulled out a tissue from a box nearby and wiped perspiration off her forehead. "I bet no one has ever made a find like this before, though." She tossed the tissue into the waste can.

Rhetta leaned over and studied the area. "Why did Chevrolet design these like this in the first place?"

Ricky smiled. "Mechanics have been asking that same question for forty years."

Rhetta returned to the workbench and stared at the old leather wallet. Time had dried out the leather, sending spiderlike cracks across the surface.

Woody examined the fender well a little longer before joining her at the workbench.

"You know we have to call the police. Why didn't you when you found this?" Rhetta said, waving a hand over the misbegotten booty.

Ricky sighed, then plopped onto a chrome and black mechanic stool sporting a Summit Racing logo across the back. "I guess I wanted you to tell me it would be okay to just ignore this."

"Why?"

"I hate the thought of putting Jeremy through anything to do with Griffith again. His dad was Griffith's former partner, Willard Spears. When Mr. Spears died last year, he'd never completely shaken off a blanket of doubt surrounding Griffith's disappearance, even though he was the primary victim."

"I really don't know much about all of that. I've only gotten to know Jeremy since you started dating him." Rhetta didn't want to add that she wasn't real fond of Ricky's new man. He struck her as conceited, and his know-it-all attitude rubbed her as painfully as though she'd used a cheese grater for a skin treatment. She decided now wasn't the time to bring that up. She had preferred Ricky's interest in Billy Dan Kercheval, an old friend of Randolph's, who was the former General Manager of the maintenance division of Inland Electric Co-Operative.

"Their joint business account for G & S Development had been drained of over a million dollars," Ricky went on, pulling Rhetta away from her negative contemplations of Jeremy Spears and thoughts of Billy Dan and Ricky together. "Half of that belonged to Willard. He was left broke when Griffith disappeared. Jeremy and his mother, along with Mrs. Griffith, firmly believe that Malcom stole the money and left with his girlfriend."

Ricky hopped from her stool and headed for the door, pulling cigarettes and a lighter from the breast pocket of her coveralls. Standing in the open doorway, she fired one up. She exhaled a plume of blue smoke before she continued. "Mr. Spears struggled to maintain the real estate development company, but when the economy took a downturn, and the recession punched a hole in the housing bubble, he was forced into bankruptcy. Eventually, he lost his upscale family home. You remember that house—it was the one Dr. Al-Serafi bought, and that your bank financed."

Rhetta's heart knocked against her rib cage at the memory of Doctor Hakim Al-Serafi. He was a customer of Missouri Community Bank Mortgage and Insurance who'd been killed in a car wreck earlier this year. His death led to the chain of events that caused Rhetta to lose Cami. She shuddered at the memory of Al-Serafi's death. She eyed Ricky's cigarette longingly. Although she'd vowed to quit smoking, she hadn't managed to succeed yet. She wouldn't, however, let Ricky or Woody know how often she gave in to her cravings.

Now, she understood Ricky's hesitation in calling the police.

"All right, I understand your concerns, but we need to call the police right now," Rhetta said, groping around inside her bulky shoulder purse for her cell phone. She glanced at her watch. "I'll stay here with you when they come, since it's my car, and all."

Woody looked up from his scrutiny of the found objects on the workbench. "Uh, Rhetta? Look at this wrench," he said, pointing to the one that Ricky had found in the fender well. "Is that dried blood?"

CHAPTER 2

RHETTA TURNED TO RICKY. "Please tell me you still had your vinyl gloves on when you picked this up?" She edged toward the discolored wrench that Woody was studying. He might be right. There was something on it that she couldn't identify.

"Of course. I already told you I did," Ricky answered, joining Rhetta at the workbench. All three locked eyes on the wrench.

Rhetta broke the stare and groped in her purse until she located her phone. "Where's your phone book?" Ricky tugged it out from under the shop phone at the end of the workbench and handed it over.

"Shouldn't you call 9-1-1?" asked Woody, his eyes still riveted on the wrench.

"I don't see where this is an actual emergency, considering Griffith has been gone over fifteen years. It's not like finding this will bring him back." She thumbed through the pages. "Here's the number." She punched the keypad of her cell phone.

"Cape Girardeau Police Department," said a crisp female voice.

"Uh, yes, this is Rhetta McCarter. May I please speak to Sergeant Abel Risko?" Rhetta had met Sergeant Risko a few months back, so his name popped into her head.

"Hold please." The dispatcher placed the call on hold.

In a minute, a gravelly male voice came on. "This is Risko."

"Sergeant, this is Rhetta McCarter. I'm not sure if you remember me. Anyway, I'm here with my friend Ricky Lane at Fast Lane Muscle Cars in

Gordonville. She's working on an old Camaro for me, and when she began taking it apart, she found Malcom Griffith's wallet inside a fenderwell."

Risko paused a moment. "I remember you, Mrs. McCarter." He cleared his throat. "Did you say Malcom Griffith? The guy that disappeared several years back?"

"That's right. I know it's Griffith's because all his ID is still in the wallet."

Risko let out a soft whistle. "As intriguing as that discovery sounds, Gordonville is in the county, so you need to notify the Sheriff's office in Jackson. Hold on, and I'll transfer you."

Rhetta should have known to look up the county sheriff. She must've allowed herself to get rattled at the discovery. Gordonville was a small community in Cape Girardeau County, definitely not in the city limits of Cape Girardeau. She sighed. She wouldn't tell Randolph she called the wrong agency. She wondered if Risko really did remember her from interviewing her after she'd found Randolph's friend, Professor Peter LaRose, dead in his apartment earlier this summer.

"Isn't Gordonville in the county jurisdiction?" asked Woody.

Rhetta glared at him. "Now, you remind me."

When the Cape Girardeau County sheriff's deputy answered, she repeated what she'd told Risko.

"Thank you, ma'am. I'll send an officer to pick it up in the morning. This is a pretty old case, so I'll check and see who will have jurisdiction. Meanwhile, don't let anyone handle the wallet, or the other items. And don't do any more to that car until we check it out." He asked her for the address and the phone number where the car was located, along with her information.

After agreeing to comply with the officer's request. Rhetta disconnected. "He sounds almost annoyed that this stuff showed up," she said, and bent over to study the wrench. "And of course, just as I feared, he said not to do anything more on the car until they check it out. That doesn't sound good."

She resisted an urge to snatch up the wrench and examine it more closely, and to pick up Griffith's wallet and tear into it. Pointing to the items, she said to Ricky, "Can you leave this stuff right here until tomorrow? He said he'd send someone to get it in the morning."

"Sure, no problem." Then, grinning, Ricky said, "Come over here and let me show you what progress I'm making." She tugged Rhetta back to the car.

"Are you sure this is progress?" Rhetta ran her hand over the sanded-down, stripped out metal shell.

"I'm nearly ready to paint, so you bet, that's progress."

Rhetta eyed the car. Would it ever look as good as Cami? She missed her two-toned blue Rally Sport with the white leather interior. She and Randolph had done most of the interior restoration themselves. She didn't want Ricky, or Woody, to think she was entertaining maudlin thoughts about losing Cami. She fished around in her purse for a tissue, and blew her nose. "Allergies are really bad this year," she said, tossing the tissue into the nearby trashcan.

"You're going to love this color." Ricky picked up a six-inch square piece of sheet metal painted an electric blue.

Rhetta nodded. She hoped she'd come to love this replacement. She knew it would be beautiful. But would it capture her heart the way Cami had? This Z28 had T-tops, and more features. Ricky promised to jazz up the interior with a custom console with cup holders, charging stations for her cell phone and an iPod dock.

"It's great," Rhetta said, and hope she sounded eager. She'd not only lost her car, but with it her purse, phone and most precious of all, a locket that had belonged to her deceased mother.

"I've been searching on eBay for a rear bumper cover, but can't find one reasonably priced, so I'm going to order a new one. Actually, the new ones are made of fiberglass instead of urethane, so a new one will look much better anyway. At first, I thought I could repair the two big breaks in the original, but I don't think it will look good patched. If it cracks again after painting, it will look really bad."

"Did the car have a rear-ender?" Rhetta wasn't keen on the idea that the car may have been wrecked from behind.

"No, I don't think so. The funny thing is, it's only the outer bumper cover that's broken. Nothing under the car, like the supports, or especially the gas tank, or the inner bumper, show any signs of being in a wreck. Frankly, it looks like some dummy pushed the car with another bigger vehicle, like a pickup." She walked to the bumper that lay on the floor, and pointed to the damaged area. "See that?"

Rhetta squatted to inspect the damage. Sure enough, even to her lesser trained eye, it appeared that something had pushed the car from behind. There were two large perpendicular cracks that went completely through the urethane. They could have been made from bumper protrusions like bumper guards. She pushed on the cracks and they yielded inward. "Maybe whoever owned this Z got it stuck somewhere and got a push from a neighbor in a tractor or pickup. No matter, I bow to your expertise. We'll toss this one."

Glimpsing the time on Ricky's wall clock, she called out to Woody. "We'd better get back to the office. LuEllen will want to go to lunch soon."

* * *

"I need to run some errands," Rhetta said as she dropped Woody off. She recognized the look Woody shot her as he got out. It was his right-eyebrow-raised suspicious look.

"I'm just going to the post office, and the bank. I'll be right back," she promised.

He turned back to glare at her. "No, you're not. I know that look. You're going to go do something about what Ricky found, and I want to go."

"No, I'm not, Woody. I'm going to the post office."

"Uh-huh," he said and got out. As soon as he stomped through the office door, she grabbed her cell phone.

"Ricky? I just got an idea. Grab your metal detector. I want to go to the barn where we got the Z and look around." She aimed Streak right back toward Gordonville.

CHAPTER 3

R HETTA BLASTED THE AIR conditioner as high as it could go. She'd set it on moderately comfortable for Woody, since he always said riding with her was like riding in a refrigerator. For herself, she loved when the fan whipped the frigid air straight at her face. She sang along to the oldies blasting on her satellite radio as she inched her way across town again to Gordonville.

Kingshighway traffic was heavier than usual, with folks who were probably running errands in anticipation of the Labor Day weekend coming up. Being Friday, and the last day before the three-day weekend, all the procrastinators in Cape had apparently decided to get their barbeque supplies at the same time. The entrance to the shopping center was as crowded as it was during the Christmas shopping stampedes. She wove through traffic lined up to turn into the shopping mall.

Once past the mall, she pushed the accelerator up to sixty and flew into Gordonville. She slammed on the brakes as she remembered the twenty-five mile per hour speed limit along Main Street. This time, the town constable eyeballed her from his favorite stakeout spot. Breathing a sigh of relief when she passed him and his blue lights didn't fire up, she coasted at twenty-five until the she passed the *Thanks for Visiting, Please Come Again* sign. Then, she floored it. Or at least as much "flooring" as the SUV was capable of. It didn't exactly burn any rubber like Cami did.

She thought about the wallet and the wrench. She couldn't conceive of a reason why they would have been in the Z28. She thought back to the day she and Ricky had taken Ricky's truck and trailer and gone after the Z. She tried to picture the inside of the barn, but couldn't recall anything unusual in or around the area when she and Ricky had finally loaded the car onto Ricky's flatbed trailer. After Ricky had backed as close as she could to the barn door, they had had to push the car to the doorway, so that Ricky could hook up the winch. When the car proved too much for the two of them, with the tires being flat and embedded into the dirt, Ricky enlisted the help of three construction workers at the highway project down the road to come and help. Offering a couple of six packs of beer was all it took to persuade the men to push the car into position, and the winch did the rest. Three brawny men and two petite women eventually got the job done.

She was so engrossed in her musings that she nearly passed up Ricky's road, and braked hard to avoid missing it. She swerved hard to the left, irritating the driver of the red Mustang convertible right behind her. He saluted her with his middle finger as he roared past.

* * *

Ricky had closed the shop and was outside waiting when Rhetta rolled up. Ricky stowed the metal detector in the back of the Trailblazer, closed the hatch and slid into the passenger seat.

"It's cold enough to hang beef in here," Ricky said, fastening her seat belt, then turning the vent away from her face. "Go back. I think I know where my parka is."

"Very funny," Rhetta said. She reached for the climate control and turned the temperature up to 73 degrees. It had been set on 60. Lately, those annoying kindnesses called "hot flashes" struck randomly, and when they did, she required plenty of cold air. Randolph had learned not to protest. He usually just carried a sweatshirt, and let her turn the air as cold as she needed, both in the car and at home.

"What are we looking for?" Ricky said.

"I'm not really sure, but there might be something else out there that could be a clue to Malcom Griffith's disappearance." Rhetta glanced over her shoulder and pulled out of Ricky's driveway. At the end of the gravel road, she turned right on to the main road going through town. After easing though, she punched it up to fifty-five.

Within minutes she turned onto another gravel road. In the distance, she spotted several huge earth-moving machines.

"Look over there," Ricky said, pointing to the equipment. "Jeremy's company is building Oak Forest Subdivision. They've got Plat One nearly ready to start installing the improvements." All of the area around where the barn was located had been cleared and platted. There were survey sticks marking lot corners, and others marking the proposed streets.

"Have they torn down the old barn yet?" Rhetta asked, turning into the tree-lined driveway. The subdivision entry used the same scenic driveway lined with tall white oaks that once led to the farmhouse.

"Not yet. Jeremy said an old boy from Arkansas wants the barn and is going to come up here and tear it down piece by piece, and haul the thing away." She clicked her tongue. "Now that's a big job. But he paid handsomely, according to Jeremy, to buy this piece of history." She made air quotation marks with her index and middle fingers as she said "piece of history."

"Hmm, I guess it's hard to find these old wood barns anymore, especially if they're in good shape," Rhetta said as they arrived at the end of the lane, parking in front of a recently leveled bare, earthen spot. She remembered the old farmhouse that had stood there. It had been recently razed.

Ricky grabbed the metal detector and waited for Rhetta to change out of her city-slicker sandals into barn-exploring tennis shoes. Rhetta kept a pair of running shoes in her car for those days when she went to Cape LaCroix Creek Park to walk the trails for a break from office stress. She wore off-white capris, probably not the best choice for barn snooping, but much better than her usual business attire—a dress or skirt.

With Rhetta's tennies tied and her sandals stowed in the cargo hatch, the two angled toward the old wooden barn.

"Jeremy is developing this whole subdivision?" Rhetta asked, scoping out the oak-lined fields around the barn.

"He isn't doing it on his own. He has two partners," Ricky said. "The partners, slash investors, are actually from California. The bulk of the responsibility is on him, though. They send the money and come out here about every six weeks to check on the progress. The company is called JS Properties."

Rhetta remembered seeing a sign as they drove down the lane. It bore a green oval logo containing the letters JSP in the middle. She recognized the logo from several billboards around town.

They stopped at the walk-through door at the gable end of the two-story wood barn and peered at a freshly installed padlock.

"That's strange," Ricky said, taking the lock into her hand, and jiggling it. "There's nothing in this old barn anymore. I wonder who padlocked it. I doubt Jeremy would have." She led the way around to the long side of the barn to a sliding door. She tugged it, but it held fast. "This one must be locked from the inside," she announced as Rhetta reached her.

Ricky glanced up. "I can climb through there," she said, and pointed to an opening approximately two feet by three feet just above their heads. She stepped back several paces, ran at the barn, and leapt, gripped the ledge and easily pulled herself over and through.

In a moment, she slid the door open.

Rhetta picked up the metal detector and ventured in. She gazed around, allowing her eyes to adjust to the dim interior. The solid old barn allowed little daylight to penetrate. Long vertical slivers of sunlight oozed through the spaces between the wallboards, casting shadows along the dirt floor. Dust motes danced in the skinny rays, and a musty, stale hay odor clung to the walls.

Inside, the temperature was significantly cooler than the late summer heat of the day. When her eyes had adjusted, Rhetta recognized the impression in the ground where the Z28 had been parked under a tarp. "Turn on that thing and check over here," she said, handing Ricky the metal detector.

Ricky began a sweeping motion in front of her as she walked slowly around the area where the car had been stored. The metal detector stayed mostly silent, with just an occasional feeble whimper.

After circling the area, and finding nothing but a few bolts and rusty nails, they stopped, and Ricky turned the machine off.

"I thought for sure we'd find something else, another clue," Rhetta said. She wiped perspiration off her forehead with the back of her hand. Her hair had begun to stick to her face. Although initially the barn air had felt cooler, there was no escaping the humidity.

Ricky propped the metal detector against a wall, wiped her face with a tissue and stuffed it into her pocket. "There's nothing much here. I guess we should go."

Rhetta eased over to the spot where the car sat for so long, and squatted to study the ground. She spotted the twin drag marks where she remembered pushing the car. The rims had dug channels into the earth. There were four deep wheel impressions on the ground where the car had rested for so many years.

She studied them, then inched her way backward, examining the ground a few feet back. "Ricky, come over here a second. Look at this." Ricky hunkered down to join Rhetta, who pointed at four faint impressions. "What does that look like?"

"It looks like car wheel impressions," Ricky answered. She stood, studied the surrounding area and stepped gingerly away. "It looks as though the car may have first sat right here for a time, and then was moved forward about a car length." She pointed to the fainter set of impressions.

Rhetta stood. "Let's not mess up these tracks."

They both stepped back.

"Grab your metal detector again," Rhetta said. "I think someone moved the car to where it was when we got it. I wonder why. Sweep the area under where we found the car one more time, real carefully. Let's do it in a grid, like they do in the detective movies. Start here." She pointed to the newer impressions. Using her foot, she connected the four dents, making a rectangle out of the area. She searched for something other than her foot when she saw how much dirt had glued to her tennies. Spotting an old section piece of a ladder rung lying nearby, she used it to scratch in the dirt and divided the whole thing into smaller squares.

Poised over the first square, Ricky flipped the switch on the detector. It hummed quietly as she started at the first square and made a thorough sweep of it before moving to the next. At the square closest to what would have been the left front wheel of where the car was parked when they picked it up, she was rewarded with a solid beep.

"There may be another tool or something in the ground there," Rhetta said, pointing to the spot where the metal detector had pinged the loudest. She bent over and ran her hand across the dry soil. She found nothing.

"What can we use to dig?" asked Ricky, peering around the empty barn. "I don't see anything resembling a shovel. In fact, I don't see anything resembling anything I can identify, except maybe some really dried cow patties." She screwed up her face at the distasteful objects.

"I've got one of those emergency portable shovels in Streak," Rhetta said. "Randolph makes me keep a whole kit in there in case I ever get stranded in winter and have to dig myself out." She rolled her eyes. "He must think we're in Montana instead of Missouri. I've never had to use it, but now's a good a time to break it in."

* * *

Rhetta returned with a flashlight and a camping-style folding shovel. Ricky took the shovel from her while Rhetta shone the beam on the spot to dig.

"Dig slowly, so we don't tear up whatever that is. It may be more evidence." Rhetta crouched and aimed the flashlight.

After removing a few shovels of dirt and making a hole about six inches deep, Ricky glanced up. "This plastic shovel can barely tear up this dirt, so I don't think we have to worry very much about it tearing any—" Before she could finish, the shovel connected with something hard, making a thud as it did. Ricky prodded again. "I don't want to mess anything up, so I think we should use our hands."

Ricky laid the shovel aside, and Rhetta propped the flashlight against it. Both of them hunched over the small hole. They carefully sifted handfuls of soil, then tossed them aside, forming a small pile.

"I feel like an archaeologist, or anthropologist, or one of those *gists*," Ricky said, and giggled.

"Oh, God," Rhetta said. She wasn't laughing. She stopped sifting to snatch the flashlight and shine it into the hole.

"What is it?" Ricky scooped another handful of dirt before she saw it. "Oh, no!"

They both stood and gaped. A gnarly finger bone wearing a heavy onyx ring protruded through the crumbly dirt.

"Can that be...?" Ricky said.

"I'm pretty sure it's a hand." Rhetta bent over the hole again.

Ricky backed away. "Whose is it?"

"I don't know, but whoever belongs to it may still be connected to it, so I think we need to call the cops," Rhetta said, turning and heading for the doorway.

Ricky dropped the metal detector and scrambled after her. "I'm coming with you. I don't want to be alone with that hand. Or whatever is attached to it."

When they reached the doorway, both women stopped and leaned against the outside of the barn. Rhetta welcomed the heat and brightness of the sun and the warmth of the barn's wood siding.

"I think we may have just discovered where Malcom Griffith has been all these years," Rhetta said.

"What? Why do you say that?" Ricky clutched her stomach. "I think I'm going to be sick." With that, she swiveled around and upchucked against the barn.

Rhetta clutched her own stomach. "I'm a sympathetic puker," she mumbled and began inhaling deep breaths until the urge subsided. "Are you okay?" she asked Ricky when her own nausea passed.

Ricky gulped, then held up her hand and nodded.

Rhetta pulled her phone from her pocket and dialed the sheriff's office. As she dialed, she whispered, "I saw two gold initials on that black ring—M and G."

CHAPTER 4

Forty minutes later, Rhetta remained outside but watched as the deputy strode toward what she knew to be a gruesome discovery. The lone officer who responded to the call told her they'd probably found the remains of a dead cow and scoffed when she insisted he'd best take a look.

"I don't know of any cows who wear initial rings," she whispered to Ricky. "In fact, I don't know of any cows who wear any jewelry at all." Ricky choked back a laugh. "Unless you count ear tags." Both women began to suffer hysterical giggles. *Not appropriate*, thought Rhetta. *I better suck it up and shut up.*

When the deputy reached the excavation, he squatted, and pulled out a ballpoint pen, which he used to prod the dirt. He shot up and slapped at the transmitter on his shoulder. Rhetta clearly heard his shrill voice calling in his location and requesting the coroner. She sighed and walked over to a still-trembling Ricky, who was puffing away at her third cigarette as she leaned against the barn. Rhetta could barely resist jerking the cigarette away from her friend and sucking until the nicotine made her head spin. This barn discovery was setting her resolve to quit smoking back a significant number of notches.

"I need to call Randolph." Rhetta resisted the cigarette craving, and pulled out her cell phone. She slid her thumb across the first name on her favorites list.

Her husband answered on the third ring. Before he could even say "Hello," Rhetta blurted, "Randolph, Ricky and I just found a body, and I believe it's Malcom Griffith."

"I think my cell phone is acting up," Randolph said. "I could've sworn you said you just found a body. And what was that about Malcom Griffith?"

"The phone isn't acting up. Ricky and I found a body, or at least a hand, so far, and I strongly suspect it belongs to Malcom Griffith. Can you come out here? We're at the barn where we got the Z28. While we're waiting for the coroner, this nice officer is going to take my statement." Rhetta nodded at the deputy who had reached her side. The sandy-haired, crew-cut-sporting deputy sheriff reached into a breast pocket and pulled out a small spiral flip notebook, tapping it against his wrist as he waited for her to get off the phone.

Randolph let out a long sigh. "Oh, God, Rhetta. What did you do now?"

* * *

Twenty minutes later, Randolph's three-quarter-ton Ford pickup roared into the driveway and screeched to a stop in a dust storm. The powdery clay swirled and glued itself to the waxed finish of the new bronze colored tuck that Rhetta named the Artmobile II. The first Artmobile, an older model pickup, had been a total loss when Randolph was run off the road earlier in the year. Randolph must've left home immediately and more than moderately exceeded the speed limit to get there so quickly. Their five-acre farmette sat on a gravel road on the other side of the county, nearly 25 miles away.

The coroner's dark blue van pulled in behind Randolph, then barreled around him and down to the barn. It was followed by a black-and-white county sheriff's sedan, plus a tan Chevy Suburban with the Missouri Highway Patrol logo on the door.

"Probably all of the Major Case Squad has been called out," Randolph said, and began coughing as the dust engulfed them from all the vehicles. Rhetta began wheezing, so she trotted away from the cluster of cars and gulped fresh air. Her wheezing subsided.

Randolph followed her, and cleared his throat. "What on earth made you come out here? And how did you find a body?" Randolph put his arm around Rhetta's shoulders. "Are you okay?"

"I'm all right." She glanced at Ricky who was talking animatedly on her cell phone. "Ricky must be calling Jeremy. This is his development, and actually, I'm not sure if he still owns the barn or not. Ricky told me Jeremy sold it to a man in Arkansas."

Before Rhetta could fill Randolph in on the discovery, she heard Ricky's voice rise. "Jeremy, what the heck do you think? That we wanted to find a body? Get a grip!" Ricky ended her conversation and thrust the phone into her pocket. She strode to Rhetta and Randolph, muttering under her breath. "Like we deliberately found a body to sabotage his development."

Before Rhetta could explain to Randolph, they were again interrupted, this time by the deputy who had initially interviewed Rhetta. "Mrs. McCarter, I'll need you and Ms. Lane to go by the sheriff's office in Jackson sometime tomorrow morning to sign the statement." It wasn't a request. "Besides the obvious issue of the remains, we received a complaint call from the property owner." He glanced at his notebook. "Mr. Jeremy Spears. Apparently someone called him and told him there were trespassers here." He glanced from Rhetta to Ricky.

"I'm dating Mr. Spears, and have been out here before. In fact, the old Z28 I'm working on for Mrs. McCarter"—Ricky jerked her thumb toward Rhetta—"came from this barn. I found it very strange that the barn was locked, so I climbed in and opened the door." Ricky took a final drag on her cigarette, then stubbed it out on the ground. She reached down and recovered the butt and held it in her hand. "I knew the barn was empty. We just wanted to look around."

Ricky went on to explain what had turned up in the Z28. The deputy scribbled furiously.

Randolph shook his head. "I can't believe it. You two found a body under that Z28."

The deputy jotted in the notebook then flipped it closed. "The area here will be blocked off until the Major Case Squad can bring in a forensic pathologist to uncover the remains. This barn is a crime scene. No one can go in or out until it's released." Deputies were already stringing yellow crime scene tape around the barn and across the opening Ricky had crawled through. They used the tape to impose a makeshift barricade across the driveway.

Ricky motioned to the deputy, who turned his attention to her and reopened his notebook, ready to take down anything she said. "When we called the sheriff's office earlier today to let them know we found Malcom Griffith's wallet in the Z28, the officer we spoke to didn't seem too impressed. In fact he said they weren't going to have anyone pick up the stuff until the morning."

Without answering her, the deputy tucked the notebook away, slapped his shoulder and stepped back. But not before they heard him say, "I'll be 10-20 in Gordonville at Fast Lane Muscle Cars, recovering evidence." He turned to Ricky. "Please lead the way, Ms. Lane. We're all going to your garage. That stuff you found in that car just might be murder evidence."

CHAPTER 5

THE PHONE CALL WITH Jeremy must've helped Ricky return to feeling like her spikey old self. When Rhetta asked her if she wanted to ride with them in the Artmobile, she declined, and instead insisted on driving Rhetta's Trailblazer to her shop. Rhetta hugged Ricky before climbing into the truck with Randolph. They pulled onto the highway behind Ricky, bringing up the tail end of the mini-caravan heading to Fast Lane.

When they were on the county road, Randolph glanced at his wife. "Why did you two go out there? Were you thinking you could do a little investigating?"

"I had no intention of investigating, as you put it. I only thought we might find more clues, and be able to turn everything over to the police, since they were supposed to come out tomorrow. I'm more than willing to let them handle it. I sure don't know anything about solving a cold murder case, or any other murder case for that matter." She pulled down the visor mirror to check her hair. Just as she feared, her short spikes had flattened against her head and were covered with a halo of clay dust. She shook her head and watched the dust cascade to the top of the dash. She also sported a streak of dirt across her left cheek. At least she hoped it was dirt, and not a crayon of dried cowpile. All the dust had made her eyes water, so she removed her contact lenses. She stared at her eyes in the mirror, barely distinguishing where green ended and bloodshot began. Groping into the back seat, she produced the tissue box Randolph kept. She snatched a handful and spit-wiped her cheek.

Randolph reached into the console and produced a packet of wet wipes. He handed her one of the foil wraps. "Here, this may work better."

She grinned.

* * *

Rhetta and Randolph edged in the crowded driveway at Fast Lane and parked behind a Cape Girardeau Sheriff's sedan. Although several police cars had crammed into the short drive, there was no sign of the Highway Patrol SUV. When they entered Ricky's shop, they spotted her perched on her stool watching a crime scene technician meticulously bag the wallet, sunglasses and the wrench. Two other deputies were scrutinizing the Z28.

"Your car's going to the lab," said Ricky, holding her hands up in surrender. "I explained everything to that nice deputy over there." She jutted her chin toward the officer who was dusting the car for prints. "There probably isn't much left of this car to process, because I've sanded and cleaned so much of it, but oh, no, they're going to gather and bag up all the pieces." She hopped down from the stool and stood in front of the car's original small block 350 engine and turbo transmission, and the rear bumper cover that lay against the wall.

"Even this stuff." She pointed to the pile of parts. "They're going to load all of it up, take it to the lab and go over everything."

Rhetta glanced at Randolph. "I guess that puts my Z28 on hold for a good long time." She took Ricky's place on the stool and swiveled back and forth.

"Sergeant," Randolph said as he walked over to the deputy. "I understand you fellas have a job to do, but since my wife and I have a lot of money tied up in this car, we'd like to have an itemized receipt of all the pieces you take. That way we can match up everything upon its return."

The deputy nodded, signed off on the evidence sheet the tech presented, then watched as the tech lugged an armload of evidence bags to his car before answering Randolph. "Judge McCarter, you know as well as I do, you may not get this car back for a very long time." He withdrew a pad of forms from a sheaf of papers he'd placed on the workbench and began filling one in. "Maybe never, if the body found has anything to do with this car and there's a trial."

Rhetta pointed to all the bags as they left and said, "That pile of bags is my car?"

Ricky patted her arm. "Don't worry, we'll put it all back together."

Rhetta's stomach knotted, as though she'd just taken a kick to her gut. Even though at first, she'd been reluctantly enthusiastic about Cami's replacement, the thought that this Z28 was now probably lost to her made a tear escape. She snuffled to mask it. "Dang allergies." She grabbed a paper towel on Ricky's workbench and blew her nose. She mumbled into the towel, and cleared her throat. Randolph put an arm around her shoulders.

The deputy called out to Ricky. "Ms. Lane, I'll need your help getting me the serial numbers and part numbers on the larger parts for my compilation." He tapped the pen against the clipboard and nodded toward Randolph. "Let's start with the Vehicle Identification Number." The deputy wiped his brow with a paper towel. "This could take a while." They trudged toward the car. Randolph followed them.

"Can I offer you a bottle of water?" Ricky asked. When the deputy nodded, she detoured to the refrigerator in the corner, grabbed a cold bottle of water, and met the officer at the car.

The tech returned and was repacking his satchel. "How long did you say this car spent in that barn?" He turned to Ricky.

"Close to twenty-five years, I was told," Ricky said.

"But the man they think was under the car has been missing fifteen years?"

Ricky nodded.

The tech shook his head. "Unbelievable. I'm heading over to the barn as soon as I finish up here. This is the strangest case I've ever been called to work." He headed for the door. "We don't get many murders here in Cape County, especially not cold cases. This one could take a long, long time."

Rhetta's nicotine craving skyrocketed.

CHAPTER 6

BEFORE LEAVING, RHETTA WROTE a check to Ricky for all the labor and parts for work done to date. The deputy's words about keeping the Z28 for evidence echoed in her ears. She didn't want Ricky out the cost of labor or any parts already purchased for the doomed car. Rhetta already thought of it as lost, seeing as how Cami's replacement would likely never get to park inside the Garage Mahal, their detached garage. She'd christened it that because she claimed it was finished as nicely inside as the house was.

"I can cancel the LS1 engine, so at least you won't be out that expense," Ricky said. "We can always find another one when we get the car back."

Rhetta nodded. "It doesn't appear that we'll have any use for it for a long time, according to the deputy. I guess the car will be held as evidence. But isn't the new motor already loaded on the truck and on its way?"

Ricky fired up another cigarette. "I don't have to accept delivery. I'll send it back."

Rhetta perched on the shop stool, elbows on the workbench. "I have to tell you, I'm getting bummed over losing this car. I can't talk to Randolph about it, because he keeps trying to cheer me up. I was on board with getting this Z28 to replace Cami, but now, with this…." She didn't finish, just sighed and gestured vaguely toward the car.

"We both thought you'd enjoy your new ride so much that maybe losing Cami wouldn't hurt so badly." Ricky blew a long slow spiral of smoke.

Rhetta stared at the various second-generation Camaro posters on the wall, and at a picture of Cami taken at a car show two years before. "I loved that car."

Ricky nodded. "Me, too. It was awesome."

The women sat quietly for a moment. Then Rhetta added, "I didn't tell you about my mother's locket that was lost in it, did I?"

Ricky touched Rhetta's arm. "No, but Randolph did."

Rhetta glanced around the garage, to the empty bay where Ricky usually kept her own car, a black 1979 Trans-Am. "So, where's the Monster?"

The Monster's moniker was earned from its shiny black paint and extra loud headers. "I've got it in the paint shop." Ricky gestured toward the addition at the back of the garage that she used for her paint booth. "I'm buffing the paint and spiffing it up to list it on eBay."

Rhetta glanced around the corner, to a car bundled under a cover. "You're going to sell the Monster?"

"Sure, you know me. I'll fix up something else. I've got a line on a 1965 Mustang that I want."

Rhetta hopped down from the stool. "I bet Monster's paint looks even more fantastic after you buffed it. Besides, if you sell it quickly, I might not get to see it again, so I should check it out now."

"Later, when it's done, I'll make sure you see it." Ricky said, steering Rhetta away from the paint bay. "There's cutting compound all over it right now, so it's not looking too great. Besides, you'll get that dust all over you." She crushed out her cigarette into a steel replica valve cover that she used as an ashtray. She looked up at Rhetta. "You haven't quit." It wasn't a question.

"No, not entirely, but I'm trying."

"I saw you eat that cigarette with your eyes. That's how I know."

CHAPTER 7

WITH A COMPLETE LIST of everything the deputies were taking, Randolph left Fast Lane as soon as the deputies cleared out. After visiting a few minutes more with Ricky, Rhetta ambled to her Trailblazer. The day had gone decidedly downhill with the grisly discovery and the presumptive loss of the Z28. To console herself, she cranked up the volume on the satellite radio, which she kept tuned to an oldies station. Today it was the 70's. As she reached her driveway, she hummed along with the Eagles. Twice along the way home, she nearly stopped to get into her secret stash of cigarettes that she kept in her console, but resisted.

Stopping to collect the mail from the oversized mailbox at the end of their gravel driveway, she waved to Mrs. Koblyk, her neighbor, who sat in a white pine rocker on her large veranda. Although shielded from the road by a copse of tall pines, the Koblyks' house sat close to the county road, directly across from the McCarter property. Mrs. Koblyk always knew everything that went on in the neighborhood. That she did made Randolph crazy at times. Rhetta didn't really mind. She found Mrs. Koblyk to be a great neighbor, especially when she brought them fresh, homemade bread. Mr. Koblyk, a retired jeweler and watchmaker, spent most of his time in his little workshop, "tinkering," as he called it. He spent hours restoring antique jewelry, which turned out to be a lucrative hobby.

The McCarter home was once a turn-of-the-twentieth-century farmhouse that sat in the center of the picturesque creek-side property. After they married ten years ago, Rhetta and Randolph spent months looking for the perfect place while living in a modest two-bedroom apartment. Rhetta had loved remodeling the house. Installing modern vinyl siding in the clapboard style kept the outside of the two-story white home looking very much like the old pictures of it that Rhetta had found in the attic. Inside, however, it was beautifully modernized.

"Sweets, I'm home," she called out as she entered the kitchen from the garage. She almost always called Randolph "Sweets," unless he left the toilet seat up. The sliding door to the deck was ajar. Rhetta spotted Randolph spooning out cat food for their four hungry felines—Pirate, Greystone, Jiggles and Smith. Rhetta said their names sounded like a law firm.

"Barn cats, indeed," he grumbled as she joined him on the deck. She brushed his cheek with her lips and relieved him of the can of food. His silver-tinged black hair flopped over one eye. He'd been so busy painting for an upcoming show that he'd let his hair grow out a little longer than his usual cut. She decided she liked it.

"I'll finish here," she said, as she bent to croon to the fur babies. "I know how much you love the smell of this canned fish." Jiggles, all white with one black paw, got his name from his strange habit of bouncing up and down every time she spooned out their food.

"I thought the cats were supposed to live in the barn and catch mice." Randolph filled their water dishes from the spigot on the deck.

"You don't see any mice in the barn, do you?" Rhetta said. "They're doing their job so well, I like to reward them."

"All right, you win. I'm outnumbered." Randolph held the door for Rhetta and they returned to the kitchen. Smith, the Siamese mix, always waited until the others began eating before he'd venture in to join them.

"I stopped at *The Golden Dragon,* and picked up supper." Randolph pointed to the take-out sacks lined up on the granite top of the new kitchen island.

Rhetta would've preferred the Golden Arches, but said nothing. She wasn't hungry anyway, so it didn't matter. She couldn't stop thinking about how they found an actual dead body. Could it really be Malcom Griffith? She shivered.

"Come on, let's eat a bite, and talk about what happened today," Randolph said, circling his arms around her waist and pulling her to him in a hug. He brushed her hair from her forehead, then patted the stool next to him at the counter.

* * *

With the meal finished, and the empty containers carried to the trashcan in the garage, Rhetta curled up in the soft leather chair in the great room. She savored the rich coffee aroma before sipping from her oversize mug.

"I hope you aren't going to get involved in this case," Randolph said as he dropped into the matching chair alongside her. Ice cubes clanked as he stirred his tall iced tea.

"I don't see where I could do anything, so why are you warning me off? It's not like the Cape Girardeau County Sheriff seeks me out for guidance." She chortled at the idea. "I'm sure the forensic pathologist will identify the remains soon enough." She swirled the remaining coffee around the nearly empty cup. "What if it's really Malcom Griffith? That means somebody killed him, and he didn't run away with a pole dancer, after all. I wonder what happened to the pole dancer. More importantly, if it is Malcom Griffith, then who killed him?" In spite of Randolph's warning, she couldn't help but think about possible suspects. The pole dancer? Griffith's wife? A disgruntled client? An agitated partner?

"Is Ricky still dating Jeremy Spears?" Randolph asked, interrupting her thoughts.

"'Fraid so." She couldn't hide her disapproval. She frowned. Did Jeremy Spears kill Malcom Griffith?

"Don't you like him?"

She returned to the conversation. "Honestly, no. I heard Ricky having a few cross words with Jeremy this afternoon. She says he's blaming her because we found the body. I wonder what he was going to do at the site after the barn was torn down. And I wonder why the old barn was locked up anyway? Ricky defended him and insisted Jeremy wasn't angry because they found the body. She said the reason he's upset is that the discovery would set his project back, and his investors were leaning on him."

"That makes sense. Especially if he's got a lot invested."

She had no desire to regurgitate the details of the chilling discovery yet again, so she changed the subject. "I have to admit, I'm disappointed about possibly losing this Z28." She drained the last of the coffee.

Randolph leaned forward. "Of course you are. You were pretty upset about losing Cami."

She stared at the remnants of coffee that clung to the bottom of the cup.

He went on. "I know people in the sheriff's department. Maybe I can get them to hurry the testing and release the car."

Rhetta peered at him over her mug. "Sweets, I know you're trying to cheer me up, but I'm a big girl. I know very well I may never see Cami's replacement ever again. Or, at least, not for a very long time." She set her cup down and stood. She kissed the top of his head. "It's all right. I was looking forward to this car, but…well, it's not Cami."

She retrieved the remote and clicked on the news. The discovery of the body presumed to be Malcom Griffith was the lead story. Video at nine. She switched off the set and noticed Randolph had left the room. She heard him talking on the phone.

She caught a single word before he disconnected—Camaro.

CHAPTER 8

THE TUESDAY AFTER LABOR Day proved to be as rainy as the three-day weekend had been. Rhetta had eagerly looked forward to enjoying some down time with Randolph at their cabin at Land-Between-the-Lakes, Kentucky, and maybe get in some quality fishing. Instead, when thunder boomed through the house and lightning split the skies and jarred Rhetta and Randolph awake before dawn Saturday morning, they decided to stay home. In the middle of Rhetta's shower Saturday morning, the power went off and the whole-house backup generator kicked on. The outage lasted until Sunday afternoon.

She felt like they hadn't had any down time at all. Tuesday made the third straight day of the heavens splitting open with storms and torrential rains.

Rhetta had forgotten her umbrella, so she sprinted across the parking lot. Woody was already parked in the slot closest to the door. "The reward for getting here early," he'd probably chirp, if she groused that she wanted that spot for herself. They'd had that discussion before. He didn't think her position as manager earned her the spot unless she got there before him.

He held the door for her. "You went looking for trouble, didn't you? Bank and post office, my broken foot." He pointed to his foot that had, until a few weeks ago, sported a walking cast.

Rhetta ignored him and carried her triple espresso mocha light to her desk, setting it down gingerly. Some splashed over the top of the cup and on to her desk. She snatched the napkin and blotted quickly. The coffee smelled heavenly. She shook her soaked hair, tossing rain droplets across her desk, then reached for her cup to savor the first sip.

"Where's LuEllen?" she said, glancing at the empty reception desk. Beyond LuEllen's desk, Rhetta had a clear view out the window at the solid sheet of rain pelting the building.

Woody ignored her question and instead, shook the newspaper at her. "It's all here in gory detail on the front page."

"How many times do I have to tell you I don't read the local paper?" She tossed the St. Louis Post-Dispatch down on her desk. "Mercifully, no one in St. Louis cares about this, so I don't have to read about it." She riffled through her desk calendar, changing the month, and tapping the date. "Is LuEllen off? There's nothing on the calendar about her being off today."

Woody dropped into the guest chair in front of her desk and laid the newspaper beside her coffee. "She called and said she'll be in late. Something about a dentist appointment. Meanwhile, I'm waiting. Spill it." He rubbed his head.

"Are you upset? You sound as though you're disappointed that you weren't there when we found the body." She rearranged her desk, set her purse down on the corner and picked up the local paper. She scanned it, then handed it back to Woody. Her arm knocked her purse over, dumping everything on the floor. "Crap." She bent over to retrieve the spilled contents.

"I'm not upset."

"Yes, you are." She stuffed her phone, wallet, notebook and an envelope of papers back into her purse. A small sheet floated to the desk. "There's the receipt for the vacuum sweeper I took to be repaired. I knew it had it." She crammed the paperwork back in her purse.

Woody tapped the newspaper. "I'm not upset, but yes, I did want to go out there with you. After all, I'm the one who suspected that wrench had dried blood on it." He held the paper up for her. "It appears I may be right."

Rhetta peered at the headlines. Front page coverage.

Cape Girardeau County Sheriff Talbot Reasoner issued a statement today about the body found in a barn last week in Gordonville. Reasoner confirmed that the remains were that of a male, but positive identification won't be made until test results are available. Preliminary lab results performed over the weekend indicated there was blood found on various items discovered by Ms. Victoria Lane inside a vintage Camaro that she was restoring. Ms. Lane had located the car inside the barn, which sits on property now being developed by Mr. Jeremy Spears. Spears is the son of the late Willard Spears, who had been partners with Malcom Griffith in G & S Development, a well-known developer in the area. Griffith disappeared fifteen years ago. Sheriff Reasoner confirmed that he did not expect test results for several days.

Before she could comment, the phone rang. Woody answered, switching to his professional voice. "MCB Mortgage and Insurance."

When the phone rang again, she answered the other line. The caller identified himself as a deputy sheriff. It seems they had a report that needed filling out. When she explained to him that she needed to be at work, instead of admitting that she'd forgotten her promise to stop by first thing this morning, the words "warrant for your arrest" made the decision easy. "I'll be right over."

CHAPTER 9

AFTER ALL THE REPORTS were signed, Sheriff Reasoner personally escorted Rhetta to the parking lot. The rain had stopped, allowing the late summer sun to peek through the parting clouds. The asphalt smelled of wet dust and sulphur.

"Give Judge McCarter my best regards, won't you?" Reasoner beamed a megawatt smile down at Rhetta, showing off bright white teeth. She decided he must've had them recently whitened. No one over thirty-five could have natural teeth that looked like Chiclets gum—perfect little squares. He removed a wide brimmed Stetson that perched squarely on his head, and then finger-combed his thick black hair. He replaced the hat carefully, and smoothed the brim. "You know we wouldn't have arrested you, of all people, Mrs. McCarter. The deputy got just a little more, shall I say, enthusiastic, than he should have."

The deputy's "enthusiasm" involved a two-hour questioning followed by a thirty-minute wait for the report to be typed. Rhetta had to call Woody to have him cover her appointment with a prospective customer.

"Oh, you can be sure I'll be telling my husband all about our little visit today," Rhetta said, beaming her best phony smile back at him, and aiming her key fob toward her ride. The headlights flashed, signaling the door was unlocked. Reasoner was up for re-election this year. In the past, Randolph had always been one of his biggest supporters. After today, she decided she didn't like the slippery-smooth politician and would convey her opinion of him to Randolph. She slammed the door shut and started the ignition.

She and Randolph usually didn't argue about politics, even though they were politically opposite. She was liberal while her husband always had an "R" after his name when he ran for judge. However, she found the sheriff way too smarmy for her liking and would tell Randolph so. It had nothing to do with any party affiliation. No party had the market on slime balls cornered.

Reasoner had acted as if he was her newest best friend, assuring her that he would do everything he could to try to get her Z28 back to her as soon as possible. He didn't realize she overheard him tell the clerk that "she'd be lucky to get that car back in time for her retirement party, right after she signs up for Medicare." Then he belly-laughed. She wanted so badly to tell Reasoner she'd heard him, just to hear what he'd say, but she decided to hold that information for Randolph to deal with. Rhetta was pleased to see that the clerk had shot the sheriff an unpleasant look, and didn't join him in his mirth.

After Randolph's accident a few months back, all of the law enforcement officers she had talked to were convinced he had been driving drunk, especially Reasoner. When she proved that Randolph wasn't drunk, Reasoner hadn't bothered to call Randolph and extend his good wishes. Now he was sucking up looking for political support. The creep.

She tried her best to squeal the tires as she left the parking lot, but Trailblazers were not Camaros. She couldn't even make the tires whimper. All she managed to do successfully was to fish-tail on the still-wet pavement. She pounded out her frustration on the steering wheel. "I want Cami back."

* * *

LuEllen was on the phone, and Woody was interviewing a young couple when she finally made it back to the office. Rhetta's stomach rumbled, reminding her that she'd missed lunch.

LuEllen hung up and turned to Rhetta. "There's pizza in the kitchen if you haven't eaten yet," she said, then swiveled back to face her computer screen.

Rhetta groaned. Although she loved pizza, she'd have to run an extra mile if she gave in and ate it. She shook her head. "Thanks, but I think I'll wait and eat an early dinner instead." Her stomach loudly protested her mouth's decision.

Plopping down at her desk, she fished out her cell phone. The deputy had asked her to turn it off when he was interviewing her. She powered it back up and three missed calls flashed on her screen. Two of them had left messages. She didn't recognize the third number.

"Call me," Ricky said in the first message, sounding out of breath. Rhetta figured that she'd probably called while sanding a car—Ricky's version of multi-tasking.

The second message was from Randolph. "Call me when you get a chance. The sheriff's office has been looking for you." His deep voice sounded serious.

She called him first and explained where she had been. "I don't like Talbot Reasoner. Don't support him in this election." She told him what happened.

"I was going to call him about getting the Z28 released," Randolph said, and she heard him sigh. "I guess that isn't going to happen."

Just then her phone beeped and she recognized Ricky's number. "I'll call you back, Sweets. Ricky is trying to reach me."

"No need, just wanted to be sure you didn't get hauled to jail." He chuckled. "Love you," he added, then disconnected. Rhetta smiled.

"What's up?" Rhetta said, answering Ricky's call.

"I listed my Trans-Am on eBay auction with a fifteen thousand dollar reserve, and I just got an email from a guy who says he wants it."

"That's great!"

"I'm pretty happy, too. I'm so excited I had to call you. I guess I'll pull down the eBay auction. He's overnighting me a cashier's check."

"So, when do you get the Mustang?"

Ricky laughed. "You know me so well. I called the guy selling it, and I'm going to go out there this afternoon and give him a deposit."

"Why don't you wait until you get the check and it clears, just in case. Your buyer might change his mind, not send out the check, and you'll be stuck having to buy the Mustang."

"You're right. I guess I'm just so excited. This is the first car I've ever listed on eBay. I didn't realize it would sell so fast. There's still five days left on the auction."

"I'm sure happy for you, although I'll miss Monster. It's an awesome car." Rhetta chuckled. "Are you sure you want to get a Ford?" They both laughed. Ricky had always protested Fords. However, she'd confessed to Rhetta in what she admitted was a moment of weakness that she'd always yearned for a first year Mustang. She vowed to paint it bright red.

That reminded Rhetta. "By the way, who do you know out your way who drives a brand new red Mustang convertible?"

"No one out my way, but Jeremy has one. Why do you ask?"

"I saw it on your road when I went out to your place the other day. I meant to ask you then, but forgot." Rhetta vividly remembered the one-finger salute, but didn't mention it to Ricky. Another reason to dislike Jeremy.

CHAPTER 10

WEDNESDAY AFTERNOON THE STREAK'S outside thermometer read 102 when Rhetta slid behind the wheel. Before she'd locked up her office for the day, she'd glanced at the weather icon on her desktop, and if it was to be believed, the area was experiencing the hottest September on record. Inside, the SUV had to be twenty degrees hotter. She cranked on the air conditioner, setting the fan to high speed and rolled down the window to blow some of the heat out. Sweat beads immediately popped out on her forehead.

Her cell rang just as she began pulling out of the parking lot. She'd forgotten to set the iPhone on the console. She stopped and groped around inside her purse, finally locating the instrument after upturning the purse on to the passenger seat. Just as she answered, the phone quit. *Crap.*

She didn't recognize the number, so she tried calling back. She didn't leave a message after hearing a generic phone company pre-recorded message. *Probably a wrong number.*

The phone rang again. Before she could speak, a bubbly sounding Ricky said, "Hey, girlfriend, what are you doing?" Ricky was perpetually cheerful.

"Putting everything back in my purse, since I had to dump it out for a call I just got and no one was on the line." Rhetta stuffed everything back in her bag and sat back, relishing the now frigid air blasting out of the vents.

"Hope you didn't cuss too bad."

"I want you to know I didn't cuss at all," Rhetta said. She didn't count *crap* as a cuss word.

"Right. Listen here, my friend, we're having a big barbeque and get-together at Jeremy's mother's swanky place this Saturday. She just got a pool installed and we're going to break it in. I'd love for you and Randolph to come."

"Isn't September a little late for a pool party?" Rhetta wiped a tissue across her sweating brow, and reconsidered. "I guess it wouldn't be, not when it's a hundred plus outside. What am I saying?" Perspiration continued to drip down her nose. Since she also felt her back and neck sweating in spite of the frigid air, she knew she was experiencing that perk of being forty-plus. As Ricky chattered on about the event, Rhetta wondered when Mrs. Spears moved into the house. She'd have to ask Ricky when she paused to breathe. According to Ricky, after losing her home Mrs. Spears had rented a two-bedroom duplex, which was a far cry from owning a luxury home and getting a new pool.

Ricky was still prattling. "The pool was supposed to be finished two months ago, but the company was way behind after its huge spring sale, so they finally got hers finished right before Labor Day."

Rhetta started to decline, since she didn't like Jeremy, and Randolph didn't like pools. However, she'd never met Mrs. Spears, so curiosity prevailed and she accepted the invite. Randolph would mutter and fuss that he wanted to spend the weekend doing anything else but sitting around a pool. He never swam in them, claiming there were too many possibilities of swimming in substances other than water.

"Sure, that sounds like fun." *Liar.* "What time and where?"

Ricky rattled off the address and Rhetta tapped it into her phone. "What can I bring?" She immediately thought about heading to *Primo Vino!* to pick up a couple of bottles of local wine. Randolph didn't drink anymore, but she was sure everyone else there would partake.

"Mrs. Spears is having the event catered, so I'd say you probably don't need to bring anything. Except if you want to stop at *Primo Vino!*"

Rhetta laughed. "Who knows who so well now?"

"*Ciao.*" Ricky signed off before Rhetta had a chance to ask her about Mrs. Spears' new fancy digs. Oh, well, she'd find out this weekend.

Rhetta placed the phone on the console and pulled out on to Kingshighway. *Hmm. I guess Mrs. Spears is recovering financially since losing her husband and her home. Maybe Mr. Spears had a big life insurance policy. A catered party and a new pool?* She recognized the address as being one of the stately older homes near Southeast Missouri State University. How did the widow Spears get a loan to buy another house so soon after the foreclosure? Rhetta knew she couldn't have gotten a loan—unless Jeremy had signed for her. He might have. He was single, and had a decent income, if she remembered more of Ricky's details about him. However, Ricky had commented that Jeremy wasn't making money on his project yet, and couldn't have financed the subdivision without help from his California investors. His credit couldn't have been good enough to buy a half million-dollar house for his mother.

Mrs. Spears must've fallen into some major money some other way.

CHAPTER 11

AT SIX O'CLOCK SATURDAY morning the thermometer was already hovering at 85, with the high expected to be near 100 once again. The local weatherman declared this would be the thirteenth straight day of 100-plus temperatures, and would thus set a new record for a September heat wave. Rhetta groaned, and poured herself another cup of coffee.

Randolph padded down the stairs from the upstairs bedroom. "Got some more of that brain juice?" Rhetta found his favorite mug and filled it for him. He joined her at the kitchen counter.

"Do we really have to go to this shindig today?" He sipped, then peered at her over the brim of his cup.

"Sweets, if you don't want to go, you know I won't insist. I'm doing this for Ricky. I know she wants me to get better acquainted with Jeremy, so I agreed. I didn't mean to obligate you."

Randolph stood and flexed his shoulder muscles, then slid an arm over her shoulder. "If it won't upset you, I think I'll stay here. I don't like being outside in this heat, and I've got a ton of work to do."

His "work" wasn't a job, but it consumed him nonetheless. Since his retirement from the bench, he'd been painting steadily. He lost several work days in the weeks following his accident. Now that he was well, he painted feverishly, preparing for a one-man show scheduled for the first week of October at the Rivers West Gallery, the art co-operative in downtown Cape Girardeau where he was a member. In addition, his paintings had been selling briskly on Etsy, an internet site for artists. "At the rate I'm going, I'm going to need to clone myself."

"Are you complaining?" she asked and he grinned.

"I remember the old saying about being careful what you wish for." He hugged her and kissed her gently. "Thanks."

She hugged him back, and kissed him solidly. "I see the cats are ready for their breakfast," she said, and headed for the sliding door to the deck. The four felines were seated side by side, staring at them, noses pressed to the glass. Although each cat was a rescue cat, all had banded together to stare inside, and thus train their people to feed them.

* * *

Rhetta cruised along North Henderson Street past the campus and turned left onto Medford Circle. The huge trees lining the cul-de-sac formed a picture-perfect canopy, while the sun sparkled through the leafy overhang. She easily located the Spears' address. The two-story brick Federalist manor was the only house on the circle with a plethora of vehicles parked in the driveway and crammed into every possible street spot. The old money upscale neighborhood homes all enjoyed large garages and paved driveways, so most likely these vehicles, ranging from Escalades to Beemers, belonged to the guests of the home she sought. She circled the circle twice without locating a parking spot, so she returned to Henderson Street and parked in the lot near the University Center. With no classes on Saturday, there were plenty of open parking spaces.

Sliding the straps of the tote bag containing the wine onto one shoulder, she slid her purse onto the other, and began the three-block trek to Mrs. Spears' home. *Crap, I forgot my cell phone.* She returned to her SUV and realized she'd forgotten to lock the Trailblazer's doors. "Good thing I had to come back," she muttered. When she snatched her phone, she noticed a missed call. She recognized the same strange out-of-state number that had called her earlier in the week. She locked the SUV, and leaned against the driver's door. A few clicks and she was online at 411.com, where she checked the reverse number locator. It was registered to an Illinois cell phone, but there was no other information available.

Who could this be? Wonder if it's a customer? Her cell number was on her business cards, and on the bank's website, so being a Saturday whoever called probably figured she wouldn't be at her office. But why hadn't the caller left a message? Either time? This second call couldn't be a wrong number again. Rhetta's answering voice message clearly indicated who she was and what her office hours were.

She was still thinking about the call and staring at her phone as she strolled to the sidewalk when a bright red Mustang convertible pulled up. Jeremy waved at her, properly this time, she noted.

"Hi, Rhetta. Let me give you a lift to the house." He swept alongside the curb, leaned over and opened the passenger door from the inside. *A gentleman would have gotten out and opened the door.* He hadn't earned any points. She thought about telling him so.

Instead, she considered Ricky and for her friend's sake, she forced herself to smile and act grateful. "Thanks. It's darned hot out here." Rhetta leaned in and placed the tote bag and her purse in the back seat. She stuffed the phone into the pocket of her white capris, and slid into the passenger seat. "Looks like there's already a crowd at your mother's. Where will you park? I circled around and had to come back to the Henderson lot to find a spot."

Jeremy's perfect lips parted, displaying teeth in what he probably thought was a winning smile. "I'll go in the back way up the alley. It's our private entrance." His arrogance oozed from every pore, but she bit her tongue. For Ricky. This day wasn't going to be easy.

He beamed a smile at her that was undoubtedly meant to disarm her. Someone had obviously paid an orthodontist a tidy sum on his behalf. Although she smiled back, Rhetta knew it was her phony one again. It was hard to be genuine with this guy. She wanted to like him for her friend's sake, but she had met too many self-important men exactly like Jeremy, and just couldn't warm up to him. His whole demeanor was cookie-cutter yuppie, from his bleached blond longish hair that he kept pushing back out of his eyes as he drove, to the loafers worn without socks. Having the top down didn't bother Rhetta. Her hair was so short it barely moved.

She studied his profile and could see why Ricky was taken with him. He was middle-aged handsome, with just the right amount of creases and lines in his tanned face to upgrade it from boyish. Apparently, he could be very appealing. He wore white chino shorts, which showed off muscular tanned legs. She remembered the middle finger salute, though, and decided his charm was all show.

As Jeremy zipped up the alley, he waved at an elderly gentleman in a security guard uniform.

"Do you have your own private security here?" Rhetta asked as she whipped her head around to stare at the guard.

"No, just for today. With so many people invited, Anjanette thought it would be best, especially to protect our neighbors' privacy."

"Who is Anjanette?"

He threw his head back and laughed. "Anjanette is your hostess, my dear Rhetta. She is also my mother."

CHAPTER 12

JEREMY EASED THE RED powerhouse into an alley and along a private rear circle drive. When he held up and aimed a remote opener, a wrought iron gate swung out noiselessly. Nestled under towering cottonwood trees behind the main residence sat a second house, a charming brick, gambrel-roofed structure with double garage doors and a massive wood entry door that took up the entire front. At the edge of the yard stood a majestic oak tree, one of the largest Rhetta had ever seen. She heard a gaggle of voices, laughter and water splashing from somewhere past the humongous flower garden that lay between where they were, and where she supposed the pool area was.

Stopping at the garage, Jeremy spoke into a voice-activated garage door opener, and one of the large wooden garage doors creaked upward.

"This used to be the stables, years ago. Then it became a garage sometime in the 1930's." Jeremy began a commentary as they sat in the idling Mustang waiting for the heavy doors to creep upward. "While it was a stable, there was a blacksmith shop, right over there near that oak tree." He nodded toward the tree Rhetta had just admired.

While driving the circle drive looking for a place to park, Rhetta had noticed a large attached garage that had been a tasteful addition to the main house in front. "So, this is a second garage?"

"In a sense, yes." He beamed at her again. "But I also live in the apartment upstairs."

Ricky hasn't told me any of this. She realized that she'd never asked many questions about Jeremy because she didn't care for him. *Wonder if*

Ricky had picked up on that and that's why she didn't rave too much about him? She'd find Ricky and ask her all about him. Now that she thought about it, she wondered why Jeremy wasn't with Ricky. Where had he been? When he began to ease the car forward, she said, "Can you just let me out here?"

"I thought you might want to see how nicely the carriage house turned out. Ricky said you remodeled your farmhouse, so I thought you might want a tour." He sounded disappointed because Rhetta wanted out of the car. She didn't know why he wanted to show her his apartment when she barely knew him.

Tour? What makes him think I want a tour? "All right. That would be nice." *No, it wouldn't.* She had to admit she was curious. Okay, nosy.

Inside the garage, the floors were painted a gleaming grey, with not a speck of dirt anywhere. In the other parking space rested a Chevy four-wheel-drive dually, also spotless. The driver's door bore a green oval with three black letters, JSP. His work truck, she guessed. *Pretty sweet work truck.* It didn't look like it had ever worked a day in its waxed and polished life. The maroon paint gleamed like new.

He motioned toward the stairs at the back of the garage. "After you."

She climbed the new wooden staircase, and waited at the top of the stairs as Jeremy eased past her with keys in hand. There wasn't much room on the three foot-square landing. When he reached around her, his arm draped casually over her shoulder. She flinched. Was he flirting with her? She needed to make a quick exit. Maybe she was over-reacting. She took a deep breath to calm herself.

The door opened, and in spite of being uneasy with Jeremy, she was in awe of the gorgeous interior. She stepped in as he waited for her to enter ahead of him, and took in the luxurious apartment. The gleaming kitchen space sparkled with new, brushed stainless steel appliances tucked into custom cherry wood cabinetry and granite countertops. Two chocolate brown leather couches formed an L around a glass top table in front of a rock fireplace. The air inside the loft was pleasantly cool. Soft lighting glowed from a back room, which she assumed was the bedroom area.

He must have noticed her looking in that direction. "Come, let me show you the master suite." He began walking toward the bedroom.

When she didn't follow he walked back to her and took her hand as though it the most natural thing in the world. She pulled back as though singed with a red-hot fireplace poker. "What do you think you're doing?"

"I know you want this as much as I do, Rhetta. Come on."

She whirled around and seized the doorknob, but it wouldn't turn. It was locked. "Let me out of here," she said, spinning back to him, her temper flaring. He'd come up silently behind her, and stood inches from her face. He reached out and seized her shoulders pulling her to him. "Stop it. Right now." She reached up and pushed against his chest.

Instead of stopping, he leaned in against her. She pushed again, but he was solidly built, and didn't move. She turned her face away.

Anger boiled over inside of her and she gritted her teeth. "Don't make me hurt you. Open the damn door." He threw his head back and laughed. She seized the opportunity and brought her knee up squarely in his groin.

His blue eyes widened in surprise as he slumped over, clutching his injury. She held her hand out. "Give me the key, Jeremy."

He reached into his pocket and withdrew the key. "Bitch," he groaned, as he handed it to her. "You'll pay for this."

She snatched it, and unlocked the door. "Thanks for the ride." She tossed the key at him and smiled as it bounced off his face. She slammed the door and bolted down the stairs.

CHAPTER 13

AT THE FOOT OF the stairway down to the garage, Rhetta paused to catch her breath. The air there wasn't nearly as cool as the upstairs apartment. She began to feel her hair dampen from the humidity. Although sweat broke out across her forehead, she felt chilled. The encounter with Jeremy combined with the odor of car tires and warm engine made her stomach queasy. Still aggravated, she jerked open the Mustang's passenger door and reached in the back to retrieve the tote bag containing the wine, along with her purse. As she did, she spotted a thick unmarked manila folder. Glancing up the stairs, making sure that Jeremy hadn't followed her, she picked it up and opened it.

She skimmed through the contents, mostly Excel spreadsheets, which she figured contained mundane accounting information on the subdivision development and started to put it back. Nothing on the sheets identified exactly what the figures represented. After another glance up toward Jeremy's door, she decided to scrutinize a couple of pages. As she scanned down the first sheet, she noted entries marked *"California,"* with large sums next to each entry. Deposits? On the next sheet were listed expenses for dirt moving, concrete, and building materials. She recognized the debit entries to the local building supply companies. The bottom line showed a modest balance, less than $50,000.00.

She flipped to the back page, which was blank, but had a stack of unsigned lien waivers clipped to it. She thumbed through them. Underneath those was a huge stack of unpaid invoices from the same companies that were marked *"paid"* on the previous page. The last page was another spreadsheet, listing all the unpaid bills.

She was looking at a set of duplicate reports. The top sheets must've been the ones he showed everyone, while the bottom one painted the true picture. And it didn't look good. The unpaid invoices meant that Jeremy had to be skimming money from his investors, if the deposits were accurate. The *"paid"* column amounts on the first set of papers matched the invoices, but on the bottom of the stack, those invoices were stamped *Past Due*. She replaced the folder on the seat where she found it and looked over her shoulder. He still hadn't followed her down the stairs. Heart thudding at her discovery, she grabbed her belongings and sprinted for the door.

Once outside the garage the enormity of everything she'd seen and just been through assaulted her stomach and she winced in pain. Not only was Jeremy bent on fooling around with other women, he was cheating his investors, too. He probably couldn't be loyal to anyone. He was no better than pond scum. She leaned against the garage and massaged her abdomen. Acid reflux kicked into overdrive. She fished around in an inner compartment in her purse for her little green pills. Tearing open the foil, she swallowed two without water. She picked her way through the yard until she located a flagstone walkway edged in a colorful abundance of zinnias, begonias and marigolds that led toward the main house. She trudged along the walk, wondering what she should say, if anything, to Ricky about what she'd seen, and about what Jeremy had done.

She needed to find Ricky and talk with her, and determine how serious Ricky felt about this jerk before she'd tell her anything. If Ricky and Jeremy weren't "in a relationship," she'd say nothing of his unwanted advances to her. If Ricky was all gaga over this creep, she'd have to find a way to tell her how sleazy he was. Her heartburn increased.

As to the folder, she decided she'd ask Randolph's advice before telling anyone anything.

* * *

Reaching the end of the walk, she encountered a tall wooden fence with an ornately trimmed gate at one end. Finding the gate unlocked, she pushed it open and discovered she was poolside among a throng of swimsuit-clad guests. Busy chatting and drinking, they ignored her as she edged past them and around the pool. Someone dove in and splashed her as she passed. A burst of laughter followed and she waved. No harm. The water felt good. She ducked under an arbor and entered a gazebo where there were more guests. These folks were somewhat less scantily clad. And from the size and shape of them, it was probably just as well.

So far, she hadn't seen anyone she knew personally. As she'd made her way around the pool, she thought she recognized some other bankers from the "big box" banks, but she couldn't be sure. They may have looked different to her since she had never seen any of them without their clothes before. The only time she saw most of them was at the Chamber of Commerce meetings, where they almost always dressed in suits. Of course, some of the women were pretty scantily clad there, too, come to think of it.

Once past the gazebo, she cut across a cobblestone patio with an open pergola. The wood slats across the top were draped in a flowering vine abundant with saucer-sized purple flowers. A custom outdoor kitchen occupied the entire west end of the patio. A mouth-watering aroma of grilling meat wafted toward her. At the barbeque pit stood a man covered in a long white apron over white jeans and sporting a chef's hat that bounced and jiggled as he deftly worked the grill. She recognized James, the chef from *Restaurant du Jour*, a favorite eatery of hers and Randolph's.

She waved at him as she pulled open one of the French doors to the house. Inside, blessedly cool air welcomed her into a sea of guests who were busy chatting, laughing and holding beverages. Many were snacking from a heavy pine table mounded with appetizers. Across the room, which was probably a gathering room, judging from the casually elegant stainless steel and leather furniture in a semi-circle in front of a fireplace, she noticed a hand waving toward her. The hand, arm, and soon the rest of Ricky emerged from a cluster of people.

"Rhetta! Over here," she called.

"Hey!" Rhetta answered, and glanced around. She held up the tote. "Where shall I put this wine?"

"Follow me," said her friend. Rhetta squeezed in behind Ricky and trailed her into the lavish kitchen that must have been renovated about the same time as Jeremy's apartment. Rhetta recognized the same high quality craftsmanship in the cabinetry along with similar high-end stainless steel appliances. She set the bottles down on a shiny granite countertop, and folded the tote into her purse.

"Let me introduce you to our hostess," Ricky said, sliding an arm through Rhetta's and leading her out to an extension of the patio, toward a silver-haired lady holding court near a water fountain. "Anjanette Spears, meet my best friend, Rhetta McCarter." As Rhetta smiled at Anjanette, she resolved to find a way to pull Ricky away and talk to her privately, and soon.

The hostess beamed at Rhetta and extended her hand. Rhetta grasped it and was surprised at the strength in the older woman's handshake. "So pleased to meet you, Mrs. Spears."

Anjanette laughed, revealing beautiful white teeth, undoubtedly the work of the same orthodontist who had worked on Jeremy. The smile was far too bright for a lady who had to be pushing seventy. "Please, my friends all call me Anjanette, as must you, dear Rhetta." When she spoke, her voice warbled as though in a song. She wore her silver hair pulled back and held by an ornate silver clasp at the base of her neck. Silver spiral earrings inlaid with diamond chips danced as did her bright blue eyes when she spoke. Taller than Rhetta, even in the flat silver sandals, her slim figure in pale blue slacks and bright print blouse belied her age.

She was gorgeous, Rhetta had to admit.

"You have a beautiful home, truly lovely." Rhetta said. It was the truth. What she didn't say out loud, was, "How the heck did you pay for all this?"

CHAPTER 14

As Rhetta and Ricky wandered among the guests, Rhetta commented that someone was missing.

"Where's Jeremy?" she asked, feigning ignorance about knowing exactly where Jeremy was. What she didn't understand was why he hadn't yet joined his girlfriend and his guests. She smiled, thinking maybe he was too sore to walk around. Maybe she could escape before he showed up, thus avoiding any awkwardness.

Ricky glanced at her watch and frowned. "He had an appointment with a client, but he should be here by now." Then she smiled. "I'm sure he'll be along in time to wolf down a steak."

Rhetta glanced at her friend. Ricky was stunning in a pair of green shorts with matching tank top, her long red locks held back with a simple scrunchie that matched her top. She needed to tell her about Jeremy. She didn't need to know whether they were a couple or not to do the right thing.

"Listen, Ricky, I...." Before she could finish, Jeremy materialized at Ricky's side. He leaned in and kissed her, cutting his eyes toward Rhetta with a cold stare. She glared back. She wanted to stick out her tongue.

Ricky threaded her arm through Jeremy's. "There you are. We were wondering where you'd gotten to."

Rhetta raised an eyebrow. She'd been practicing that one-eyebrow raising thing that Woody did so well. She discovered it came in really handy. That Jeremy had changed into tan chinos from his white shorts was not lost on her. She smiled.

Anjanette joined them. "Jeremy, darling, would you be a dear and check in with the chef to be sure he has enough steaks for all of our guests?"

"Of course. Come with me, Ricky," he added, steering her toward the patio. He leaned in and whispered something and Ricky giggled.

Oh, crap, she has it bad.

"Don't they make a lovely couple?" Anjanette asked. "I'm so glad that we called Ricky when we were looking for someone to list our lots out in the new subdivision."

So, that's how they met.

"Yes, lovely."

Anjanette took Rhetta's arm and walked her away from the guests until they stood alone in the foyer. Rhetta wondered what the woman wanted.

"Such an unfortunate incident at the barn," she began. *Unfortunate incident? Yes, indeed, finding a body was quite unfortunate—especially for the dead guy.*

"I'm told that your husband is a former judge. I was hoping he would be here with you today."

Huh? "Well, actually, Randolph—" Before she could finish, Anjanette interrupted, laying her slim hand on Rhetta's arm. Each of her fingers bore heavy jeweled rings as though to camouflage the age spots and rather gnarly fingers.

"I so want to be able to move quickly past this incident and continue the project. This is such an inconvenience. I imagine the deceased is some derelict who chose to die in that barn. Now we must put our project on hold. I was so hoping Judge McCarter could help us with this."

Holy crap. This woman is nuts. I guess the derelict buried himself there, too. Doesn't she get it?

"I understand only the barn is off limits for now, until the investigation is over," Rhetta said. "What's so critical about the barn?"

"The barn needs to be taken down immediately so that we can pour a slab there for the tennis courts."

"I see. That's critical, all right." She deliberately tried to sound sarcastic.

Clearly, it went over her hostess' head. Anjanette tossed her superbly coiffed head back and laughed. "Well, not just the tennis courts, of course, but the pool and the clubhouse will all be in that area. We must have those amenities in place to lure builders to build the type of homes Jeremy is planning for the lots. So, you see, it is critical to get the barn removed as soon as possible."

Rhetta just shook her head. While she was hoping for several mortgage loans from the subdivision, she couldn't fathom this woman's coldness about the "derelict" who chose to die in the barn. This conversation was totally off the wall.

To get away from the Ice Queen, as Rhetta now thought of her, she asked," Is there a bathroom nearby?"

Anjanette motioned toward the hall with her jewelry-laden hand. "Down there. Second door on the right." As Rhetta moved away, Anjanette returned to her guests.

Rhetta meandered down the hallway, peeking into the first door on the right. Inside was a beautifully appointed office. She scoped the hallway and finding no one around, eased open the door and entered. She closed the door softly behind her. Against one wall was a large oak roll-top desk, modernized to hold a computer and all the peripherals, like a printer and scanner.

A polished oak gun cabinet stood against the opposite wall. Alongside the cabinet, the wall was decorated with framed awards. She tiptoed to the glass-fronted cabinet and spied several cleaned and blued rifles lined up like sentries in their slots inside. When she glanced at the awards she was surprised to learn that Anjanette Spears was an expert shot. This was definitely not the bathroom.

She sidled to the desk where she marveled at the sleek flat-screen monitor, wireless keyboard and accessories. The computer itself was out of sight. Curious about the type of computer, Rhetta began looking for the unit. It had to be pretty small to be concealed inside this desk. She wondered what brand it was. She needed a new one at the office and would love to have a small CPU, or one that was altogether with the monitor. She glanced around the top of the desk without spotting it, so she opened a few of the doors.

One side door opened to a series of drawers behind it. She pulled the top drawer but it stuck. She tugged it harder, and the drawer sailed out. When she knelt to retrieve the contents that had spilled on to the carpeted floor, she was eye level with the empty space where the drawer had been. She peered into the cavity. Something was lodged at the back, probably the reason the drawer was sticking. She reached for it.

She stared at a handwritten envelope bearing an old postmark. Even with squinting, she couldn't make out the date. She fished out her glasses from her purse and tried again. If she wasn't misreading it, this envelope was postmarked nearly sixteen years ago.

Using her thumb, she opened the flap on the envelope open and withdrew the letter.

"To my dearest Anjie," it began. What followed was obviously a love letter. As Rhetta scanned to the bottom, she thought how sweet it was that Mrs. Spears had kept this letter sent to her by her late husband, probably when he was away on a trip. She felt guilty for invading the woman's privacy.

Then, she spotted the signature line: "All my love, Malcom."

CHAPTER 15

RHETTA BLINKED IN SURPRISE and then re-read it. Malcom? Malcom Griffith, Willard Spears' partner? Had Anjanette Spears been having an affair with Malcom Griffith at the time of his disappearance? If that was so, then who was the exotic pole dancer everyone talked about?

The ramifications of what she held in her hand hit her squarely between the eyes in an instant headache that shot outward to her temples. She dropped the letter back into the envelope, and tucked it into the drawer with the rest of the contents. She pushed it to go back in place, but it resisted. She shoved harder, wanting desperately to leave the office that she'd carelessly entered to investigate.

As she struggled with the desk, she heard two people talking as they walked down the hall, their voices growing louder as they neared the office. She slammed both palms into the drawer, and this time it yielded, and slid into place. Her headache pounded as the voices got closer. She closed the door that concealed the drawers, then jumped as it clicked loudly when it latched. She desperately prayed that the two people, who sounded like they'd stopped in front of the office door, didn't hear it. Frantically, she eyeballed the room for a place to hide. The voices grew louder as they disagreed. Rhetta couldn't quite make out their words, but she could tell a man and a woman were arguing. She spotted a closet and streaked for it, tugged open the door and shot inside, only to discover that instead of a regular closet containing articles of clothing or coats, she thudded against steel filing cabinets. More noise. Her heart hammered as she turned around, sucked in a breath and pulled the door closed. She could barely fit.

In her hasty retreat, she'd forgotten to turn off the light. She began to sweat.

Her hiding place had louvered doors, which allowed her to peer through the slats. Had a light been on inside the closet, she would have been seen. Luckily, that side of the room was dim—the vertical blinds at the window were still closed. She prayed she wouldn't be spotted. Her heart thudded so loudly that not only was she afraid they'd hear it, but also that they'd feel the vibration all the way across the room, like a 6.2 earthquake on the Richter scale. She'd managed her escape just in time to watch Jeremy and Anjanette enter the office and stop in front of the desk in the exact spot she had just vacated.

Anjanette's pleasant disposition had disappeared. When she spoke, she fairly hissed. Rhetta saw her face contort in anger.

His response was caustic. "All right, *Mother*," he said, with a dripping dose of sarcasm on the word *mother*. "I'll make sure this situation gets cleared up."

"See to it that you do, or there might be consequences."

He threw his head back and laughed. "Consequences? Of course there's going to be consequences. The first of which will be that we won't be able to build anything there anytime soon." He sidled over to an elegant stuffed chair, one of a pair that faced each other across a marble top coffee table. He dropped into the chair and draped a leg lazily over one of the arms.

Anjanette sat primly at the edge of the leather desk chair, pulled open a middle drawer that Rhetta had not previously noticed and withdrew a business checkbook. She scribbled quickly, tore out a check, then stood and handed it to Jeremy.

"This needs to last you a while. I don't know how much more I can give you."

He leapt to his feet and in one stride stood directly in her face. "I," he said, poking her in the chest with his index finger, "will be the one to decide that." His voice dropped in pitch, and sounded like a snarl as he snatched the check from her, then strode toward the door.

Rhetta's hand flew over her mouth. *Oh, God, how am I ever going to get Ricky away from this slime bucket? And what the heck was going on?*

Why was Anjanette giving money to Jeremy? From what she saw of his books, he was getting plenty from his investors.

After he closed the door, Anjanette slumped into the desk chair, buried her head in her arms and began weeping.

Lordy, she'll be here awhile. I'll be stiff as a board smashed in this closet. Rhetta needed to move, to change positions. Her butt muscles began to cramp, then her legs. She dared not move and risk exposure. She was a fast talker, but she'd never be able to convince Anjanette Spears that she got lost looking for the bathroom and wound up in a closet. A muscle spasm vibrated down the back of her leg, followed by a searing pain from a sciatic nerve as she continued cramping. She wanted to whimper. She stuffed her fist into her mouth. Tears from the pain began to trickle down her cheek. She tried to take deep breaths, but was terrified of being discovered, so she sucked in jerky little gasps instead.

Anjanette reached for a tissue and dabbed her eyes, then rose, closed the checkbook and held it to her chest. She glanced around the room, then took the checkbook with her and went through a doorway that must have led into the bathroom. Rhetta heard water run.

Rhetta slid open the louvered door, and stumbled for the doorway leading to the hall. She snatched it open.

And stood face-to-face with Jeremy.

Jeremy paled when he saw her. He grabbed her by the shoulders. "What were you doing in the office?"

"Take your hands off me, and right now," she said, stage whispering into his ear and totally ignoring his question. She shrugged emphatically as he released his grip. She sidestepped him without answering, and trotted briskly down the hall to rejoin the guests. Let him figure out what, if anything, she was doing in there.

Her stomach had turned to jelly, and her hands began to shake. Perspiration covered her forehead, and dripped down her nose. Now she really had to use the bathroom. As soon as he could get herself together, she had to find Ricky.

CHAPTER 16

AFTER SUCCESSFULLY FINDING A restroom, but being unsuccessful in locating Ricky, Rhetta wandered out to the patio and sidled up to James. His fluffy white chef's hat bobbed as he grilled. "Have you seen Ricky Lane?"

"Not in the last fifteen minutes or so," James answered. "She stopped with him to check on the food, then went out to the pool area." When he said *him*, he rolled his eyes with much exaggeration.

"I guess you mean Jeremy?" Rhetta laughed when he nodded. "Thanks a bunch, James." Rhetta finger-waggled a backward wave at him, and headed to the pool. Rhetta was still unable to locate Ricky even after threading her way once again through the assembled poolsiders. She decided not to go back to the house in search of her friend. She wanted to leave and go home to her sane and normal husband. She had known dysfunctional people before, but these folks ranked right up there amongst the worst. She was amazed that Ricky couldn't see through them. In fact, Ricky was probably having a big time somewhere inside the house. Rhetta couldn't stand any more time there of any kind, so she trotted to the back of the yard.

The air hung muggy and close, without a breeze to moderate the humidity. The late afternoon sun bronzed the glistening bodies. Many guests already wore bright red patches of sunburned skin on shoulders, cheeks, backs and noses. They'd be paying tomorrow for their fun today. As she walked, she riffled through her purse, pulled out her cell phone and dialed Ricky's number. The call went straight to voice mail. She left a message as she walked down the flagstone path, going back to the alley the way she'd come in. "Ricky, I had to leave, and couldn't find you. Call me when you get a chance." Rhetta hit END and dropped the phone into her purse.

She passed Jeremy's garage/house, and couldn't tell if anyone was there. The garage doors were tightly closed. Arriving at the gate leading into the alley, she leaned a shoulder against it. After a great effort, she managed to shove it open. She wondered why it was so hard to push until she noticed the spring-loaded hinges. And a tiny red flashing light. It was designed to be opened electronically. With her luck, she probably set off a burglar alarm. She didn't care. Ignoring the sun beating down on her, she walked briskly toward Henderson, and her car. She nodded to the watchman on her way out. And swatted away the drops of perspiration that ran down her nose.

* * *

Rhetta turned on the radio and the air conditioner. Sweat had plastered her hair against her scalp then dripped down her forehead and her nose after the uphill hike to her car. Inside the car, she located a box of tissues, and wiped down her face. Makeup smeared onto the tissue. She glanced at her watch. It was still early, barely five o'clock. Her stomach grumbled. The steaks had smelled so great when she first inhaled the mouth-watering scent of James' grilling. She'd head home and throw a couple of steaks on their gas grill and cook for Randolph.

Maybe she should call Randolph and tell him she was on her way home early. She pulled up to a red light, and groped in her purse for her cell. Sometimes when her phone was buried in her bag, she couldn't hear it ring. She found it and glanced at the screen. No messages. She called Randolph and when he didn't answer, she left him a message. "Hi, Sweets, I'm on my way home. If you'll take a couple of steaks out of the freezer, I'll grill them."

Her mind returned to Ricky. How should she approach telling her about Jeremy? Rhetta badly wanted to know more about Jeremy and Anjanette Spears. She tapped her favorites list for the one guy who kept up with everybody and anything Cape Girardeau—her personal information resource that she'd nicknamed Woody-the-Answer-Man-dot-com.

He answered on the second ring.

"Is this Woody-the-Answer-Man?" She reached over to crank the air conditioning on high and turn the radio off.

Woody chuckled. "So what do you need to know about the Family Spears?"

"How did you know that's why I called?" The light changed and she edged over to the right lane.

"I know you."

"I know you know me, but how do you know I wanted to ask you about the great American dysfunctional family?"

"It's Saturday afternoon, and you were going there for a pool party, to which I wasn't invited, by the way, and now you call me. It's a given."

"Hey, I wasn't in charge of the invites." Rhetta stopped for another red light at the corner of Broadway and Kingshighway. "I wish I hadn't gone."

"That bad?"

"Yep. Worse. I'll tell you about it Monday. I don't want to talk about my experience over a cell phone."

Woody whistled. "Since when?"

"Look, things were pretty weird, and I promise I'll fill you in, but first some info. How was Mrs. Spears able to buy that house?"

"What happened to not wanting to talk about stuff on a cell phone?"

"This is different."

Woody sighed. "Uh-huh. If you say so. Anyhow, the details are public record by now. Agnes Dalton-Evers with Tri-County Realty told me that Mrs. Spears paid cash for the house. Agnes handled the sale as both the buyer's and sellers' agent. It closed real quick for a short sale. You know how long it usually takes for a bank short sale. In fact they should call them long sales." Woody chuckled at his own joke. When banks sold homes through short sales, they could sometimes take up to a year or longer to close.

"Must've been a local bank that owned it, and not one of the big national bad boys," Rhetta said.

"Yep, our competitor, Cape First Bank."

"How short was it?"

"I'm not sure about that, but Agnes said Mrs. Spears paid right at a million for the place."

Rhetta nearly swerved into a Honda. "Did you say one million? Dollars? Where in God's name did she get that kind of money?"

"I don't think the name on the policy was God's." Woody chuckled. "I heard she collected two point five million bucks from her husband's death."

"Did you say million? With all the zeros? How come you never told me about this before now?"

"You didn't ask."

"Woody, you know Jeremy is dating Ricky. You should've told me."

"You should've asked."

He's right. I should have asked. Woody always knows this stuff. "That explains how she got the big bucks."

The light changed to green and Rhetta accelerated. "Woody, exactly how did Willard Spears die?"

"He had a stroke or a seizure or something like it. Went pretty quickly."

She resolved to check the newspaper obits to find out more.

CHAPTER 17

AS SHE ZOOMED WESTWARD out of Cape toward home, Rhetta tapped her phone, pulled up her recent calls, and hit redial on Ricky's number. Again it went straight into voice mail. Ricky must've turned her phone off. Rhetta dropped her phone into her purse.

As she made a left turn, she heard her phone ringing. Certain that Ricky was calling her back, Rhetta plunged her arm into her purse and managed to locate the phone in time to answer it.

"Ricky, I've been trying to call you. I need to talk—"

Before she could finish, an unfamiliar voice asked, "Is this Rhetta McCarter?"

Rhetta pulled the phone away from her ear and glanced at the number displayed for the caller. It was the Illinois number.

"This is Rhetta McCarter." Rhetta said as she slowed, then turned into a convenience store parking lot. If this gravel-voiced woman wanted a loan, the conversation might get lengthy. Rhetta didn't think she could focus on driving and talking to a customer at the same time.

"My name is Mylene Allard," the woman said, then paused.

Rhetta did a rapid scan of her memory and was sure she didn't know her caller. "What can I do for you?"

"I need you to meet me at Jeremy Spears' barn at nine o'clock tonight. Come alone, and do NOT mention this to anyone, do you understand?"

Rhetta's stomach flipped. *Who the heck is this Mylene Allard? And why on earth did she want me to meet her at the barn?* In spite of having been uncomfortably warm in the late afternoon heat, especially after her recent trek to her car, goose bumps erupted on her arms.

She blurted, "I don't think so. I'm not going out there alone at nine o'clock tonight. You just need to tell me what you want, or I can call the police and have them meet you out there instead."

Before she could ask Mylene Allard how she got her phone number, and why she wanted her to meet her at the barn, Mylene disconnected. *Crap. I'm not a very good detective. Good thing I'm a banker.* Rhetta pounded her hand on the steering wheel. *Now I'll never know what she wanted. She'll probably never call back.* Rhetta was mad at herself for not playing a little cozier with Mylene. Then again, who knows who this person is? She may be a serial killer.

Rhetta quickly dialed Randolph. His call went to voice mail. She called Ricky, and again the call went to voice mail. *Doesn't anybody answer the phone?* She thought about the call for a few minutes, and even started to call back. Good sense prevailed for once, so she didn't call.

Rhetta glanced at her watch. It was only 5:30. She pulled back on to Kingshighway, passed a truck loaded with logs, and punched the accelerator for home.

* * *

Fifteen minutes later, she pulled into her driveway, after waving to Mrs. Koblyk. When she opened the garage door, she found the spot that was normally occupied by Randolph's truck empty.

If he'd left, she wondered again why he hadn't answered her call. She spotted his cell phone on the kitchen counter, plugged into his charger. If he went off without his phone, as he sometimes did, that would explain why he didn't answer. She picked it up and glanced at it, seeing the missed call from her number.

Rhetta set her purse on the countertop and peered out the sliding door, and didn't spot any of the cats. They'd show up magically as soon as they started to fire up the grill. Peering around, she glimpsed the Artmobile alongside the Garage Mahal. Randolph's art trailer was hooked to it. He must've gone down there to load up some paintings to take to the gallery, and forgotten to take his cell phone. *That's probably where the cats are, too.* She hadn't bothered to call their house phone. She didn't think about calling it, since they seldom used the land line. In fact, she'd decided to have it disconnected, since the only reason she kept the house phone was because she'd occasionally call the house and leave herself a message about something she might need to remember at home. She used her cell phone for everything else.

She jogged down the circular path to the garage. Not finding him around the truck or trailer, she stuck her head inside the garage and called to him, but got no reply. After a quick scan inside, she returned outside and began circling the garage, calling out again. Still no answer. *Where could he be?* Then she heard the distinctive meowing of the cats. She followed the sound to the back of the barn. The cats were lined up staring at something on the ground, their tails swishing. A couple of them were meowing. She jogged over to the cats, and spotted a jeans-clad leg and a foot wearing one of Randolph's boots on the ground behind the dumpster.

Her heart sunk to her stomach in fear as she bent over his still form. "Oh, God, Randolph. What happened? Are you all right?" He moaned then, and began to move. The side of his head bore an ugly, blood-soaked welt. "Are you all right?" Rhetta asked again, caressing his face. He groaned, then tried to sit up.

She put a hand on his shoulder. "Don't move, Sweets. I'm calling an ambulance."

His eyes fluttered open, and although he appeared to be dazed, he recognized her. "Rhetta," he said, and closed his eyes again.

"What happened?" she asked.

He mumbled something she couldn't understand. She patted his arm, desperately trying to remain calm. "Sweets, can you understand me?"

He mumbled, "Yes."

"Do not move." She spoke slowly, and with as much authority as she could muster. She realized her phone was in the house, in her purse, which was on the counter alongside his cell phone. "I'm going into your studio to call 9-1-1. I'll be right back." She stood and made sure he remained quiet. He did. She raced to the barn, which sat behind the garage. Randolph's new, larger studio was a finished area inside the barn. She snatched the phone extension.

Once she'd given the Emergency Operator the necessary information, Rhetta ran back to her husband, thankful for the phone in the studio. She resolved to keep the land line service.

CHAPTER 18

THREE HOURS AFTER TESTS and scans in the emergency room at St. Mark's Hospital revealed nothing more serious than a mild concussion, Randolph insisted on going home—in spite of the emergency room physician's recommendation that he spend the night for observation. Rhetta had informed the doctor that Randolph had been out cold when she found him. Randolph insisted that he wasn't.

When they were alone, Rhetta took her husband's hand. His head bore a serious bandage across the welt and his face had been cleaned up.

"I know you want to go home, but because of your last head injury, Doctor Marinthe wants you to spend the night to be sure everything is all right. He remembers your previous accident."

"This does hurt," he said, touching the bandage on his head, and wincing.

"Do you remember what happened" She pulled the sheet up and tucked it around him. *Why are emergency rooms always so cold?*

"The Dumpster lid got me." He smiled crookedly, then flinched. "I guess I shouldn't have tried holding the lid open and swinging the trash bag in at the same time. Next time, I'll know to make sure it's all the way open first." He shivered, and Rhetta reached for the thermal blanket folded on the table. "The next thing I knew, you were standing over me."

She kissed the side of his face. "I agree totally with Dr. Marinthe. You're going to spend the night."

"All right, if you say I was out, then I guess I'll stay." He grasped her hand, and squeezed.

"You were indeed out, and yes, I insist." She squeezed back.

"Your wife is right, of course," said Dr. Marinthe, sliding the privacy curtain aside and walking toward the gurney. Marinthe's limp was evidenced in his shuffling gait. He pulled a stool out from under the counter and sat by Randolph. "We will have a room ready in about ten minutes." His French accent lent a musical lilt to his words.

Marinthe, who hailed from French West Africa, was Randolph's hospitalist following his wreck. The slight-framed doctor rolled the stool to a nearby computer station and keyed in his notes. He tucked the stool away, and returned to Randolph's bedside. "It is good to see you again, my friend, but I am sorry it is because of another *calamité*." He smiled and turned to Rhetta. "His head is very hard, *non*?"

"That's true in more ways than one, Doctor," Rhetta said and smiled.

"I will check on you later, my friend," Marinthe said, patted Randolph's shoulder, then left.

Rhetta had just begun gathering up her husband's clothes, wallet and personal items when an orderly arrived to take him to a room. Rhetta accompanied them on the trip upstairs, and waited while the staff got him settled in.

"The doctor would prefer that you have only liquids until tomorrow morning." The orderly broke the news to him as he tucked a warm blanket around Randolph.

Rhetta's stomach growled. She hadn't stayed at the pool party long enough to eat, nor had she been able to grill steaks at home. The memory of the wonderful scent of the grilling steaks made her stomach rumble. She realized she was famished.

"That's all right, I'm not hungry," Randolph said, as he wriggled down into the covers.

"I'm hungry enough to eat a couple double cheeseburgers by myself," Rhetta said. Her stomach growled in agreement.

"You go on and get something to eat. I'm in good hands here," Randolph said.

She leaned in and kissed him, then headed for the door. "I love you. Be a good patient," she admonished wagging an index finger at him.

Walking down the hall to the elevator, she realized that in all the excitement she hadn't told Randolph about the party, or about the strange phone call. *Oh, well. It can wait until morning.*

She checked her phone. Still no call from Ricky. She dialed again. Voice mail. Now, she was worried. *Had that scumbag of a boyfriend done something to her?* Although Ricky claimed Jeremy was "younger," Rhetta wasn't sure who Ricky thought he was younger than. Certainly not her or Ricky. Methuselah, perhaps. During their close encounter, she spotted telltale crows' feet that indicated he was on the long side past forty. Probably the Botox was wearing off. In fact, her rapid mental calculations determined that Jeremy was an adult when Malcom Griffith "disappeared." Might he have had something to do with that, should the body turn out to be Griffith's?

* * *

As Rhetta pulled out of the parking lot, she dropped her visor down to temper the glare from the setting sun. She paused at the exit and groped through her console for a pair of sunglasses. The daylight, although waning, was still bright enough that she had to squint. Glasses in place, radio blasting, she began singing along with the Beach Boys as she cruised to the hamburger stand. McDonald's sat just a hop across the interstate on the Gordonville Road.

Although nearing eight, the drive-thru lines were slow going, filled to capacity with university students crowded into vehicles snaking around the restaurant. She glanced at her watch. If she could get her food quickly enough, she might have time to drive by the barn, just to see if someone showed up there. She was pretty sure that this Mylene Allard, whoever she was, couldn't know what kind of vehicle she drove. Decision made, she'd drive past the barn and scope it out.

CHAPTER 19

TEN MINUTES LATER, AFTER suffering through two teenage girls working at the window, followed by a pimply-faced boy with a nose ring, and finally the assistant manager, they finally got her complicated order straight—two double cheeseburgers, ketchup only, no pickles or onions. She tossed the bag of food on to the passenger seat. She eased into the last parking space available and unwrapped the food.

She hadn't eaten all day, so she'd ordered two. No fries, although she dearly loved the famous sweet-salty skinny fries. She sighed. *Two cheeseburgers means I'll have to run an extra mile or two tomorrow.* She inhaled the distinct aroma of the McDonald's temptation and took a gigantic bite. It was heaven. While she chewed and dabbed at the grease dripping from her chin, she tried to remember the last McDonald's burger she'd eaten. It had to be over a year ago. She'd been working hard not to eat fast foods and ran to stay in shape. She sipped her diet Coke, and folded up the first wrapper. Appetite partially sated, she set the second burger aside and backed out of the parking slot. She decided to wait until she finished the soda to see if she was still hungry enough to eat the second one. Maybe her eyes had been bigger than her stomach, as her mother would have said.

Recalling her mother's expression made her heart ache, as it did whenever she remembered how an aneurysm resulting from cancer claimed her nearly ten years before. When that happened, her father was nowhere to be found, and hadn't attended the funeral. He'd abandoned them when

Rhetta was only two, only to show up mysteriously a few months ago, giving her a locket that had belonged to her mother. She lost the treasure when she lost Cami. She wasn't hungry anymore. She rewrapped the second burger, placed it back in the sack, and tossed it all into the trash container as she left.

The sun was nearly down, its orange dome mere minutes away from sliding over the horizon. Behind her, to the east, the inky night sky was too cloudy to see the stars. She pointed Streak straight for Oak Forest Subdivision. The crime scene tape that had earlier barricaded the entry was gone. Stopping at the gate, she drummed her fingers on the steering wheel. Now that she was here, she wasn't so sure about going in. Then she reasoned that the Allard woman not only didn't know what she drove, she undoubtedly wouldn't know what Rhetta looked like, either. She pulled in.

Winding her way slowly along the lane to the barn she reflected again on the strange phone call. Who was Mylene Allard, and why did she want to meet at this barn? How did she get her cell phone number? Then Rhetta realized her name had been in all the news reports about the gruesome discovery, so it would've been easy for someone to find her. Especially since her cell number was on all her business cards and in some of the advertising, too. However, that didn't explain why she wanted Rhetta there.

Rhetta stared ahead through the near dark. The barn stood like a sinister custodian guarding deathly secrets. This wasn't a good idea. She would turn around as soon as possible and leave. She didn't see any other lights or vehicles along the driveway. When she reached the barn, she was alone. She pulled up alongside and turned her radio down. She listened carefully, but heard nothing. The call from Mylene Allard, or whoever she was, was probably a hoax. She eased forward past the barn to turn around. As she did, she spotted a vehicle behind the barn—a maroon dually bearing a green oval logo on the door. She recognized Jeremy's work truck.

That settled it. She didn't relish bumping into Jeremy. Just the thought of another encounter with him made the burger in her stomach flip and her reflux kick in. She swallowed bile and quickly made a Y-turn, and headed back down the lane, grateful that Jeremy didn't come out and catch her cruising around his barn. His truck was the only vehicle there, so Mylene, whoever she was, hadn't shown up. Rhetta zipped back to the county road wondering now what Jeremy was doing out here at this time of evening. Did this Mylene know Jeremy would be at the barn? She puzzled again at the call.

Back on a paved road, Rhetta slowed, grappled through her purse for her cell phone and called Ricky.

This time, her friend answered. "Where are you, Rhetta? Why did you leave so early?"

"I, uh, am on my way home, again." That part was the truth. "I tried calling you when I left, but I guess your phone was off."

"I turned it off when I put my purse in the closet at Anjanette's house. I didn't turn it on until just a few minutes ago, after I got home. Jeremy and I had a terrible fight before I left. I thought maybe he'd call, but, no, he hasn't." She sighed. As though just realizing what Rhetta said, she answered, "What do you mean, on your way home, again?"

After Rhetta told her about Randolph, Ricky asked, "Is he all right?"

"He's just staying the night because he conked his head. Doctor Marinthe felt it would be best, considering his past head injury."

"Sure, that would be best. By the way, guess what I got today from Fed Ex? It was at my door when I got home." Ricky could change topics with lightning speed. Sometimes, it caused Rhetta mental whiplash trying to keep up.

"I give up. What?"

"I got a check for my Trans Am. But, it's kinda weird."

"What's weird about it?" Tiny alarm bells began tinkling in Rhetta's brain.

"It's for a thousand dollars more than the price of the car, with instructions for me to immediately send the extra thousand dollars by Western Union to their shipper, a man by the name of Trevor Brinkman in Paducah, Kentucky. The instructions say that Brinkman is waiting for me to send the funds. Why would I have to send money to the shipper?"

"Ricky, don't deposit the check, and especially don't send out any money. I think you've been scammed."

"What do you mean?"

"For one thing, eBay cautions against dealing with anyone who pays you outside of eBay channels, and especially, not to send anyone any funds via Western Union. Didn't you read all the selling instructions eBay provides?"

"I guess not. But this Brinkman sent me a business check. It looks legit. Except there are a couple of discrepancies."

"How so?"

"The guy who was emailing me said his name was Herman Epson, but this check is drawn on a commercial farm account in Corinth, Mississippi—Valley View Farms, Inc. with a different signature, which looks like Rita Wilson, while the Fed Ex envelope was sent from an address in Paducah. Isn't that strange?"

"You should turn this over to the FBI. This smells like an interstate scam. Shippers don't get paid in advance, and especially not by the seller. Let's look at this tomorrow, and see if we can figure it out."

* * *

After disconnecting with Ricky, Rhetta decided to check in on Randolph before going home. Even though Dr. Marinthe assured her that keeping Randolph was strictly for observation, she was worried, especially since Randolph had suffered a serious head injury earlier in the year.

When she reached his floor, a nurse rose from the station and greeted her. "Sorry, ma'am, but visiting hours are over."

"I wanted to check on my husband, Randolph McCarter before I go home."

The nurse, a statuesque woman of perhaps thirty, brushed an errant strand of mahogany colored hair from her eyes. "He's right in here," she said, pointing to a room across the hall. "He was resting when we checked on him a few minutes ago." She left the desk and led Rhetta across the hall. She pushed open the door and Rhetta leaned in. Randolph was sleeping peacefully, so she stepped back without going in.

"Thanks, I won't bother him. Dr. Marinthe said he should be able to leave in the morning, so I'll be back then."

The nurse nodded, and returned to her desk.

Rhetta skipped the elevator and bounded down the stairs. She'd also jogged up the two floors on her way in, hoping to get a head start on burning up the hamburger calories.

CHAPTER 20

MONDAY MORNING, RHETTA FLEW through the drive-through at Subway, and grabbed an egg-white-only sandwich on a wheat wrap, and a large cup of coffee. Traffic was especially light and she made it to work an hour early. This time, she noted with satisfaction, she beat Woody there, so she snagged the parking spot closest to the door. Grinning, she unlocked the office. The coffee aroma wafted tantalizingly. She set the steaming cup down carefully and unwrapped the sandwich. While waiting for the computer to boot up, she turned on the radio, then sat back, savoring her coffee and enjoying her breakfast.

This was going to be a great week, she just knew it. There were several loans that would be closing soon, plus this morning the fresh air smelled sweet with low humidity for the first time in weeks. With the clear sky and the songbirds chattering, the morning couldn't have been better.

When she had picked up Randolph from the hospital yesterday morning, Dr. Marinthe cautioned him to take it easy for a few days. Rhetta had hovered over him most of the day, much to his annoyance. Finally, she relented and didn't follow him out to his studio, where he said he just wanted to paint and unwind. She smiled as she watched the cats follow him to the studio. He tossed them treats along the way. He was acting like his old self.

Humming a song she'd just heard on the radio, she headed straight to the kitchen area to start a pot of coffee. One morning cup wouldn't suffice. The Subway coffee was only a tide over.

Returning to her desk, she caught the tail end of a local radio news report.

... Police were called to Oak Forest Subdivision after a report that the body of a man was found in a barn scheduled to be torn down. The identity of the dead man hasn't been revealed pending notification of next-of-kin. This is the same barn where unidentified remains were found earlier this month. Stay tuned for updates on this developing story.

Rhetta sat down hard and stared at the radio.

The coffee turned to acid while the egg wrap curdled in her stomach. She scanned the computer for the local television station's website and stared at the scrolling headline. It said the same thing.

Woody came in just then, waving a newspaper at her. "Did you see this?"

She didn't answer.

Woody stopped at her desk. "Rhetta, are you all right? You look like you're sick."

With that, Rhetta tuned and bolted for the restroom. Woody's assessment proved correct. She flushed the breakfast down the commode and splashed water on her face.

When she returned, still drying her face with a paper towel, Woody was seated in front of her desk. "Woody, I was at that barn Saturday night, and saw Jeremy's truck there. That body—it has to be Jeremy. Maybe he was already dead when I was there. What could've happened? Did he have a heart attack? Oh, God, was he murdered?" She whispered this and buried her face in her hands.

"What do you mean, you were out there Saturday night? Why were you there?'

She filled him in on what had happened to Randolph and the phone call from Mylene Allard.

"I have to call Randolph," she said and grabbed her purse. "I think Mylene Allard may have had something to do with this." Frustrated and shaking, she couldn't find her phone. She snatched the desk phone and punched in his number. It rang until his voice mail kicked on.

"Please call me as soon as you can." She disconnected.

Her phone buzzed from the depths of her purse just as she set the receiver down.

"Rhetta, oh my God, did you hear?" Evidently, Ricky had heard. Her voice caught in a choking sob. "I can't reach Jeremy on his cell phone. There's no answer at his house or at Anjanette's. I think that it might be Jeremy they found out at the barn. Oh, God, Rhetta, I'm scared."

Rhetta didn't know what she could say to comfort Ricky. Her head swirled with the memory of driving past the barn and seeing Jeremy's truck. And of not wanting to stop because she wanted to avoid Jeremy. "I'm sure you are, honey. Please, stay strong. Let me try to reach Randolph again. He knows the coroner. I'll try to find out something."

As she disconnected, Woody, who had left her desk to answer the ringing phone at his own desk, waved frantically at her. "Hold on, Randolph, she's coming." He gestured for Rhetta to pick up.

She punched the hold light. "Randolph? Did you hear?"

"I did, Rhetta. Are you all right? How's Ricky?"

Rhetta paused. "Ricky is frantic. Is it Jeremy? The radio didn't say."

This time it was Randolph who paused. "Yes, Rhetta, it's Jeremy. He's dead."

CHAPTER 21

RHETTA RECOILED AS THOUGH kicked by a mule. "Dear God." She ran her hands through her hair. "How did he die? Was it from natural causes?" Although she asked, and prayed it was so, deep in her gut she knew it wouldn't be.

"Matt said it appears to be from a blow to the head, although he couldn't confirm until after the autopsy."

"When will that be?" Rhetta began to swallow, hoping to keep the nausea at bay.

"Matt isn't a physician, so the autopsy will be done in St. Louis, by the medical examiner there." Matthew Clippard, the Cape Girardeau County Coroner, was an undertaker, not a doctor. In second-class counties like Cape, no medical license was required to run for coroner. Typically, the post was held by funeral directors.

"Isn't that where the other body was taken, too?"

"It was. By the way, Matt said they have a cause of death on the first remains, but are waiting for testing to confirm the identity. The first victim also died from a blow to the head."

Rhetta shuddered. "Two people killed in that barn each by a blow to the head? Do we have a serial killer on the loose?"

Randolph grunted. "I think it's a little premature to suspect a serial killer. There's been a great deal of time between the two deaths. But since there've been two men killed in that same barn, I'm sure the police will be looking at all angles."

"I was there Saturday night, Randolph," Rhetta whispered. Her eyes welled. Why in the heck had she gone out there? She could kick herself.

"There? You mean at the barn? When did you go there? And why?"

She told him about the strange phone call, and her decision to drive by out of curiosity, then what she saw when she drove past the barn.

"I'm coming to get you, and we're going straight to the Sheriff's office. You may be a witness. Don't talk to anyone. I'm on my way." He disconnected.

She nodded, although she knew he couldn't see her. She stared at the phone.

Woody appeared by her desk. "You're in it up to your eyeballs, aren't you?" he said, shaking his head. He lowered himself into her guest chair and began massaging his slick head.

"I didn't see anything, Woody, only Jeremy's truck." She pushed a file away from her. She couldn't concentrate on work, now. "Maybe I should have stopped at the barn when I was out there."

Woody shook his head, stood and began to pace. "If you would've stopped, how do you know you wouldn't have been hit over the head, and be dead now, too?"

That thought made whatever was left in her stomach churn, and she bolted again for the bathroom.

* * *

She came out of the restroom just as Randolph walked through the front door. With him was LuEllen, reporting for work, her expression somber. Her grey hair was pulled back into a knot at her neck and her normally dancing blue eyes were huge and questioning.

"I heard the news on the way in here," LuEllen began, dropping her purse on the table and continuing to Rhetta's desk. "What in heaven's name is going on?" She stared from Woody to Rhetta.

Rhetta patted her arm. "LuEllen, I'll be out of the office for a while. I'm going with Randolph to make a statement at the Sheriff's office."

They nodded. Rhetta grabbed her purse. Randolph held the door.

"Let me drive, Randolph, I don't think you should be driving today. Dr. Marinthe said not to for a few days, remember?" He ignored her and held the truck's passenger door open. She climbed in.

He hurried to the driver's side, and slid in behind the wheel. He leaned over and kissed her cheek. "I may have a knock on my noggin, but I think you may be too upset to drive. Let me be the pilot, okay?"

Rhetta fastened her seat belt. "I'm not as upset as I am shocked. I'm worried about Ricky. Does she know about Jeremy?"

Randolph maneuvered into the northbound lane on Kingshighway before answering. "She knows. I called Talbot Reasoner on my way here, and told him you would be coming in for a statement. He told me they had Ricky there and a detective was questioning her."

"Questioning her? What do you mean?"

Randolph reached over and squeezed his wife's hand. "They found her metal detector by the body. It had fresh blood and other DNA evidence on it. They suspect it may be the murder weapon."

"The metal detector?" Rhetta flashed on her last memory of the thing. She couldn't remember whether or not Ricky had taken it with her when they left the barn the day they found the body.

"They've pulled prints off it, and are waiting for the results," Randolph continued, turning right into the Cape Girardeau County offices.

"I had to be fingerprinted to work for the bank," Rhetta said, squeezing Randolph's hand. "They're going to find my prints on that metal detector, too."

CHAPTER 22

THE CAPE GIRARDEAU COUNTY Sheriff's office occupied a concrete afterthought of a building adjacent to the county jail. Vertical bars enveloped its small gloomy windows on the outside, as though to prevent anyone from breaking in. The county had painted the building battleship grey with a red stripe encircling it, giving the impression it was held together with a big rubber band. *Someone's idea of art moderne*, Rhetta thought. It was one of the ugliest buildings she'd ever had the misfortune to see. The interior wasn't much prettier.

The tiny waiting room was chaotic. Reporters clamored for an interview with a spokesperson, if not Sheriff Talbot Reasoner himself. Media people chattered on cell phones, scribbled in note pads, or lit up the drab interior with flashes from cameras. The floors were littered in paper from the overflowing waste cans. Most of the litter was generated by empty Styrofoam coffee cups. A television station from Paducah, Kentucky had their evening news anchor and her cameraman in attendance. No one had been granted an audience with the sheriff, and everyone was complaining. All six waiting room chairs were filled, so the media types crowded together as best they could. The noise level from their clamoring was deafening.

Randolph held Rhetta close to him while he edged his way past the herd to the harried-looking desk sergeant, a beefy veteran of an officer who sat at a metal desk safely behind a bullet-proof glass partition. His short, unkempt hair that looked as though rats had nested there, evidenced his rough morning.

After Randolph waited for over a minute, the sergeant slid open a small glass partition, much like Rhetta used to see in her doctor's office. "Yes?" he said, his brusque manner displaying his impatience. He ran his hand through his hair, the action explaining why tufts stood out all over his head.

"I have Rhetta McCarter here to give a statement."

"Are you her lawyer?" the sergeant asked, head bent over a list on his clipboard, finger running down a list of printed names. "McCarter, here it is," he said, before Randolph could answer. "I'll let you in."

A loud buzzer sounded at the metal door alongside the partition, and the media surged forward. "Folks, you'll have to stay back while I let these people in, or I'll have the deputy come out and start arresting you," the sergeant said, waving everyone to stand aside.

As Rhetta and Randolph started toward the still-buzzing door, reporters jabbed microphones in front of them, firing questions. Neither she nor Randolph answered. Safely on the other side, Rhetta exhaled. "That was pretty scary," she said, threading her arm through her husband's. "I'm glad you're here with me."

They were instructed to follow a young deputy down a grey hallway. "I bet Sears had a sale on grey paint," Rhetta whispered to Randolph.

"What?" Randolph said, and looked around. Then, he smiled. "I think you're right."

At the end of the hall, outside a door bearing a brass nameplate, which read, *Lieutenant J. Adams,* Rhetta and Randolph were instructed to take a seat and wait until they were called. They had their choice of six folding chairs lined up along the wall. All were empty except for one.

A short, plump woman who appeared to be in her late sixties, maybe early seventies, sat primly in the chair closest to the door. She was wearing a pale blue polyester pantsuit, her feet enclosed in white diabetic shoes parked close together and flat on the floor, hands folded in her lap. When she nodded as Randolph and Rhetta walked to take a seat next to her, her short grey curls bounced.

Rhetta looked over at Randolph, who was studying the woman. He surprised Rhetta by walking up to the grandmotherly-looking lady.

"Mrs. Griffith?" The woman turned, and glanced at Randolph, a quizzical look on her face.

"Yes. Do I know you?" She tilted her head and studied him.

"Randolph McCarter," he said and extended his hand.

"Of course, Judge, I didn't recognize you." She gripped his hand in return.

Turning to Rhetta, Randolph, said, "May I introduce my wife? Rhetta, this is Mrs. Malcom Griffith."

CHAPTER 23

R HETTA FELT HER MOUTH open, but she closed it quickly.
"Mrs. Griffith. How do you do?" Rhetta managed, shooting her husband a penetrating look over the top of Mrs. Griffith's head. He should have warned her that's who this lady was. Maybe Mrs. Griffith hadn't seen her mouth flop.

"Please, call me Adele," she said, grasping Rhetta's hand. Her grip was frail.

Randolph sat in the chair closest to her. "I suppose you're here about Jeremy Spears too?" He leaned back and crossed his legs. "A terrible thing."

Rhetta's brain clicked feverishly. *Why would Mrs. Griffith be here about Jeremy Spears?* What did Randolph know that he hadn't told her?

Mrs. Griffith shook her head. "Jeremy? No." The curls bounced. "Lieutenant Adams called me this morning and asked me to come and identify some items he thinks belonged to my husband, Malcom." Then, turning to Rhetta, a puzzled look on her face, Adele Griffith added, "What's wrong with Jeremy?"

Rhetta stared wordlessly at Mrs. Griffith, not knowing how to answer. Then she glanced at Randolph, pleading with her eyes for him to say something.

He was saved from answering when the office door opened. Adams' wrinkled golf-style shirt hung out over faded blue jeans, partially hiding the badge hanging on a leather badge holder on his belt. His police revolver nestled in a leather holster on his hip. He escorted a sobbing woman from his office. Rhetta recognized a grief-stricken Anjanette Spears.

Adele Griffith jumped to her feet when she spotted Anjanette. "What is she doing here?" she cried, leaping with an agility that shocked Rhetta. Moments earlier, Rhetta had thought of her as frail. Randolph reached for Mrs. Griffith's arm.

Anjanette Spears didn't look anything like the well-put-together matron Rhetta had met mere days ago. Her silver hair clumped against her head; her eyes and cheeks were distorted with tears. Her tan slacks were wrinkled as was her white blouse. Her hands trembled as she reached for Lieutenant Adams.

Randolph gently touched Mrs. Griffith's arm. "Mrs. Griffith, Anjanette just lost her son, Jeremy. Please, sit here." He steered her back to the chair.

Adele Griffith looked confused. "Jeremy? She's not here about Malcom?"

"No, ma'am." Randolph eased his arm away from her and glanced at Rhetta. Adams guided Anjanette down the hall. Her shoulders shook from sobbing. Anjanette hadn't appeared to recognize Rhetta, but then, Rhetta hadn't stepped forward to speak to her. It was obvious that the woman was distraught. Rhetta was uncomfortable in this kind of situation. When her own mother had passed away, she absolutely hated people offering mealy-mouthed words of sympathy. As a result, she could never find the right words to console anybody.

Adams handed Mrs. Spears off to a deputy, who led her toward the back of the building, presumably to the rear exit to avoid the media.

Rhetta glanced at Mrs. Griffith. The woman had regained some of her composure, smoothing her slacks, and patting her hair.

Adams walked up briskly and asked Mrs. Griffith to step into the room.

As soon as the door closed, Rhetta said, "I didn't know that you knew Mrs. Griffith."

"You forgot I'm the judge who declared her husband dead."

"I should've asked you about her instead of Woody-the-Answer-Man-dot-com." Rhetta gave herself a headslap.

"She seems like she's gone downhill since the last time I saw her, about five years ago. She was so vibrant then. I wonder why she was so upset at seeing Mrs. Spears?" Randolph said. He reached for Rhetta's hand and kissed it. "She's been through a lot, and now, after those remains...."

Rhetta thought she had the answer as to why Adele Griffith was upset. She'd tell Randolph about the letter, but later, when they left. She didn't want to risk Anjanette overhearing her. She leaned against her husband. She was so relieved he was there with her. He kept her calm. She whispered, "What do you think they want to talk to her about?"

"They probably have the things you and Ricky found and want her to identify them, like the wallet and ring."

"After all this time, can they can still use DNA to identify the body?"

"More likely they'll have to rely on dental records. I think the body was way too decomposed for any DNA, except for the type found in bones. Since Malcom Griffith was local and had a local dentist, I would think dental records would be the easiest and fastest way to identify him. I think that's what they'll start with, then go from there."

* * *

Ten minutes later, the door opened and Mrs. Griffith emerged, looking paler and frailer. She no longer looked plump and healthy.

Randolph stood and offered his arm. "Are you all right, Mrs. Griffith?"

When she nodded, a tear slipped down her cheek. She brushed it away. She patted Randolph's arm, but didn't take it.

"All those things," she angled her chin toward the door, "are my Malcom's. I signed some papers to allow them to get his dental records." She sighed heavily. "I guess he truly is dead after all." She pushed her purse up on her arm. Another officer took her arm, and began leading her. "Thank you, officer, for driving me. I just don't drive anymore," she said and shuffled alongside him down the hallway.

After Adams introduced himself to Randolph and Rhetta, he invited them to follow him. His office was painted in the same drab grey as the rest of the building. The small space was filled nearly to capacity with his county-issued metal desk, which faced the door, two metal guest chairs squeezed in front of the desk, and a row of four mismatched filing cabinets along the wall. Behind Adams' chair, certificates and awards filled the brag space on the wall.

Rhetta and Randolph sat and waited while Adams opened a thick file and thumbed through it.

"Mrs. McCarter, it seems like you wind up in the middle of things, don't you?"

Rhetta glanced at Randolph, not sure how to answer. First of all, the question was rhetorical, and second, she found him rude. "I came here voluntarily, Lieutenant Adams. You don't have to be rude. I know my husband already notified you I was out by the barn Saturday night, so let's just skip the asinine observations. Do you have pertinent questions for me?"

Adams snapped the folder shut so suddenly that Rhetta blinked. Still staring at her, he retrieved a yellow legal tablet and reached for a pen.

"All right, ma'am, no offense." He held up his hands, palms out in an exaggerated mock surrender. "Let's begin by you telling me, Mrs. McCarter, exactly what time you were out at the barn at Oak Forest Subdivision last Saturday night." Pen poised in midair above the pad, he awaited her answer.

"It was just getting dark, so probably around 8:45."

"Did you see anyone in or around the barn?" He began to jot.

"No. I did see Jeremy's truck, but I didn't see him." She squirmed uncomfortably. Randolph slipped his hand into hers. She relaxed.

"Why did you go to the barn in the first place?" He scrawled feverishly as she spoke, firing his questions while barely looking at her.

"I received a strange phone call, asking me to go out there." Rhetta groped in her purse for her cell phone.

Adams stopped writing. He stared at her, his dark eyes revealing nothing. "Strange phone call? From whom?"

"A woman who said her name was Mylene Allard. " Rhetta said. She passed her iPhone across to him, and pointed to the number on the recent call list.

He set the pen down and took the phone, staring at the display. "This Mylene Allard, how did she know how to reach you?" He continued examining the phone while he waited for her answer.

Rhetta shrugged. "I have no idea."

Randolph interjected. "My wife's picture and information about where she works and the barn's location were all in the media recently, if you recall, Lieutenant."

Adams nodded, set the phone aside and resumed writing. Rhetta and Randolph sat in silence for a minute while he wrote. Abruptly, Adams lay his pen down and leaned forward. "May we borrow your phone, Mrs. McCarter? We'd like to record that phone list."

Rhetta frowned, and turned to Randolph.

"No, you may not have the phone. If you'll excuse me, I need to confer with my client." Randolph guided Rhetta a few feet away and whispered, "Is there anything on that phone that he shouldn't see?"

"No, it's just got my recent personal calls and a few business calls."

Randolph led Rhetta back to Adams. "We'll let you look at the call list only—no browser history, nothing else. Understood?"

Adams picked up the phone and held it in one hand while he punched a button on his desk phone with the other hand. He barked an order, summoning a deputy. As he disconnected, he answered her. "Just for a few minutes. We can pull that list from here, right now."

Adams handed the iPhone to the deputy who had arrived clutching a sheet of paper, which he slid across the desk toward Adams. Adams snatched the sheet and scanned it.

"We have the results of the fingerprints found on the metal detector. There were two sets." He tapped the paper. "Yours, Mrs. McCarter, and those of Miss Victoria Lane." He set the paper aside, stood, then came around the desk and propped a slender haunch up on its corner. He examined his fingernails and as casually as though asking what she had for dinner last night, asked, "Did you two ladies murder Jeremy Spears?"

CHAPTER 24

RHETTA'S HEAD SPUN. GRABBING the edge of Adams' desk, she stood and whirled around.

"Where's Ashton Kutcher?" She swiveled her head and looked back at the door. "I'm getting punk'd, right? There's no other explanation for that kind of question."

Randolph stood when she did, and lay his hand on her arm. "Rhetta, please, sit down and be quiet." His voice was firm, professional. She had never heard him use that tone with her before. Turning to Adams, he said, "I'm no longer just Mrs. McCarter's husband. I am now her attorney. She isn't going to answer any questions like that unless you arrest her and Mirandize her. In fact, you made a serious mistake. You can't use anything you get off her phone, since you haven't Mirandized her. That phone can't be used as evidence."

Rhetta grabbed Randolph's arm. "For God's sake, Randolph, don't give him any ideas!"

Adams spread his hands apart, palms out, and shook his head. "Hold on, Judge. I'm not going to arrest your wife, I mean client." He cleared his throat. "It's just a question I needed to ask, to get it out of the way. We weren't looking for evidence on her phone."

"Either ask what you need to know to determine if she's a witness, or my client and I will be leaving. As she told you, she's here voluntarily. That means she's free to go."

Rhetta's heart hammered against her ribs. Did this cop really think she had anything to do with Jeremy's death? Her head broke out in beads of perspiration. She had an immense dislike for Jeremy Spears, but unless she'd had an out-of-body experience, she hadn't killed him.

"Are you warm, Mrs. McCarter?" Adams asked, obviously noticing her glistening brow.

"As a matter of fact, I'm burning up. Doesn't the air conditioning work in this place?" She snatched a nearby magazine and began fanning herself.

Randolph took her hand and gave her The Look. She shut up.

Adams cleared his throat. "All we need to see is her recent call list. We need to find this woman who supposedly called your wife." He paused to scan his notes. "Mylene Allard."

Randolph again asked Rhetta to point out Mylene Allard's phone number on the list. "Write this number down, Lieutenant." He rattled off the number, then lifted his head and addressed Rhetta.

"I don't have any further questions, Mrs. McCarter, so yes, you're free to leave." Adams motioned to the door. He didn't bother escorting her to the door or down the hall like he had with the two previous women.

Probably because they weren't murder suspects, like me.

They walked a few steps, then Randolph turned back to Adams. "You sure you got that number, Lieutenant?" Adams nodded. "Good, then have a nice day."

Randolph held the door for his wife, then followed her into the hall.

* * *

"The nerve of Adams accusing me of killing Jeremy Spears. Especially after we came down here voluntarily to try and help," Rhetta fumed.

"He's only doing his job." Randolph opened the passenger door of his truck. Rhetta climbed in. "I wish you hadn't gone back to that barn." He shook his head. She began to protest and he raised his hand to silence her. "What's done is done. I know you didn't have anything to do with Jeremy Spears' death, or with Malcom Griffith's. With these two deaths, the sheriff's department has its hands full now, no doubt about it. I guess we could cut them a little slack."

While Randolph and Rhetta were elbowing their way out through the waiting room amidst an even larger gaggle of reporters and media people, through a tangle of wires and laptops, cell phones and microphone stands, Sheriff Reasoner had announced over a public address system that he'd be giving a news briefing in thirty minutes. The media folks had surged forward when the door from the back had opened and were visibly disappointed when they spotted Rhetta and Randolph instead of the sheriff. Grumbling, they returned to scanning their iPhones, iPads and whatever else "i" that abounded.

Randolph maneuvered the Artmobile 2 out of the crowded parking lot and onto Highway 61, and aimed it for home. After cranking the air conditioner on high, Rhetta sank back against the plush comfort of the seat and headrest. She closed her eyes for a moment. Then she snapped them open. "What about Streak? It's still at my office."

"Text Woody to lock it up and leave the keys in your desk. I'll take you to work tomorrow. We need to go home."

"Good idea." Rhetta searched out her iPhone and texted Woody. She received an immediate answer. He'd take care of it. "Woody's a lifesaver," Rhetta said, and sat back again.

Randolph fiddled with the radio until he located the local all-news station. "Maybe we can catch Talbot's press statement."

"I'd rather listen to oldies music than that windbag," Rhetta said, closing her eyes and savoring the cool air.

"I had always had respect for Reasoner, but I've changed my mind. You have me convinced. I'm not going to support him this next election. He didn't bother to come in and talk to you and me himself while we were there. Just hid away in his office, and let Adams do all the interviewing. He's a real rodent."

Rhetta cut her gaze across to Randolph. He never said ugly things about people. That Sheriff Talbot Reasoner hadn't troubled himself to speak to his supposed friend must have spoken volumes to Randolph.

Just as they pulled off on the gravel county road that led home, the station broke in with a live news feed to present the press conference. Talbot Reasoner cleared his throat, then tapped the mike. "Good afternoon ladies and gentlemen. First, off let me tell y'all, this won't be a question-and-answer session." A collective groan vibrated from the reporters in attendance. Following the murmuring, paper rattled loudly into the mike, probably the sheriff scanning his notes. Reasoner continued. "As you know, the body of Jeremy Spears was found early this morning in a barn on property he was developing into a subdivision in Gordonville. The murder weapon has been identified, and we now have a suspect in custody." The crowd murmured.

Randolph and Rhetta stared at each other.

"We've arrested Mr. Spears' girlfriend, Victoria Lane. That's all for now." The clamor that followed was interrupted by the studio feed "Kool Kape Radio will bring you the latest developments as they break," warbled a deep-voiced announcer.

Randolph punched the radio off, and shook his head. "I hope she knows a good lawyer."

CHAPTER 25

"THIS IS JUST PLAIN crazy. Nuts!" Rhetta fumed as she slammed the newspaper on to Woody's desk the next morning.

He rolled his chair backward and raised his arms in surrender. "I didn't write the story, Rhetta. I just brought in the paper."

She paced between their desks. "I know. I'm sorry. It's not your fault. It's not even the newspaper's fault for reporting the news. And it seems to be very big news." She pointed to the headline splashed in bold type across the top third of the paper: *GIRLFRIEND ARRESTED IN LOCAL DEVELOPER'S DEATH.*

"There is absolutely no way on God's green earth that Ricky could have hurt Jeremy or anybody else. She's the softhearted one who rescues animals. Last year, she made a pet out of a baby 'possum she found, remember?"

Woody only nodded.

Rhetta plopped down at her desk, and blew across the top of her coffee. Randolph had dropped her off earlier, so that she had plenty of time to get the coffee made and all the computers started before Woody came in, local paper tucked under his arm. When he mentioned the arrest was all over the front page, she'd insisted on reading the story. She hadn't bought the St. Louis paper. She didn't want to know if the news had reached the Big Lou.

"Oh, no!" Rhetta said, leaping up.

Woody's head swiveled around. "What? What's wrong?"

"Speaking of rescued animals, Ricky has two house dogs. I don't know who she'd get to go over there to let them out. She always calls me to check on her dogs if she's going to be gone overnight. She didn't call me, and I forgot all about Taffy and Tater." Rhetta grabbed her purse, and searched for her keys. Unable to find them, she turned her purse over and dumped everything on to her desk. A tube of lipstick rolled off the desk to the floor. "I can't find my keys. Where are they?" she groused as she riffled through the checkbook, her wallet, her set of office keys, and miscellaneous papers before stuffing everything back into her bag. Still no keys. She looked around frantically.

"Uh, Rhetta? Did you look in your desk drawer? You asked me to lock up your car and leave the keys in your desk."

She yanked open the top middle drawer. "I found them." It was too late to avoid feeling really foolish. As soon as he told her, she remembered texting him.

"I'm going out there and take care of her dogs. I'll be back soon."

LuEllen arrived just as Rhetta was sailing out the door. She rested her hand on Rhetta's arm, stopping her boss. "Wait, Rhetta. Are you leaving again? You know you have two closings today, don't you? Mrs. Gentry really didn't like talking to me yesterday about her loan. She wants you to be at her closing." For emphasis, LuEllen tapped on the wall calendar, which had two notations circled on it. Rhetta glanced at her watch. "What time are they scheduled?"

"Mrs. Gentry's reverse mortgage closing is first, at 10:30. The Rigdon purchase isn't until 2:00." She sat at her desk, tucked a tiny purse away and brought her monitor to life. Rhetta had often asked herself how the woman could get by with a purse that was smaller than Rhetta's wallet.

"You're right, LuEllen. I need to be here with Mrs. Gentry. The dear old soul is frightened enough of all this paperwork. I'll go out to Ricky's later." Rhetta returned to her desk, stuffed her purse into the bottom drawer and adjusted the height of her chair, a daily requirement. Every night the chair sank all the way down which necessitated Rhetta adjusting it upward every morning. When she forgot, her chin would nearly touch her desktop.

Woody stood and rolled his chair to park it in front of his desk, then headed for the front door. "I don't have any appointments until late this afternoon. I'll go out there for you and let the dogs out and feed them, too."

"Thanks, Woody, you're a doll. Her keys are under a grey faux rock by the back door. The rock has the words "The Rock" painted on it. Don't let them out without their leashes. They don't know you and may try to run off. Their kibbles are in the pantry on the back porch."

"Got it," he said, digging in his pants pockets for his car keys.

"And don't forget to give them fresh water," Rhetta shouted as he was leaving.

He turned around and sighed. "Really? I hadn't thought of that."

She waved him off. "I'm sorry. Of course, you know that." He merely nodded as he closed the door. Woody was the proud daddy of Lela and Lottie, two gorgeous Boxers that he'd adopted. He and Jenn were childless, like Rhetta and Randolph. Woody's dogs were his kids. Rhetta and Randolph's fur babies were feline.

* * *

Woody returned just as Mrs. Gentry was getting ready to leave following her closing. He held the door for her. She paused to give Rhetta a hug. "Thank you, Rhetta. Thanks to you, I can keep my home."

"Thanks for bringing us brownies. I'll be by soon for some more, Mrs. Gentry," Rhetta said, and glanced at the plate of chocolate brownies beckoning to her from the closing table. She mentally calculated how many calories were in each one. Her mouth watered.

Once the door was closed, she turned to Woody. "Did you run into any trouble at Ricky's?"

"No." Woody rolled his desk chair out and sat. He touched the mouse and his computer sprang to life.

"Just, 'no?' Are the dogs okay?"

"The dogs are just fine." He began tapping on his keyboard.

Rhetta looked at LuEllen, who shrugged.

"So, what did happen out there?" Rhetta cocked her head and watched Woody.

He turned slowly. "What makes you think anything happened?"

"Because you said you didn't run into any trouble out there, but you were gone a long time. What happened?"

He threw up his hands. "Taffy escaped. Took me forty-five minutes to round him up."

"I told you not to take them out without a leash."

"The silly mutt rocketed through my legs the instant I opened the door." Woody's gaze returned to his monitor. "But I lured him back with the promise of my hamburger."

Rhetta grinned. "Did you have to give him your lunch?"

"Yes." He ignored Rhetta's laughter. "While I was there a delivery truck came and I signed for a motor the driver wanted to unload." He obviously wanted to change the subject away from his dog adventure.

Rhetta groaned. "I think that's the LS1 for my now-police-evidence-Z28. Did you see the waybill?"

"Nope. The driver wanted to take it into the shop where it would be safe. I finally found the shop keys and let him leave it inside. It took a while for him to get it off the back of the truck. At that, he grumbled the whole time for me to help him."

Woody spun his chair around. "By the way, didn't Ricky sell her car? I saw her Trans Am was still in the shop, all polished up. There was another car there, too. I was checking out where to leave the motor and saw it in the paint booth. Looks like another second generation Camaro."

"Are you sure about the other car being a Camaro?"

"Pretty sure. You and Ricky have educated me on the body style of those cars." He pulled up a web page devoted to Camaros between 1970 and 1981. "Yep, it looks like this." He swiveled the monitor so she could see what he pointed at. It was a 1979 Camaro. "Wasn't Cami a '79 Camaro?"

Chapter 26

Rhetta turned off the office computers and set the phones to the answering machine. She had wondered all afternoon about the other Camaro that Ricky had in her shop. Maybe she was working on one for a customer, even though she hadn't told Rhetta. That puzzled her, though, because Ricky knew that Rhetta enjoyed watching the transformation of these cars under Ricky's superb craftsmanship. Ricky usually gushed about her projects.

As Rhetta turned off the last of the office lights and reached for the keys to lock up, her cell phone jingled from the innards of her purse. She managed to find it before it quit ringing. She didn't recognize the local number.

"Rhetta, it's Ricky. Can you come and get me? They let me go. I'm using the sheriff's office phone." That explained the unfamiliar number.

"Sure, I'll be right there. But how...? Just tell me you didn't grab a deputy's gun, hold him hostage and threaten his life to get out. Did you?"

"No, of course not." Ricky chuckled, but with little mirth in her voice. "The prosecutor and the sheriff got into quite an argument, and the bottom line was the prosecutor said there wasn't enough evidence to arrest me in the first place, so I've been downgraded from a suspect to a person of interest."

"That's great, Ricky. Of course, there's no evidence. You didn't do it. I'm on my way."

Rhetta called Randolph.

"That doesn't surprise me one bit," Randolph said. "Sheriff Reasoner has been called Sheriff Unreasonable by several of the assistant prosecutors. He's got a history of jumping the gun. He's ruined many cases for Prosecutor Fox. Reasoner wants to call the shots about charges, and Sylvio Fox doesn't want him interfering. It's a mess."

"Great. Just ducky. A turf war. Does that mean if Reasoner solves these murders that Fox won't prosecute?"

Randolph laughed. "They don't call our prosecutor *Sly Fox*, for nothing."

Rhetta shivered at the thought that a killer was still on the loose. And that someone might be building a case against Ricky.

"I'll be home after I drop Ricky off. Can you get the grill ready? I thawed some steaks that need to be cooked tonight."

"Yep. And I'll feed the cats, too. Love you. And, Rhetta?"

"Yes, Sweets, I'll be careful."

* * *

Ricky appeared to have aged ten years since Rhetta last saw her. Her normally vibrant red hair hung limply in a ponytail held by a brown rubber band, probably one she'd pilfered from a county desk. Her jeans fit loosely, as though she'd lost weight, even though she'd only spent a day in lockup. Ricky, sitting in the sheriff's department waiting room with her hands folded primly on her lap, clutching her purse, gazed up at Rhetta with puffy eyes in a tear-stained face.

Once safely belted in, Rhetta asked, "Why don't you come to the house and have supper with us?"

Ricky shook her head. "No, but thanks, anyway. I need to go home and hug Taffy and Tater. I missed them so much." Rhetta told her about Woody tending to the dogs. She didn't tell her about Taffy's escape.

"Woody said he signed for a motor delivered to you. I told him that was the one you wanted to send back. I'll pay you for it, and we can keep it for whenever my Z28 gets released from the evidence garage."

"Okay, no problem." Ricky stared out the side window. Rhetta glanced at her friend as she cranked up the air. She spotted fresh tears spilling down her cheeks.

They rode in silence the rest of the way. Whenever Ricky wanted to talk, she would. Rhetta wouldn't push her.

After pulling into the driveway and parking, Rhetta walked Ricky to the back door, and waited as Ricky found her key and unlocked it.

As Ricky pushed the door open, Rhetta said, "Keep all your doors and windows locked. There's a murderer still on the loose." With that, Ricky turned and fell into Rhetta's arms, sobbing openly.

She pulled away and rubbed the tears from her cheeks. "I didn't kill him Rhetta. But, I'll tell you the truth. Saturday night I was so mad at him, I wanted to."

CHAPTER 27

They sat at Ricky's antique round kitchen table, Taffy and Tater each vying for their mom's attention by jumping up on her lap. Ricky hugged them both, and set them down. Taffy, a terrier mix, immediately jumped back into Ricky's lap, while Tater, a Labrador-Golden Retriever cross, lay by her feet, tail thumping on the floor.

"Can you get us a soda?" Ricky asked, hugging and petting her fur babies.

Rhetta located two cans of Diet Coke in the refrigerator and returned with two glasses of ice. She set a coaster under each glass.

"Do you want to tell me why you were so mad at Jeremy?" Rhetta asked as she popped the tab on their sodas and poured for each of them.

Ricky sighed and stared at the beverage as it crackled over the crushed ice.

"I caught him with another woman in his apartment." Ricky finally said, as she circled the rim of her glass with her thumb.

Rhetta flashed back to her experience with Jeremy on Saturday. She hadn't yet told Ricky about it. Maybe if she would have, Jeremy might not have been at the barn, and gotten himself killed. Had he arranged to meet someone out there? This newly discovered other woman?

Rhetta sipped, waiting for Ricky to go on. She'd gauge when would be the best time to tell her.

New tears began dribbling down Ricky's cheeks. She sniffled, then reached across the table for a tissue and blew her nose. "I guess I didn't know what he was really like. I went looking for him at the party, and when I couldn't find him, I jogged upstairs to his apartment. I walked in on him and some bimbo. He yelled at me, and called me everything but free and over twenty-one, as though it was my fault he was cheating on me. I slammed the door after yelling something like I hoped he rotted in hell, or some such, and then I left the party."

"Do you know who he was with?" Rhetta asked, thinking that this woman could be a suspect in Jeremy's murder.

"I didn't recognize her big white behind," Ricky smiled.

Rhetta patted her arm. "I know this is all terrible about Jeremy getting killed, but you really are better off without him."

"What's really terrible is that I'm a suspect." Glass in hand, she slid to the floor and cradled the dogs, hugging their necks and enveloping them into her lap.

"Did you tell the detective about this white-butted woman?"

"I did. But, frankly, I bet we never find out who she is. Most, if not all the women at the party, were there with their husbands or at least with their significant others. I'm sure none will want to come forward." Ricky stood, and the dogs wound through her legs.

"Well, I'll come forward," Rhetta said.

"What?" Ricky nearly dropped her glass. "You?"

"Wait, no, I wasn't the white-cheeked woman, if that's what you're thinking." Rhetta twisted around to examine her rear. "My butt's not big! What I mean is that Jeremy made a move on me, too, but I kneed him in the groin." Rhetta gathered up the two glasses and headed for the sink. "I'm surprised he wanted to make a move on a woman so soon after our confrontation."

Ricky burst out laughing. "I can just imagine how that went." Ricky dropped into the chair, snatched a tissue and dabbed her eyes. This time, her tears weren't from sadness. "You were right, Rhetta, he's nothing but a big jerk. Or was....Who could have killed him, and why?"

"That, my dear friend, is the million dollar question." Rhetta headed for the door. "If you're not going to come home with me, I'd better take off. Randolph was getting the grill started."

She started out the door but turned back to Ricky. "By the way, Woody said you have another Camaro in the shop. Is that a new project?"

"Woody talks too much," Ricky said under her breath. Rhetta, however, had excellent hearing. "No," Ricky continued. "that's just an old Camaro I had in the other shed that I'm using for parts." Ricky cleared her throat, and waved dismissively. "Now that your Z28 may be held captive for a while, I want to strip this car and sell the parts. If I can do that, and sell my Trans Am, I may be able to pay for a lawyer." Ricky sighed. "There goes my dream of a restored '65 Mustang. I may need the money for my legal defense fund, instead of a hot car."

"Now that you mention your Trans Am, let me see that so-called check you got for payment." In all that had happened, Rhetta forgot her promise to check out the suspicious check.

Ricky pulled open the top middle drawer of an antique oak sideboard, withdrew the Fed Ex envelope and handed it to Rhetta. "Do you really think this is a scam? " Ricky looked wistfully at the envelope as Rhetta took it.

"Yes, and we may have to get to the bottom of this. I'll have Woody help. He's a computer whiz."

Ricky smiled. "That's why you call him Woody-the-Answer-Man, right?"

"That, plus he always has his finger on the pulse on everything going on in Cape."

Rhetta tucked the envelope in her purse, hugged her friend again, and left.

Poor Ricky. First a scam for her Trans Am and now her man gets murdered. Boy, when things go south, they go in a hurry.

CHAPTER 28

"RHETTA, YOU DON'T NEED to be sticking your nose into this murder investigation," Randolph said as he forked two thick sirloins onto the grill and stood back as they sizzled. Sniffing the delicious odor of the cooking steaks launched Rhetta's stomach into a growl that made one of the cats meow in response.

She crossed the patio and placed two foil-covered potatoes and fresh ears of corn wrapped in their husks alongside the steaks. "I'm not the least bit sticking my nose in. But, if you remember, Sweets, my fingerprints are also on that metal detector they think is the murder weapon. I have to be prepared to defend myself in case Sheriff Unreasonable decides to come after me, too."

"Reasoner will definitely be pushing for an arrest. Ricky may still be the one they agree to charge, but they need more evidence. I hope she's not planning on leaving town, and I hope she gets a lawyer."

"Can you represent her?" Rhetta asked as she stirred seasoned oil and vinegar into a fresh salad she'd assembled in a large olivewood bowl.

"No. I don't practice law at all anymore, and I don't keep malpractice insurance since I retired."

"Can you find someone for her?" Rhetta asked.

"I already did." Randolph winked at her.

She hugged his neck. "Thanks!"

She set plates on the red and white checked tablecloth on the outdoor patio table. Although the temperature was still high, a light breeze whispered through the weeping willow that shaded the patio. A perfect evening for an outdoor meal.

With the steaming food on a platter, and tall glasses of tea at the ready, they sat to enjoy the meal. Rhetta cut her steak meticulously, trimming away all the outer fat. Then she forked a piece of the tender meat into her mouth, and murmured with pleasure. "Umm, this is absolutely heavenly. Steak, baked potato, salad and corn on the cob is my absolute favorite meal in the whole world."

Randolph nodded his agreement.

When they'd eaten enough to resume conversation, Rhetta said, "Ricky told me she and Jeremy had a bad fight the night he was killed."

"Is that right?" Randolph said, and swallowed some tea. He stirred some sweetener into his drink, then sampled it again.

"Ricky caught him with another woman." At her words, Randolph stopped chewing to glance at her. "I think Jeremy made a habit out of seducing any woman he could," Rhetta said. "He made a pass at me, too."

Randolph resumed chewing and then chuckled. "I bet he regretted that pretty quickly."

Rhetta smiled. "Yep, I'm sure he did." She told him what happened.

Randolph's smile turned to a frown. "Rhetta, that could have been a dangerous situation for you. Why didn't you tell me about this sooner?"

"It was nothing at the time and ever since then everything's been chaotic."

"I wouldn't call what he did, *nothing*."

She shrugged. "You know I can take care of myself. Well, most of the time, anyway. Especially with a jerk like Jeremy." She stabbed at an ear of corn, and brought it to her plate. "I wonder if he made arrangements to meet another woman out at the barn, and he made an unwanted pass at her, too, and she conked him on the head. Maybe she's too frightened to come forward."

Rhetta said, "My money's on Mylene Allard!"

"Why her?"

"Maybe she was the one who was at the barn. And, maybe she had already killed Jeremy before I got there."

He shook his head. "That doesn't make any sense. Why would she call you if she was planning to meet Jeremy?"

"Who knows? When the cops catch up with her, they can ask her that question." She gulped the last of her tea.

"At the rate the cops are going, I wouldn't look for them to be checking her out anytime soon," Randolph said, and began scraping his leftovers into a plate. "I honestly think they won't even check out this Mylene, since they don't see a connection. I feel that they're going to try to pin this on Ricky. And if she told them about the fight, that may make it look worse for her."

Rhetta's head swirled with what Randolph just said. She began clearing away the dishes. Randolph carried the platters and remaining food into the house. At the other side of the kitchen, four feline faces pressed against the glass.

"I'll give a few of these scraps to our poor starving cats," Randolph said, and squeezed out the door. The cats surrounded him.

Rhetta snatched her phone and dialed Woody. "I have a challenge for you," she said when he answered. "We need to find an address for this cell number in Illinois" She repeated it twice.

"Why?"

"I want to personally ask Mylene Allard why she called me. I've tried calling her back, and she doesn't answer."

"Does Randolph know you want me to do this?"

"What do you think?"

"That's what I thought."

"Woody, don't you tell him."

"I get the parking spot for a month." He hung up.

CHAPTER 29

Woody's Jeep sat prominently in the primo slot next to the door when Rhetta pulled in.

She parked next to his ride, then reached in the back seat for her bag of overdue books from the library. She hoped to persuade LuEllen to take them back for her. Sliding the canvas book bag up on to one shoulder and her purse on the other, she balanced her coffee in her left hand and tugged the door. It didn't open, and the force of the resistance caused a middle fingernail to bend backwards and snap. "Oww," she whimpered, not wanting to see the damage to her finger. It would only make it hurt worse. Her mother used to tell her not to look at her scrapes and cuts when she was a kid, telling her that if she looked, it would hurt more. She still believed it.

She rapped on the door glass and stuck her finger in her mouth to assuage the pain. She didn't want to have to set everything down to fish for her keys.

Woody appeared and unlocked the door.

"Why is the door still locked?" Rhetta said, sliding past him and dropping her books near LuEllen's desk. After making sure her coffee and purse were safe on her own desk, she held up her injured finger. "I pulled that door so hard I broke this nail down into the quick." She worked up the courage to look at it. New pain throbbed up her finger. Her mother was right.

"Why did you do that?"

"Never mind, I'll live. It's too far from my heart to kill me." Honestly, sometimes Woody asked the silliest questions.

Woody ignored her wounded finger. "I got here really early and was so absorbed in searching for your Mylene Allard that I forgot to check the time. Sorry." He had returned to his desk. His fingers flew over the keyboard.

"You found her?" Rhetta reached for her coffee.

"Yep."

Rhetta leapt up and danced around, high-fiving Woody. He glanced around as though embarrassed, afraid that someone might come through the door any moment and catch her ungainly duck dancing.

The printer whirred and he snatched the page it spit out, handing it to her. His wide grin split his whiskers. "Here it is. When do we go?"

Rhetta scanned the address. "Jonesboro, Illinois, isn't very far, about an hour's drive, right?" She glanced at her watch. LuEllen would be here in a few minutes. "We can go when LuEllen gets here. Do you have anything going on this morning?"

"Nope." As he rubbed his head, something sparkly fell to his shoulder. Rhetta glanced at it, then back to his shaved head.

"Is that glitter on your head? And on your shirt, too?" She sidled over to his desk. "There's even some in your beard." She began chuckling. "What kind of kinky game were you and Jenn playing?"

Woody rubbed his head, swiped his shoulder and tried finger combing his beard.

"It's Jenn's fault. She had a top with sparkly stuff all over it and she dried it with the towels." He swiped furiously. "When I took my shower, I must've grabbed a towel she dried with that top."

He swatted his head and face as though bees were after him.

"I'm going to run home and change clothes," he said, and galloped to the door.

Rhetta laughed so hard she forgot about her broken nail.

LuEllen arrived just as Woody flew out the door. "Where's he going?"

"So much glitter," Rhetta said, and cracked up. LuEllen glanced from Rhetta back to the door Woody just exited through, shrugged and sat at her desk.

"What's this?" LuEllen asked, picking up Rhetta's tote, and wagging it in her direction.

"I have some overdue books. Can I talk you into taking them back for me? I put the money in an envelope inside the tote. They always look at me like I'm a criminal when I'm late."

LuEllen merely smiled and placed the tote next to her purse. "I'll put it next to my purse so I won't forget," she said, and turned on her computer. "You really ought to get an eReader," she added. "I have one and I love it." LuEllen was always on the cutting edge of electronics. Rhetta, not so much. Most days even the copier challenged her.

* * *

It took Woody nearly an hour to change clothes. Rhetta had been so tempted to move her car into his space while he was gone, but decided against it. She didn't want Woody tattling to Randolph.

When he finally returned he was rubbing the side of his head. Rhetta glanced at him as he strode by. He had on the same shirt and slacks.

"I thought you were going home to change?"

"I decided to go to the car wash instead."

She sidled over to him, giving him the once-over for glitter. She didn't see any, but noticed the whole side of his face and the top of his shaved head were red and swollen.

"What happened to your head?"

"I told you, I went to the car wash."

"What has that got to do with your head?"

Woody patted his head instead of rubbing it. "I thought I could use the power wand at the car wash and rinse my head off with it."

"Wait, you used the high powered rinse on your head?"

"Yeah, after I used the soap, I needed to rinse it off."

Rhetta couldn't help herself. She erupted into laughter and collapsed into her chair so hard she nearly knocked her chin on the desk.

LuEllen was much more sympathetic. She rushed to Woody's side. "Oh, my goodness, Woody. Why didn't you use the gentle rinse? You could have peeled your head with that power wand. My nephew, Franklin, complained that it took the paint off his car's bumper last year."

"Now, you tell me," Woody said.

By now, Rhetta was laughing so hard, she made a beeline to the bathroom.

When she returned, Woody was trying his best to shoo LuEllen away and stop her fussing over his head.

"It'll be all right. I'm fine," he grumbled. "At least I got rid of the glitter."

"Not all of it," Rhetta said, flicking a silvery morsel from his shoulder.

"Okay, keep that up, and I won't tell you who I saw at the car wash."

Still chuckling, but trying not to, Rhetta said, "All right, I'll quit picking on you. Who did you see?" She sat at her desk and reached for her coffee. She tried to stifle her giggles.

Woody straightened his tie, swatted at any possible remaining glitter, visible or invisible, then sat. He swiveled slowly around to an expectant Rhetta. "When I got done, and was driving out, I glanced over to see who was in the next bay. A lady was rinsing off the muddy wheels of a high riding pickup truck complete with gun racks, one of which held a rifle and scope."

"Okay, so a woman was rinsing off her vehicle. At least she wasn't rinsing off her head." Rhetta couldn't control her laughter any longer. She went back to her desk and picked up her cup.

"Then I won't tell you it was Adele Griffith."

CHAPTER 30

RHETTA NEARLY SPIT COFFEE across her desk.

"Adele Griffith? Are you sure?"

"Yep. Her picture was in the paper this weekend."

"Still, how do you know it was her for sure?"

"Well, besides the lady looking just like her picture, her license plates are personalized. They say A-D-E-L-E."

"Holy cow. I overheard her tell the deputy she doesn't drive."

"Well, maybe she doesn't drive much, but that doesn't mean she can't drive."

Rhetta thought about that. "Yeah, maybe she was too upset in the sheriff's office." She told Woody about seeing her there, and how she'd confirmed that the belongings they found were indeed Malcom's.

"Have you just changed your mind or are we still going to Illinois?"

"We're absolutely going to go look for Mylene Allard. Checking out Mrs. Griffith will just have to wait."

"Do you want to drive on this person hunt, or do you want me to?" Woody asked, jingling his keys at her.

"I need air conditioning, so I'll drive," Rhetta said, withdrawing her keys from her purse, then sliding the purse up her arm. She gulped the last of her coffee.

"My Jeep is air conditioned. All natural air when the top's down."

"I know how that works. No thanks. Let's take mine." She aimed her keys at Streak, clicked the opener and unlocked the doors.

Woody jumped in quickly and was strapped in by the time Rhetta slid behind the wheel, set her phone on top of the console and inserted the keys in the ignition. She turned and studied him. "You sure got in quickly."

"Last time I got in with you, you took off so fast, you nearly threw me out on the pavement," he said. His lips twitched in a faint smile.

"Dang, Woody, you make it sound like I did that on purpose."

He shot her a sideways look, but said nothing. He pulled out his notepad containing the page he had printed with the information, along with his iPhone. "I mapped the address, as well as printed it." He held up the phone. "Let's roll."

* * *

Twenty minutes later, they'd crossed the Emerson Bridge over the bank-full Mississippi River. The drive normally took about five minutes, but today, thanks to a load of produce that had been dumped in the middle of Kingshighway, and a minivan that sideswiped a police cruiser, traffic was snarled all the way from their office to the bridge.

Early persistent summer rains had pushed the river up against the Cape Girardeau, Missouri, floodwall during several months of high water, resulting in swamped fields on the unprotected Illinois side. The flooding was still evident in the water-soaked land that bordered each side of Route 146, making the highway look like a causeway through a giant lake. No crops this year. As they rounded a curve near the small village of East Cape Girardeau, Rhetta spotted the local notorious bar and hot spot, The Pink Peacock. A single car sat in the parking lot. Although the business appeared closed, she knew the bar didn't open until evenings, and that later, the lot would be full. She and Randolph used this route when they went to the Lake. According to the blinking roadside sign in the parking lot, the club featured pole dancers, strippers and various other forms of entertainment that Rhetta didn't want to think about. About a quarter mile past the Peacock, Rhetta pulled over and began to turn around.

"What's up?" Woody asked, swiveling his head to look back to where they'd just come. "Why are you turning around?"

"The sign back there said the Pink Peacock has strippers and pole dancers. Just for grins, let's go and see if anyone there knows Mylene Allard."

"There doesn't seem to be anyone there right now, and what makes you think anyone there would know her?"

"There's one car in the lot. Someone's there, maybe the manager. I'm thinking Mylene's our missing pole dancer."

Woody gazed back at Rhetta. "If she is, she'd be a little old to still be pole dancing, don't you think?"

"That depends. Nobody seemed to know exactly how old she was when she was supposedly carrying on with Malcom Griffith. She could be barely in her forties now. Not too old for the Peacock, based on the pictures I've seen of the entertainers there," Rhetta said and chuckled. "It isn't Las Vegas. Besides, the interior is dim and they serve alcohol, so all the women are bound to look good." Woody just shook his head, and said nothing. "I'm wondering why she wanted to meet me out at the barn. Now Jeremy is dead. It's much too coincidental."

Woody continued staring at Rhetta. "I know—you hate coincidences. You think she might be the killer?"

"I don't really know what to think. That's why we need to find her and talk to her. The cops don't seem in a big hurry to find her. They're too busy looking at Ricky for this."

"Then we should try going to her address first. It's only about ten miles from here. Besides, if we ask about her at the Peacock, word might get back to her. Not to mention what might happen to us for asking."

Rhetta made a left turn into the Peacock's pothole-riddled parking lot. The only car near the building was incongruous in the surroundings—a magnificent late-model Dodge Viper. She pulled in beside it and shut off Streak. She climbed out and wandered around to the front of the spotless red machine. The personalized plate read MYVPR. "Hmm. *My Viper*. I'd take it in a heartbeat." She glanced at the plate again and noticed it bore a running horse across the top. Not an Illinois tag. The car must belong to a wealthy Peacock customer from Kentucky.

Rhetta returned to her vehicle and leaned on the passenger door. Woody had rolled down the window, but was still buckled in. She pointed to the bar. "This is the only strip joint in a fifty mile radius of where you say her address is. All the more reason to stop here and check it out." She eyed Woody, who still hadn't unfastened his seat belt. "Aren't you coming with me?"

"I want to know how you know this is the only strip joint? You make a habit of going to strip joints? Does Randolph know about this?"

She glared at him. "You're not the only person who knows how to use Google."

Woody wasn't swayed. "This isn't a good idea. This is a rough place, Rhetta. We have no business being here." She knew he was referring to the stories they'd heard about unsavory happenings at the Peacock. Tales of abundant drugs and hard-boiled mobsters, prostitution rings, and you-name-it made the news many times over the years. "That snappy red Viper probably belongs to a hit man out of Chicago," he added.

She turned so he wouldn't see her roll her eyes with impatience as she headed for the entrance. He threw open the car door. She was already striding toward the building. "Hold on, I'm coming, since you're determined to go in and ask about her." He loped toward her. When she saw he was following, she waited for him to catch up. He placed a hand on her arm. "Just what, exactly, are you going to say?"

"I don't know yet. I'll play this by ear." Woody groaned and Rhetta shot him a withering look. At least she hoped it was. She felt like she was the one withering, standing in the heat arguing with him.

The Peacock was housed in a sixty-year old, flat-roofed concrete block building in a shade of yellowish green that hadn't been popular in over forty years. An eight-foot peacock in chipped pink paint and trimmed in neon tubing adorned the front. At night, the lighted neon peacock strutted across the face of the building. By day, it merely looked worn out.

Rhetta cupped her hands around her eyes and peered through the frosted glass on the locked entry door. Although she couldn't see anyone, lights glowed from inside. "Someone must be here. There are lights on," she said as she banged on the door. The heat had already caused sweat droplets to pop out on her forehead, and made Woody's head shine. Wiping his head with a handkerchief he'd pulled from his rear pants pocket, Woody stopped alongside her. She'd forgotten her sunglasses in the car, so she shielded her eyes as she swept them across the parking area. Unless there was additional parking in back, there were no other cars.

At the sound of her knocking, a shadow slid from behind the bar and made its way to the door. "Someone's coming, but I can't tell if it's a man or a woman," Rhetta whispered, just as the figure reached the door and unlocked it. A tall, slim brunette woman of indeterminate age greeted them.

"Yes?" she asked. Her voice sounded much older than her face appeared. Probably from the years of smoking as evidenced by the lit cigarette she carried, the smoke coiling toward the ceiling. She took a deep drag, then said, "What can I do for you? The bar doesn't open until seven." She turned her head and blew the smoke out of the side of her mouth.

"We're not looking for the bar. I'm trying to find someone, and I wonder if she may have worked here at one time."

"Maybe. Who wants to know? Are you guys cops?" She scrutinized them from top to bottom. "Or the IRS?"

"Us, IRS? No. Not cops, either. We're bankers." Rhetta glanced at Woody. He was staring at the redhead. His hand went to the top of his head.

The woman threw her head back and laughed. "That's a new one. Bankers." Her laughed turned to a choking cough. When she caught her breath, she said, "The last two nuts that showed up here were carrying Bibles. They were a husband and wife team from some little reform church over in Marble Hill. They stopped the girls on their way in. They did that for a couple of days, and finally gave up. Tried to get the girls to quit working here. Didn't have another job for 'em, but wanted 'em to quit so they could get saved." She took another long drag, then tossed the still burning cigarette out into the broken asphalt parking lot. "So, are you guys going to lend 'em money instead of trying to save 'em?" Her laugh turned to a rattle, and then she coughed again. After a wheezy breath, she folded her arms across her chest. "All right, who are you looking for?"

Rhetta shot Woody a glance, and he nodded.

"Mylene Allard," he said. "Do you know her?"

The woman stepped to within inches of Rhetta. With hands on her narrow hips, she studied Rhetta from top to bottom, then performed a similar appraisal of Woody. When she was apparently satisfied, she stepped back and held the door open, gesturing for them to follow her. "Come in," she said, jutting her chin toward the interior. Once inside, she closed and bolted the door. Rhetta spun around and stared at the locked door. At least she had Woody there for protection, although she wished she had her .38. The locked door made her decidedly nervous. More than one person had been shot at the Peacock. She glanced around the dim interior. The air was stale with cigarette smoke. Tables with chairs stacked on top were crowded together on the hardwood floor. Along one side of the huge open room was a long bar, with stools lined up close together, like soldiers awaiting orders. Across the opposite wall was a raised stage where Rhetta spotted several poles and a few cages on platforms. Cages? Were those handcuffs attached to the bars? She shuddered.

The brunette whirled around.

"I'm Mylene Allard."

CHAPTER 31

WOODY, WHO'D BEEN LEADING the way, stopped so suddenly that Rhetta bumped into him. She scrambled around him. The woman's expression had hardened as she stood there facing them.

"Now that you know who I am, would you mind telling me who you two are?" Mylene stepped back and from somewhere that Rhetta couldn't have guessed, she produced a pistol and took aim directly at Woody.

Oh, crap. Didn't see that coming.

Rhetta held up her arms, palms out. Woody was quick to follow suit.

"Wait, that's not necessary," Rhetta said, directing her chin toward the weapon. "In fact, you've been trying to contact me. I'm Rhetta McCarter, and this is my associate, Woody Zelinski." Woody nodded.

Mylene scrutinized them both for a long minute before tucking the pearl-handled .38 into her waistband at the small of her back. Her large chambray shirt, worn outside the denim capris had provided a perfect hiding place for the weapon.

When she did, Rhetta and Woody lowered their arms. Rhetta had a sudden urge to use the bathroom, but decided she could do that later. Her bladder was probably contracting from fear.

"Well, this is a surprise, Rhetta McCarter. How did you know to find me here?"

"How about if you tell me first, why you were trying to reach me?"

"Is this what's called a standoff?" Mylene chuckled and reached in a breast pocket for a package of cigarettes.

As she went through the process of withdrawing one and lighting it, it was Rhetta's turn to size up Mylene. Although the woman possessed a smoker's voice, her pale facial skin, evidence of a life spent mostly indoors, was remarkably free from wrinkles. Aside from a few tiny crows' feet at the corner of her eyes, her face was smooth, and dotted with tiny freckles. A quick glance to her thick, shoulder length hair didn't reveal any grey at the roots. Rhetta guessed they were about the same age.

Mylene stopped at a table sporting upside-down chairs and deftly grabbed one, turned it over and set it on the floor near the table. As she reached for another, Woody and Rhetta stepped up, grabbed one apiece, and joined the first chair. The three sat, and Rhetta glanced at Woody. His head was shiny.

Mylene began. "All right, Miss Rhetta, I'll go first. I wanted to meet you out at the barn where you found Malcom Griffith. After I spoke to you, I decided that you might actually call the cops, so I decided not to go." She paused and took a deep drag. Another coughing fit followed. Rhetta eyed the cigarette. Although she powerfully wanted to light up and join in, the coughing and raspy voice reminded her of why she needed to stay away from smoking. Was it already too late for Mylene? That didn't do much to quell her nicotine craving, which got stronger when she was stressed. Like now.

Woody coughed and fanned the smoke away. He scooted his chair back.

"I'll put this out, if it bothers you," Mylene said, and ground the cigarette out on the concrete floor.

"Thanks," Woody mumbled. He didn't pull the chair back up.

"What on earth did you want to meet me for?" Rhetta continued. "Did you know Malcom Griffith?" Rhetta's mind began racing with possibilities. Could Mylene be the missing pole dancer?

Mylene nodded slowly. "I knew him. I wanted to see where he died. I wanted to make sure he was dead. Your information was in the paper, where you worked, etc., so you were easy enough to find."

"Were you the pole dancer?"

"I was a pole dancer. I manage this place, now." When she saw Rhetta nod, she continued. "Which pole dancer were you referring to?" In spite of accommodating Woody earlier, she fired up another cigarette.

Rhetta decided she must be a chain smoker. The stale air and cigarette smoke began affecting her, too. She coughed and dared a look at Woody before answering. His head had been swiveling back and forth as the women spoke, as though watching a tennis match.

"I, uh, we, that is, we had heard that Malcom had made off with a lot of money and a pole dancer. Of course, that was before he was found murdered," Rhetta said, squirming uncomfortably. She didn't want Mylene getting angry and whipping that gun out again.

Mylene threw her head back and laughed.

Rhetta and Woody exchanged glances. This was funny?

"Did you go out to the barn anyway, Saturday night?" Rhetta asked. Woody coughed suddenly, and glared at Rhetta.

Ignoring him, she went on. "Did you happen to run into Jeremy Spears while you were there?"

"Let's go, Rhetta." Woody said, jumping up and grabbing her elbow. "The smoke is really bothering me."

She jerked her elbow back, and glared at him. "I'm just asking a question here, Woody."

"I didn't go to the barn. And I certainly didn't kill Jeremy Spears, if that's where you're going," Mylene answered softly. "Although I couldn't stand the little creep."

Woody sat, and put his hands up in surrender. "I give up. I don't know why she's asking you this."

Rhetta glared again at Woody, hoping that he'd just keep his mouth shut if he couldn't contribute anything worthwhile.

"The Cape Girardeau Sheriff's Department has your phone number, so if we were able to find you, I'm sure they can, too," Rhetta said, hoping to imply that the cops would know where to come looking for them, should they not return home.

"What do you mean, we?" Woody asked.

Rhetta ignored him, and leveled her gaze at Mylene. "I think you killed Jeremy Spears and Malcom Griffith."

Woody groaned and buried his head on his arms.

Mylene took another drag, this time without coughing. She blew a long spiral upward, then followed that with little round puffs that morphed into smoke rings.

"My father taught me how to blow smoke rings," she said, almost wistfully. "He and I used to sneak out to the barn and smoke together. Probably not the best thing for a father to teach a thirteen-year-old. I guess I can thank him for the emphysema I have now." She ground the cigarette out in the same spot on the old floor where she'd extinguished the other.

Rhetta glanced around. Now that her eyes had adjusted to the dim interior, she observed several other dead cigarettes scattered around the floor. She decided that cleanliness wasn't a top priority in the Pink Peacock.

Mylene shook her head. "No, my dear, while I give you credit for finding me, your investigation is totally on the wrong tangent. I didn't kill either one of them." She stood and ambled to the bar where she poured herself a tall drink of deep amber liquid from a decanter on a glass shelf. She reached for two more glasses. "Can I offer you a drink? On the house, of course."

Rhetta and Woody shook their heads.

She carried her drink back to the table and sat. "I didn't kill Jeremy, although I hated him. And I didn't kill Malcom, because I loved him." She tilted her head back and downed most of the beverage.

Of course, she's the pole dancer! Even though she hadn't run away with Malcom, she really was his missing lover! Rhetta's stomach quivered in excitement. She couldn't wait to tell Randolph.

Mylene smiled. "You see, Malcom was my father. Jeremy Spears was my bastard brother."

CHAPTER 32

"I COULD USE THAT drink now," Rhetta said. Mylene smiled and headed for the bar. Rhetta wasn't that surprised to hear that Jeremy Spears was Malcom Griffith's son, especially after finding the love letter in Anjanette Spears' desk. She hadn't told Woody about her find, so he looked completely ambushed.

"You want one, too?" Mylene asked Woody, raising a glass. He shook his head.

She returned with a heavy whiskey tumbler and handed it to Rhetta. Rhetta sipped, swallowed, and coughed. Straight, strong rye whiskey. Maybe she needed a cigarette instead.

Just as she was working up the nerve to ask Mylene for one in front of Woody, whom she had tried to convince that she had quit, a loud thumping on the door interrupted them. She badly needed to bolster herself with nicotine so that she could question Mylene's story.

"We don't open until seven," Mylene said, as she made her way through the tables to see who was assaulting the door. Rhetta was sure that whoever was there was pounding so loudly they couldn't have heard her.

Rhetta peered at the frosted glass door, seeing only general shapes of the group assembled there. A small cluster, determined to enter, if the knocking was any indication. As soon as Mylene opened the door, five men dressed in black stormed through.

Rhetta wasn't sure who they were, but the weapons in their hands captured her full attention.

"Hands on your heads!" barked the leader of the contingent, a square-built man of average height, wearing a black, bulletproof vest over black T-shirt and cargo pants. A black ball cap pulled low over his eyes completed the ensemble and a badge hung from a belt at his waist. All Rhetta could tell of his face was that he wore a thick black mustache. As soon as Rhetta and Woody stood, Woody placed both of his hands on top of his head. Mylene had already obeyed.

"Rhetta, put your hands on your head," Woody said in a very loud whisper.

"But, we haven't done—"

"Do as I tell you ma'am. I won't be telling you again," the mustache said as he sidled up alongside her. She made out the letters "ACSD" on his cap.

"Okay, okay, but what's going on?" No one answered her.

Mr. Mustache took both of Rhetta's wrists and in one swift move, wrenched them behind her back and snapped shut a pair of handcuffs.

"Look here," she protested, "what do you think you're doing?"

Again, he didn't answer her, but turned and shouted orders to the remaining lawmen. "Make sure you look everywhere, including the damn toilet this time." They fanned out. One disappeared into the washroom area.

Woody and Mylene were also cuffed. Mylene snickered. "It's Alexander County's finest, screwing up my life again."

Mustache walked by and fairly hissed at her. "You're going down this time, Mylene, and I don't mean with a customer." He laughed at his own joke, and pushed her forward. He began chanting, "You have the right to remain silent. Anything you say can and will be used against you in a court of law. You have the right to speak to an attorney, and to have an attorney present during any questioning. If you cannot afford a lawyer, one will be provided for you at government expense." He shook her. Rather roughly and unnecessarily, Rhetta thought, before adding, "Do you understand?"

Mylene didn't answer. He shook her again. "Yeah. I understand. By the way, Dick Tracy, you forgot to remove the .38 at my back." He stopped at the door, and relieved her of the weapon, stuffing it into his own belt.

"This time, I want my gun back, understand? You guys got enough weapons from me now to outfit the whole force of six. By the way, who's not here?" She glanced over her shoulder. "Oh, yeah, Mr. Big Cheese, the duly elected sheriff isn't here this time. Is he too busy playing golf?" She laughed. The deputy gripped her arm and led her out of the building.

Rhetta and Woody remained standing while the other lawmen ransacked the area, overturning chairs, stools, and dumping out the contents of nearly every open liquor bottle—and not into the sink. A dark stain from the alcohol mixture pooling on the floor spread to the side of the bar. The officers emptied the bowls of chips into the mix and ground it in with their boots, laughing as they created a huge mess.

The stench of liquor wafted across the room, filling Rhetta's nostrils and making her stomach queasy.

As though finally remembering they had two people in handcuffs, a young deputy strode over, pulled out a laminated card from his shirt pocket and began reading, "You have the right to remain silent...." Rhetta realized with absolute clarity that the place was being raided, and they were being arrested.

The deputy shoved her in the small of her back, urging her out the door and toward a waiting police vehicle—a black and white four-door sedan with *Alexander County Sheriff Department* splashed along the side, and red and blue lights swirling overhead. She stole a glance at Woody. His face was ashen and his head shiny with perspiration. As they marched, she remembered her purse was still inside the club. Her phone was in her purse. She stopped walking, turning to face her captor. "Officer, please have someone get my purse."

He ignored her request, and urged her forward. He pushed her hard enough that she stumbled. "Get into the car, ma'am." He opened the door, placed a hand on her head, and began to force her to sit.

She resisted. "I'd just hate to have my husband and lawyer, Judge Randolph McCarter, have to bring theft charges against you."

He shoved her all the way into the car, locked the door, and went around to the driver's side. Punching a radio on his shoulder, he said, "Jack, bring my prisoner's purse, will you? I'm trembling with fear out here. Her husband is a judge."

He said the word Judge like it had two syllables, *ju-udge*.

Not a good sign.

CHAPTER 33

Woody made the trip home in silence until they had crossed the Emerson Bridge and were once again on Missouri soil. A deputy had deposited them in the Pink Peacock parking lot next to Rhetta's unlocked SUV. She was amazed Streak was still there. The dark parking lot was empty except for her car. The Viper was gone. Either someone had made a choice between stealing a Viper or a Trailblazer, and the Trailblazer lost, or the Viper belonged to Mylene, and she had driven it home. Evidently the raid had been bad for business. The bar was closed.

Woody glanced at his watch, sighed and leaned his head against the headrest. "Jenn was mad at me because we got arrested. Like it was my fault. I tried to explain that it wasn't my fault. It was your fault."

Rhetta shot him a look, which he probably couldn't tell much about in the dark. She chose not to answer him. No point in arguing. Instead, she felt along the top of the console for her cell phone, and glanced down long enough to speed dial Randolph. "Yes, we're fine. I'm dropping Woody off at the office, then I'll be right home." She disconnected, then returned the iPhone to the console. She couldn't just let his remark slide past. "What do you mean it was my fault? I'm not the one who had drugs stashed. Anyway, if it's any consolation, I think Randolph is mad at me, too. I don't think I've ever heard him strangle on words like he did when he asked me to repeat where I was."

"He ought to be plenty mad. I know I am." When Rhetta started to protest, Woody held up his hand in a stop gesture, and didn't let her speak.

"We had no business being at the Pink Peacock, no matter what time of the day. That is Sin City, and today, we were the sinners."

"Woody, how can you say that? We didn't do anything wrong. I'm sure this will all be cleared up." She fiddled with the radio, turning it on, then off. "Besides, we needed to find Mylene Allard. We had nothing to do with her operation, and this will all be straightened out." She dared hope her bravado rang true. Of all the places to be caught in a drug bust, Alexander County, Illinois had to be the worst place on earth. She had heard nothing good about any of the officials or cops there. In fact, what she always heard was how crooked they all were.

"Sure it will. I heard the deputies say they found a huge stash of drugs, and there you were, sitting and enjoying a drink with the woman they'd come after. There's going to be plenty to have to clear up. I don't think we looked too innocent, even to me." He sighed and rubbed his head three times. "I should've known better than to go with you on a hunt for that woman."

Rhetta turned into the now dark office parking lot and stopped alongside Woody's Jeep. "I'll wait to make sure your car starts before I leave." She didn't like that the parking lot didn't have any night lighting.

He cut her a look, started to say something, then apparently thought the better of it. He just shook his head and climbed out of the car.

Within a minute, the Jeep pulled out on to Kingshighway. Rhetta followed, turned the opposite way and aimed Streak for home. She glanced at her watch. It was nearly 9:00 PM.

Although Randolph remained calm when she'd finally got hold of her purse and phone and was able to call him to tell him what had happened, she heard the edge to his voice. It reminded her of her mother's tone whenever Rhetta called home after staying out past curfew. Her mother always reprimanded her when she got home. Rhetta braced for a scolding from Randolph, too.

She turned up the Oldies. It would take much more than the DJ, Cousin Brucie, playing Andy Kim, the Beach Boys or the Righteous Brothers to cheer her up. She had to be back in court in Alexander County in one week to face arraignment. She turned the radio off and swerved into a convenience store parking lot, and stopped near the trashcans. Opening the console, she rooted around under her tissues and sunglasses and pulled out her secret stash. Leaning against the front fender, she slipped on her plastic gloves, fired up a cigarette and inhaled a deep, lung-filling jolt of nicotine. She stood and smoked the cigarette down to the smallest nub she'd ever managed to smoke a butt down to. When there wasn't enough left for a single drag, she ground out the stub, peeled off the gloves and tossed them and what was left of the pack of smokes into the trashcan. Disgusted with herself, she climbed back in the SUV and headed home.

* * *

The motion sensor light over the garage door clicked on, spilling daylight quality floodlighting into the driveway when she pulled up. That reminded her to ask the landlord about installing lights in their parking lot at work.

The door took forever to fold upward. It probably didn't, really, but her dread of going in made the door appear to move slowly. After she parked Streak, she slipped into the kitchen from the garage. The house was dark and silent. She listened intently and couldn't hear any sounds from the television. Switching on the overhead recessed lighting, she called out cheerfully, "Sweets, I'm home," hoping to make light of the situation. Her heart, however, wasn't so light.

From the deck, Randolph slid open the glass door, and padded into the kitchen. He was wearing his slippers and the blue robe she'd bought for his birthday. Her heart melted. He carried in an empty iced-tea glass, and set it gently into the sink. Guiltily, Rhetta thought about smoking the cigarette. Randolph could've easily used the occasion as a reason to justify mixing himself a drink, but chose iced tea instead. Hearing that your wife was arrested in a neighboring state for possession with the intent to distribute drugs would have driven anyone to drink. He had really quit drinking. She vowed she'd never buy another pack of cigarettes.

He rinsed the glass, opened the dishwasher and set it carefully inside. Then he turned around to Rhetta and opened his arms. "Come here." She melted into his embrace. They stood silently, Rhetta soaking up the love she felt from her husband.

He led her to the kitchen table and sat her down. "Do you want some coffee?" She shook her head. "Are you hungry?"

When she nodded, Randolph went to the refrigerator and brought out ham, condiments and a fresh loaf of wheat bread. She watched him as he unwrapped the ham, her mouth watering at the sweet smoky fragrance of the meat. He placed the food on the table, then sat across from her, taking her hands in his. "Want to tell me how this happened?"

She told him everything. Except the part about smoking.

CHAPTER 34

"I CAN'T UNDERSTAND WHY Mylene Allard posted bond for us, but I'm sure grateful she did." Rhetta guided a knife through the boneless ham. She arranged the slices on a small platter along with wheat bread, and retrieved a couple of plates from the cabinet. Now that she was home, she was ravenous. She and Woody had been incarcerated right through the supper hour. She returned to the table with the plates and a tin of chocolate chip cookies. She couldn't fathom what Alexander County would have served them. Probably bread and water. Or nothing.

Randolph poured them each a glass of milk while she prepared their sandwiches. He returned the milk to the refrigerator. "Maybe she just wants you out of her hair, so she can get back to work. Mylene is probably selling drugs at the Pink Peacock." He eyed the cookies.

"Heck if I know about any drugs. I didn't see any, even when the deputies were tearing the place apart. She was just about to elaborate on Malcom Griffith and Jeremy Spears when we were, ah, interrupted." Rhetta stuffed a bite of the ham sandwich into her mouth. She swallowed, then studied what was left. She found a piece of fat still clinging to the ham, so she carefully peeled it off. "She did tell me that she and Jeremy were half-brother and -sister. Malcom was their father. She managed to get herself out of jail almost immediately, while we sat around for a couple of hours." She took a long drink of milk and wiped the cat whisker off her upper lip. "I wonder why she posted bail for us? Maybe she knew the officers wouldn't let us make any phone calls. By the way, isn't that unconstitutional?"

"Apparently not in Illinois. They have their own ideas. That ought to teach you to stay away from there permanently." Randolph finished one sandwich and began preparing a second for himself.

"I hate to hear that about Illinois. I still like Chicago," Rhetta said, and took another bite. She dabbed at her lips with a paper napkin. "Umm, this is delicious. I'm so happy to be home."

Randolph had to smile. "Then stay out of Alexander County, will you? I'll call the State's Attorney in the morning and see if we can work something out." He finished his sandwich, and snatched a paper towel to dab his chin.

"Her lawyer looked pretty sharp. He wore a dark green suit that looked like it was silk. And his shoes were those European, loafer-style, with tassels in a sort of cordovan color. Is cordovan still a color? Anyhow, he didn't wear a dress shirt, but had on a pale green T-shirt and no socks. He looked more like a rapper than a lawyer. Or a member of the Chicago Bulls. He was the tallest man I've ever met." Rhetta wolfed the rest of her sandwich and eyed the remaining two pieces of ham on the plate. Randolph snatched one and left one for her. She scarfed the last piece. Randolph popped open the tin of cookies and nabbed several. Rhetta reached for a cookie, then changed her mind. *No cookies.* Still, she eyed the cookies longingly.

While he sat there nibbling, Rhetta gathered their plates for the dishwasher. "At any rate, Mylene may be my new best friend, especially if she sent her lawyer to bail us out." Rhetta veered to her purse sitting on the island. "I have his card." After digging around, she waved it triumphantly. "His name is Matthew Elias."

Randolph sniffed and held up a cookie for closer inspection. "Mylene may now be your new worst enemy, especially if she's a murderer selling dope." He plopped the cookie into his mouth.

"I don't think she killed anybody. And I have a hard time believing she's peddling or using dope."

"Then why does she have the most powerful lawyer in Illinois representing her?"

"You know Matthew Elias?" Rhetta filled the soap dispenser in the dishwasher and pushed the start button. The dishwasher began filling with water.

"You ever heard of Kill-R-Dogg, the rapper?" Randolph closed the cookie tin and carried it across the kitchen to the pantry.

Rhetta cleaned the sink and gathered up the morning newspaper that was spread out on the countertop. "No, can't say that I have. Sixties on Six doesn't play much rap." The dishwasher began sloshing its way through the cycles.

"He's the singer-slash-rapper that was accused of killing that thirteen-year-old girl last year."

Rhetta turned from the dishwasher, and dried her hands on a kitchen towel. "I remember that." Rhetta vividly recalled the horrifying story of the raised-in-the-hood success-story rapper who'd been accused of kidnapping and molesting, and finally killing a young girl who'd gone to a concert. She had been missing for nearly a month when police arrested Kill-R-Dogg and charged him. He denied any wrongdoing, even after they found her brutalized body buried on the grounds of his country home outside Evanston, Illinois.

"Uh-huh. After getting him off, Elias is now the most sought-after criminal defense attorney in Illinois. Now you tell me he's Mylene's lawyer."

"Oh, crap."

CHAPTER 35

RHETTA WAS THE FIRST to arrive at the office the next morning. The sun shone brilliantly in a cloudless cerulean sky. Although the day was picture perfect, her mood didn't match it. She replayed the events of the previous day, still worried about Woody. From the way he acted on the way home, she wasn't sure if it was because of his PTSD or if he was totally peeved.

For a moment she thought about snatching the coveted parking spot, since technically, she felt the agreement was off, since Randolph knew everything, leaving Woody with no ammunition with which to tattle on her to Randolph. She'd confessed everything to Randolph about their lunatic trip to Illinois in search of Mylene Allard. Plus, she'd arrived first. Instead, she decided to treat Woody especially nice, since he blamed her for them getting arrested. So, she let him have the spot. She still, however, couldn't follow his logic on the getting arrested business. All she'd done was stop to try and find Mylene Allard. She didn't know anything about any drugs, presuming there really was a stash of drugs seized in the raid.

She'd cruised through Starbucks and ordered two grande light cappuccinos to go. It was going to be a double caffeine morning. Woody liked these, so she wanted to bribe him into making up. The unique fragrance wafted to her from the cups sitting in the cup holders by the console. That reminded her that she'd never been able to carry drinks in Cami. People driving in the seventies must have never thought about eating or drinking anything while they drove. None of the cars of that era seemed to be equipped with drink holders. Come to think of it, most of the population was thinner back then, too. Was there any correlation? She decided to ask Ricky about the possibility of a custom console for the Z28, should she ever get the car back from the sheriff's department. She decided she needed cup holders.

She enjoyed the quiet time in the mornings when she managed to get to the office early. There was something strangely comforting about hearing the ticking of the oversized clock, and turning on the lights to start the day.

After setting Woody's beverage on his desk, she adjusted her chair, then sat and stared at her files while the computer booted up. The single chime sounded, indicating the booting process was completed. As the computer did its thing, Rhetta turned to gaze out the large window to the parking lot. LuEllen had parked her spotless white Honda Accord at the very end of the lot. No wonder the woman looked so healthy and stayed so slim. She walked at every opportunity. Rhetta almost felt guilty about wanting to park so close to the door. She sipped her sinful coffee.

LuEllen called out to Rhetta as she walked in. "I took your books back." She unloaded her purse and her lunch tote on to the table near her desk.

"Thanks a million. I promise I won't make you return any more late books for me." Rhetta really meant it, this time. She hated taking back late books, and vowed not to make her wonderful LuEllen do her dirty work anymore. She glanced at LuEllen's lunch tote and figured it probably contained something healthy, like a salad. She spun around to her computer and opened her email.

LuEllen tucked her purse into her desk drawer, and pulled out her computer chair. "Woody called me and said he isn't coming in this morning. Said he's not feeling well."

Rhetta stopped reading her email. "Did he say what was wrong?" She knew that Woody was terribly upset last night. Maybe he just didn't want to have to deal with Rhetta this morning—probably why he'd called in sick to LuEllen and not Rhetta. Rhetta felt guilty about possibly taking Woody to the brink of an episode.

"Nope. Just said he'd try to come in later. He has an appointment with a customer this afternoon." LuEllen turned on her own computer as she strolled by her desk, picking up her lunch tote on her way to the kitchen. Rhetta heard her humming while she made coffee.

She needed to quit feeling guilty so much. As she reached for a file, she spotted the FedEx envelope that Ricky gave her containing the check payment for Monster. Had that just been a couple of days ago? So much had happened since then.

She'd scanned the TV news this morning to hear if any funeral arrangements had been announced for Jeremy, but there was nothing. Woody might bring the paper with him, so she'd check it when he came in.

She dumped the contents of the envelope on to her desk. The check appeared to be a typical business type check, drawn on a Regions Bank in Corinth, Mississippi. Yet, when she read the hand-written FedEx label, the shipper's address was from Paducah. She snatched the phone and dialed her local FedEx office.

Carol Hartwell, a customer Rhetta had closed a loan for a few months ago, worked at the FedEx depot south of Cape. She answered on the second ring. After asking her for information about the account, Carol promised that she would call Rhetta back on her lunch break with the information. Next, Rhetta Googled the number for the bank in Corinth.

After explaining to the clerk who answered the phone that she wanted to verify funds in an account, the manager came on the line. "You're about the sixth or seventh person that's called checking on the validity of this same check number on the Valley View Farms account. I'm sorry to inform you that the check is a forgery, and that the account, while valid, has been frozen. Someone stole a Valley View Farms check and is trying to forge copies of it to buy stuff from all over the country. I'm afraid the check is no good." The woman sounded genuinely sorry.

"I understand. I was pretty sure it was bogus, too. Thanks for your help." Rhetta returned the phone to the cradle. This was the real deal as far as scams went. Was "real deal scam" an oxymoron?

It was eleven-thirty when Carol Hartwell checked in. "That FedEx account number you gave me belongs to Crimson Peripherals in California," she said.

"Crimson Peripherals in California? That means someone is using their account number to commit fraud. CP is so huge I bet they never go over each and every charge on their account. Can you report it?"

Carol promised she would.

Poor Ricky. She'd definitely been scammed. Someone who stole a check had somehow gotten Crimson Peripherals' account number. It could be a former FedEx employee, or someone who had seen the account number written out on a label. At least Ricky hadn't sent the shipper the thousand dollars.

Rhetta tapped Ricky's cell number from her favorites list. Ricky's voice mail picked up. "Hey, Ricky, I did some checking, and the check you received for the Monster is for sure a scam. Good thing you didn't send money to the phony shipper. Call me and I'll fill you in."

Two minutes later, Rhetta's iPhone played *Little Deuce Coupe*, the oldies tune Rhetta had programmed as a ringtone for Ricky's number.

A distraught Ricky blurted, "Too late, Rhetta. I sent the money this morning via Western Union."

Chapter 36

"Oh, no." Rhetta couldn't fathom what Ricky was telling her. What on earth was she thinking? Rhetta had pointedly advised her not to send any money until she researched it. "I told you not to do anything until I could check it out."

Ricky sniffled, as though she might cry. "I know what you said, but I kept getting emails telling me that I needed to send the money right away, so that the buyer could make arrangements to get the car. They said it was urgent that I do it immediately. I emailed them back and told them I wanted to check it out first, but they told me that I had their money and that they expected me to live up to my side of the deal. They convinced me they had really sent me the money." Ricky blew her nose. "In fact, they threatened to report me to the FBI if I didn't send them the money, because they said they verified that I received the funds." Then she added in a small voice. "Rhetta, they are so convincing. Are you positive that the check was no good?"

Rhetta couldn't believe Ricky sent a thousand dollars via Western Union to the supposed shipper in Paducah, Kentucky after Rhetta had specifically warned her not to. No use in chastising her anymore. She could tell her friend felt terrible. Nobody likes to lose a thousand bucks. "I'm calling the FBI. We have to get your money back."

Before Ricky could argue, Rhetta disconnected and searched for the phone book. After riffling through three drawers, she found it under the desk phone, where it was logically supposed to be. The girl who cleaned the office must have put it there. She hated when that happened.

After thumbing through the endless listings for the Federal Government, she finally located a toll free number for the FBI. She tapped it into the desk phone and waited while the number rang. When the number finally auto answered, she was invited via voice prompts to select a destination for her call. None of the choices was what she needed, so she repeatedly punched the zero button. Finally, a human came on the line. "Federal Bureau of Investigation, how may I direct your call?" asked a very bored-sounding young female voice.

"I want to speak to an agent, please."

"What is the purpose of your call?"

"I just told you, to speak to an agent."

"Hold, please." Rhetta was treated to a tinny instrumental version of "Light My Fire" before an agent finally came on the line.

"Agent John Wa…" He mumbled the last part of his name so that Rhetta didn't really catch it. Was it Waxman? Whitman? Whatever.

"Agent, I want to report an interstate scam. It started with a phony offer to buy a car my friend had listed on eBay." Then Rhetta told him the story. To his credit, he never once interrupted her.

"Did your friend lose any money?"

"Yes, I told you, she sent a thousand dollars via Western Union to someone who claimed to be a shipper in Paducah, Kentucky."

"Well, ma'am, I'm sorry she did that, but the only thing I can tell you to do is to go on line to *wwwdotIC3dotgov* and file a complaint to the internet crimes unit."

"File a complaint online? Are you telling me she has to go online and do this? You can't help her?"

"Ma'am, if we took the time to investigate every one of these kinds of reports we get, then that's all we'd be doing. There are thousands of cases like this."

Rhetta felt her blood begin to simmer and her temperature shoot up. "Maybe if the FBI would start going after these people and prosecuting them, they wouldn't continue to operate so blatantly. Then there wouldn't be so many, and you might put a stop to it. They probably know you don't care about stopping them."

"Yes, ma'am. She needs to go online." Rhetta swore she heard him yawn.

"No, agent whatever-your-name is, we won't go online and file a complaint. I think that's what you get paid for. It's not our job and it's obviously a waste of time, since this type of crime is so rampant. Have a nice day." She slammed the receiver.

Why the heck hadn't Ricky listened to her? She cradled her head in her hands, hoping to ward off the headache she felt crawling across her forehead from her temples and squeezing her head. She headed to the kitchen for water to down some Advil.

She rushed back to her desk and snatched her iPhone from her purse and called Ricky. She had an idea.

"When did you send out the money?"

"Uh, around eight this morning."

Rhetta's heart began to thump with excitement. "Did Western Union say how long it would take before the recipient could pick it up?" Somewhere in the back of her mind, Rhetta thought she remembered that it took up to six hours to get the money to its destination.

"They said it wouldn't be ready before two this afternoon."

"Do you still have all the information and the address of the pickup location?"

"Yes, of course."

Rhetta glanced at her watch. It was 11:35. They had time.

"Fire up the Monster. We're going to Paducah."

CHAPTER 37

RHETTA PAUSED AT LUELLEN'S desk on her way out. "Please call Woody and tell him I'm not in the office. He may come in sooner." Although LuEllen regarded her quizzically, she didn't ask what that statement meant. Rhetta didn't take time to explain. "I need to go to Paducah, Kentucky, but if you need me, call me on my cell." LuEllen nodded and Rhetta swore she heard her "tsk" under her breath. She'd explain later. She was the boss and could leave whenever she wanted to, but still, she liked to be there if anyone needed her. She knew Woody wouldn't need her; he was extremely efficient. Did Obsessive Compulsive Disorder go hand in hand with Post-Traumatic Stress Disorder? If not, then Woody manifested both. It didn't matter. He was the best agent she could ask for.

* * *

Streak's fuel tank required replenishing, as did Rhetta's caffeine, so it was twenty minutes before Rhetta made it into Ricky's driveway. Ricky sailed out her back door, locking it and sliding the key under The Rock. She loped toward the garage where she kept Monster.

Rhetta honked and stuck her head out her window. "Let's take Streak. I just filled it, it's got air conditioning, and we won't have to worry about getting dust all over your car."

Ricky gave her a thumbs-up and slid into the passenger seat. She shivered.

"I know, I know. It's cold enough to hang beef in here." Rhetta turned up the temperature so Ricky wouldn't catch a chill. Ricky had dressed for hot weather in a pale blue T-shirt, white Capris and sandals. She hadn't brought along a sweater or a sweatshirt. Rhetta knew that she was probably the only person whose passengers consistently carried outerwear with them whenever they accompanied her during the summer.

"So tell me what we're going to do in Paducah." Ricky set her Dr. Pepper can into the beverage holder, and snapped her shoulder and seat belt harness into place.

"Here's my plan. We go to this Trevor Brinkman's address, then park where we can watch the house. We follow him as he goes to pick up the Western Union MoneyGram." Rhetta tucked her purse into the back seat, and made sure her phone was handy.

"Then what do we do?"

"We ask him for it back, of course."

Ricky groaned. "He's not likely to give it back without a fight. The guy is probably ten feet tall and bulletproof. How about we get the cops to back us up?"

"Sure, we'll ask them. Good idea." Rhetta thought the local cops wouldn't care a whit about helping them get back interstate fraud money. And she already knew what the feds thought.

As they approached the Emerson Bridge that took them into Illinois over the Mississippi River, Rhetta realized that she hadn't crossed that bridge as many times in a month as what she had the past two days. At least this time she could enjoy the view. Bright sunshine sparkled on the water below them, creating the illusion of a dancing firefly festival. Two tugs were languidly pushing their strings of barges upriver. It was amazing those little boats could push or pull the long rows of barges. They were little, but mighty.

Once across the bridge, Rhetta shivered, not from the cold air, but because she remembered Randolph's warning to stay out of Alexander County. And here she was again. She slowed to five miles under the speed limit, in case any deputies were out seeking to fill any quotas.

"How long will it take us to get to Paducah?" Ricky sipped from her soda.

"Normally it takes about an hour and a half, but today it might need to take a little longer." She glanced at her speedometer, making sure she was still obeying the speed limit. "I don't want to get arrested in Illinois again."

"What do you mean, again? When were you ever arrested in Illinois?"

"Yesterday."

Ricky was in mid-gulp and nearly choked on the soda. She set the can down and wiped her chin. "You got arrested yesterday? What on earth for?"

"Woody and I got arrested at the Pink Peacock. Over there." She pointed to the bar, which was coming up on their right. Rhetta slowed, turned right and eased into the empty parking lot. No Viper today. In fact, the windows on the bar were boarded up.

"Holy blazes, did you shoot someone?" Rhetta was known to carry a .38 from time to time. And the Peacock had a reputation for gunfights.

"No, silly. Woody and I were in there talking to Mylene Allard when the place got raided, and we were arrested along with her."

"Who's Mylene Allard?"

Rhetta realized she hadn't caught Ricky up on her adventure from the previous day. "Boy, have I got lots to tell you."

Rhetta turned Streak around to exit the parking lot, but as she drove by the door, she spotted a sheet of paper taped to it that might be a note. She stopped, got out and read the neat handwriting. "Gone Quilting."

CHAPTER 38

"WHAT ON EARTH DOES 'Gone Quilting' mean?" Rhetta muttered the question almost to herself, knowing Ricky wouldn't have a clue. In fact, Ricky hadn't known anything about what had happened yesterday until Rhetta filled her in.

"Oh, blazes, Rhetta, what will you do? You have to go back to court in Cairo?" Cairo, the county seat for Alexander County was nothing more than a forgotten, burned-out shell of a former elegant river city. And infamous for its corruption.

"Randolph is calling the State's Attorney to try to get charges against us dismissed. Woody is totally ticked at me. I'm afraid of a PTSD episode. He got really upset in jail." Woody had sat alone in a holding cell across the hall from her, staring off, saying nothing. When the deputy came to tell them they could leave, he walked like an automaton to the office to collect his things, and didn't speak until they got back to Missouri. She prayed Randolph would be able to convince the State's Attorney that she and Woody were victims of circumstance, and not dope pushers.

Rhetta kept Streak at a sedate 50 miles per hour until she pulled on to Interstate 24 at Vienna. From there she floored it to 70, crossed the Ohio River into Kentucky and exited just west of Paducah. She cruised along at the speed limit until the Paducah city limits sign came into view. The trip from Cape had taken them close to two hours.

They pulled over into a convenience store to use the facilities and restock on Diet Coke and Dr. Pepper. Rhetta set the address Ricky had given her into Streak's GPS. "That's funny. The GPS can find the street, but not that number on the street. Let's drive that way, and see what we can figure out."

"Shouldn't we contact the Paducah police before we go there?" Ricky glanced back and forth from the paper in her hand with Trevor Brinkman's address, to the GPS screen.

"We don't need to bring them in on a wild goose chase. Let's make sure that the address is bona fide. Then we can call them."

"Okay, that's a plan. Let's go." Ricky agreed. She and Rhetta buckled up and Rhetta followed the turn-by-turn directions to the street. They began searching for the house number Rhetta glanced at her watch. Fifteen minutes to two.

Although they easily found the street, finding the number was a different matter. Instead of a house or office being at the location where the number should have been, there was only an empty church parking lot.

Rhetta checked the time again. Five minutes had elapsed. "Maybe we'd better just drive to the supermarket where he was supposed to pick it up. We'll go in and see if Trevor Brinkman shows up to collect his money."

"Rhetta, let's call the police to meet us there. This is making me nervous."

"You're right. I'll call on the way over." Rhetta reprogrammed the GPS for the address of the Shop 'n' Save at 11439 Hickory Hills Boulevard. It was less than a block from the church lot.

They sat in Streak in the parking lot outside the supermarket while Rhetta called 9-1-1. The dispatcher couldn't seem to figure out what Rhetta was trying to tell her. Frustrated after trying two different ways of explaining, Rhetta finally said, "Please, just have an officer come to the Shop 'n' Save on Hickory Hills Boulevard. A man there is about to steal a thousand dollars." Then she disconnected. "That dispatcher couldn't make any sense out of what I was trying to tell her. Maybe if she thinks there's a robbery, she'll dispatch a car."

"I wish we knew what this guy Trevor Brinkman looks like," Ricky said.

"Let's go in." Rhetta figured that Brinkman would be standing near the customer service counter just waiting for the money to arrive. She didn't want to miss him.

Ricky scrambled out of the SUV. Rhetta snatched her purse and keys, locked the door and jogged after Ricky. The only thing Ricky carried was a handful of papers with the information and the receipt.

The sole person standing at the customer service counter was a stocky woman in jeans and a plaid shirt carrying a baby in an infant carrier. No Brinkman. Scanning the nearly empty store, Rhetta could find no one else showing any interest in the customer service counter. After cruising up and down the aisles, Rhetta joined Ricky at the front of the counter. They stood behind the woman and baby and waited for her to complete her transaction.

The young man behind the counter consulted his watch. "Not yet, ma'am. Give it another fifteen minutes, at least. These things sometimes take a little while." The woman nodded and shuffled aside.

"What can I help you with?" the clerk asked as Rhetta and Ricky stepped up to the counter.

"Has a Trevor Brinkman been in to pick up a MoneyGram?"

The clerk, a look of confusion blanketing his acne covered face, glanced from Rhetta to the woman with the baby. "Ah, no. No Trevor Brinkman." He shook his head. Rhetta nodded and began to move aside. "But this woman, over here, said her name is Treva Brinkman, and she's waiting for a MoneyGram." He pointed at the woman and baby.

Rhetta and Ricky spun toward the woman, but were a fraction of a second too late. In a burst of speed, the woman reared back and flung the baby carrier. It hurtled toward them. Ricky cried out and caught it, clutching the carrier to her chest, like a wide receiver catching a pass. With a heavy thud, she landed on the floor flat on her back. Miraculously, she still clutched the baby carrier. Rhetta stumbled over Ricky and sprawled to the floor. She picked herself up and, knee throbbing, scurried after the fleeing baby-tosser. She spotted the woman halfway across the parking lot, and hobbled toward her. With each step, her knee shot out a bolt of pain.

Rhetta spotted the woman, and just as she prepared to tackle her, the woman turned. Rhetta stopped in mid-tackle. To her amazement, it was a different lady—a woman Rhetta guessed to be in her late sixties carrying a walking stick. She was definitely not the woman who had rushed out of the store, but was dressed similarly in light blue jeans and a baggy plaid shirt. The old woman raised her three-toed aluminum cane and was about to slam it over Rhetta's head when Rhetta threw up her arms in self-defense. "Please, I wasn't going to hurt you. I was chasing someone else. A thief," she panted. The woman cautiously lowered her clawed weapon. Rhetta doubled over to catch her breath. She massaged her painful right knee while the old woman voiced her opinions about young hooligans.

As Rhetta mumbled apologies to the frightened elderly woman, a black, late model, high-riding pickup truck with tires as tall as Rhetta, burned out of the parking lot. Fishtailing while it smoked rubber, it nearly collided with a blue and white police cruiser careening into the lot. While the truck roared off, the police car screamed to a stop at the front door of the Shop 'n' Save. Rhetta limped back to the market, huffing to catch her breath. *What the heck was going on? That crazy woman inside the store just tossed her baby at us. What kind of person would do that?*

A crowd began to gather and murmur. Several young men stood menacingly near the police car, pointing toward the cops who had their weapons drawn as they stormed the store. God, she hoped a riot wasn't about to break out. How would she explain that to Randolph?

CHAPTER 39

IT TOOK TWO MORE squad cars, an officer with a megaphone, two television camera crews—one from Paducah, and one from Cape Girardeau—three newspaper reporters with cameras, and a Girl Scout selling cookies to subdue the crowd of over fifty angry people who'd gathered. The locals chanted they weren't going to put up with any more police profiling.

Rhetta spoke up early on, trying to convince the crowd that no persons of color were being arrested. She couldn't speak for the other minorities, like the Irish, Scots or French-Canadians. In fact, no persons at all were being arrested, since the baby-tossing woman had fled in an overgrown pickup. She gave up trying to explain anything to the crowd and retreated into the safety of the supermarket.

It took a lot more explaining to two burly police officers before Rhetta convinced them about the eBay hoax and the involvement by Trevor or Treva Brinkman, or whoever this person was. Rhetta wasn't entirely convinced that the woman with the baby had even been a woman. The stocky build combined with the testosterone-fueled pickup led her to believe it was a man disguised as a female in this scheme. She described Brinkman as best she could. The customer service manager was able to verify the story. Finally, the cops shook their heads, took out their notepads and began to write out everyone's statements.

The baby in the carrier turned out to be a doll covered in blankets, lending more credence to the story about the scam. The store manager, who was called in from a round of golf on his day off, was only too glad to hand over the Western Union money to Ricky, if she and Rhetta promised to leave, never come back, and take the crowd with them. He was not convinced that any of the publicity would benefit his store.

Rhetta steered around the panel van from the Cape television station. She recognized the cameraman/newsman as the one who'd been to her office interviewing Woody about low mortgage rates last spring. He was one of the "stringers" that the Cape station sent out to cover Paducah and Southern Illinois. Those areas are part of the Cape Girardeau viewing and advertising reach, since they were within a hundred mile radius as the crow flies. She waved as she went by. He smiled and gave her a thumbs-up as he rolled the camera on her departure. She decided to call Randolph and warn him that she might appear on the evening news. Again.

* * *

Luckily, Randolph didn't answer his phone before the voice mail picked up. Rhetta left him a short message summing up their Paducah trip. "I'll tell you all about it tonight, Sweets. The good news is that we got Ricky's money back and we didn't get arrested." She clicked the left turn signal as she pulled out from the Wendy's Restaurant where they had picked up lunch at the drive-through.

Rhetta wolfed down her two plain chicken wraps, and sipped an icy Diet Coke. She envied Ricky who scarfed two cheeseburgers with fries and a chocolate milkshake. Ricky never worried about her weight. Rhetta sighed.

"How's your back?" Rhetta asked as she eased into traffic. "You took quite a fall trying to save that baby."

Ricky rubbed the small of her back. "I'll probably be black and blue tomorrow, but I'm okay."

"That was quite a production back there, but at least the manager gave you your money."

"I really owe you for this, Rhetta. I can't believe I was bullied into sending the money in the first place."

"Kris Williams with First News out of Cape said they wanted to do a story with us about the eBay scam." Rhetta stopped for a red light. "I think it might help expose both eBay and Craigslist scammers. I'm all for it."

"I'll let you be the one on TV, Rhetta. I don't want to be high profile with Jeremy's death still hanging out there." Ricky turned her attention to the side window.

Rhetta thought she caught a tear sneaking down Ricky's cheek. She reached across the seat and squeezed her hand. "On second thought, let's not either one of us do anything on TV."

After a few seconds, Rhetta asked, "When is Jeremy's funeral?"

Ricky shook her head. "I still don't know. I think the coroner will notify Anjanette when they release his body. Might be a few more days."

Rhetta patted her friend's hand.

Ricky's head swiveled sideways as she glanced out the side window. "I don't remember coming in this way. Are we lost?" She scanned the mostly commercial area. "None of this looks familiar."

"I think we can go out this way," Rhetta answered. They headed down a one-way street directly toward the elaborately painted floodwall along the river that reminded her of the one in Cape Girardeau. She turned left on Water then another left on Jefferson. "I'll pull into that parking lot over there and re-configure the GPS." Making a right turn landed them in the parking lot at the National Quilt Museum.

Rhetta re-set the GPS, then paused to admire the building. "Wow, I guess I never realized that the National Quilt Museum was in Paducah. My mother had several quilts belonging to my grandmother. I still have them." She had them packed in tissue paper inside a camelback trunk she'd bought at Annie Laurie's Antiques in Cape. Thinking about the precious hand-made quilts made her want to get into the trunk and caress them again. When she buried her head in a fold, she swore she could still smell the sweet lingering lavender fragrance that her mother wore.

Rhetta put Streak in gear, adjusted her seat belt and cut across the parking lot to exit on Jefferson, heading west. Just as she passed the side of the two-story sprawling compound that was bordered by a perfectly manicured lawn edged in reproduction gas lamps, she spotted a large sign near the entrance to the building. It announced the dates for the upcoming National Quilt Show next spring. The show's theme, written in two-foot-high blue lettering read, "Gone Quilting!"

CHAPTER 40

Rhetta braked hard, then slammed Streak into reverse.

"What's wrong?" Ricky asked as she gripped the entry bar over the door to keep from sliding off the seat. She was in the process of fastening her seat belt when Rhetta stopped abruptly.

"I think I know where Mylene Allard might be." Rhetta dug her phone out of her purse and dialed Mylene's number. It went directly to an automated message stating the number was not a working number. "Just as I thought. Her cell phone in Illinois is disconnected. She placed a sign on The Pink Peacock that said 'Gone Quilting.' That was a message."

Ricky scooted back up on her seat and pointed to the museum sign. "That's what this sign says."

"Right. 'Gone Quilting' means she's here in Paducah. Locals in Illinois or Missouri probably wouldn't understand the significance, but folks who know Mylene, like her regular customers will understand what it means. She put up that innocent sounding message to tell anyone looking for her where she is! I bet she's lived here in Paducah all along, perhaps shuttling back and forth between The Pink Peacock and a business or her home here. And I'll just bet the business really does involve drugs. That Viper I saw in the parking lot had to be hers. Those babies aren't cheap. Now that I think about the personalized plate that said MYVPR, it wasn't an Illinois plate. There was a stylized running horse across the top of it. That's a Kentucky plate. And MY could mean either "my," as possessive or M-Y as in the first two letters of Mylene." She slapped her forehead. "We need to find her."

"Oh, no. No, no, no." Ricky threw up her hand in a palm-out stopping motion. You just finished telling me what happened the last time you found her. Do you want to try again to get arrested, this time in Kentucky? This afternoon and the Shop 'n' Save wasn't enough? Randolph will kill you."

"Okay, you're right, but I bet we can find her car. That Viper should be easy to spot. We can at least tell the Cape authorities where to look for her, just in case they start acting like cops and pursuing another suspect in their investigation."

Ricky sat back against the seat and closed her eyes. "Besides me, you mean." She opened her eyes and stared earnestly at Rhetta. "Where do you suggest we start?"

"Paducah isn't any bigger than Cape, so I bet if we cruise around downtown, we'll find her." Rhetta hoped she sounded more confident that she felt.

"Sure, that's a good plan. I wonder how many bars are in Paducah?"

"Wait a sec, maybe she won't be in the city limits. I don't know, but I bet Paducah is like Cape and doesn't allow pole dancing and all-night drinking. Let's go back through Mayfield and Wickliffe. More than likely she'll be on the outskirts somewhere."

Ricky swallowed the last of her soda, and tossed the empty into the small trashcan Rhetta kept on the back seat floorboard. "Let's do this."

* * *

Back out on Jefferson, Rhetta headed west. She was concentrating on the GPS directions and watching for road sign markers, when Ricky said, "Hey, look over there. It's a topless bar, and the sign says they feature pole dancing and lap dancing."

"So much for my theory about topless bars not being allowed within the Paducah city limits." Rhetta swerved to the curb. The place wasn't open yet, but the outside seemed pretty seedy-looking. They could assume the worst for the interior. She pulled into the parking lot and headed for the back of the brown, shingle-sided converted house. No cars back there either. "This one is about as ratty-looking as the Peacock. But no Viper." She parked Streak and grabbed her iPhone. "I'm going to Google strip clubs in Paducah and see what I get." She tapped her phone. Within seconds a list appeared. "There are five listed here," she said, handing the phone to Ricky. "Call out the addresses and I'll put them into the GPS."

Once all five were programmed, Rhetta calculated that four of them were within a twenty-block radius. The fifth was at the west edge of town. They'd already eliminated the one they were at, since there was no red Viper in the parking lot. That left three in town and one outside town.

"What if Mylene Allard isn't driving the Viper today? Does that mean we have to double back and actually go inside those places? " Ricky shook her head. "I'm no prude, but I'm not going in any of them to ask about her, and neither are you." She folded her hands across her chest.

"I have no intentions of going in any of them either." She couldn't look at Ricky because she knew that was a bald-faced lie and Ricky would be able to tell from her shifty eyes that she was lying. "If we see the car, we get the heck away from Paducah. And let the cops in Cape deal with talking to her somehow."

Ricky nodded enthusiastically.

Rhetta began planning a way to talk Ricky into going in if they found the car.

None of the remaining downtown establishments had a red Viper in the parking areas. Some had other vehicles, but no super-hot sports car.

"I kinda hope I get to see the car close up," Ricky said. "I've only seen two ever, and those were at the River Tales Car Show in Cape last year. A doctor owned one, and a dentist owned the other one. And they had them corded off so we, the peasants, couldn't get too close."

Rhetta detoured into a nearby Dairy Queen, stopped and studied her GPS. "I think I know how to get over to the last one when we leave. What did you tell me the name of the place is?" She pulled to the drive-up. "Besides, I need a Dilly Bar."

Ricky studied the list she had copied from Rhetta's phone on to a napkin. "The Pink Partridge."

"That has to be it." Rhetta said, paying for their treats. After carefully removing the paper from the frozen bar, Rhetta aimed Streak for The Pink Partridge. The GPS indicated it was about five miles from where they were at the Dairy Queen. Rhetta gulped her ice cream. Her adrenalin kicked in, and she began to sweat. *Maybe I'll sweat off these calories.* She didn't turn the air on high.

Ricky put her window down. "First you get me ice cream I gorge so fast I have brain freeze, and now you're turning Streak into a sauna. What's wrong with you?"

"Nothing," Rhetta said, and switched on the air and fan. She'd run an extra mile in the morning.

By the time they caught sight of the two-story Victorian style home with a wrought iron double gate entryway bearing a rather elaborate pink partridge on each gate, Streak's cab temperature was back down to beef hanging range. Rhetta stopped in front of the closed gate and stared through the iron grille toward the elegant home. A circular driveway wound around an artificial pond with a three-tiered waterfall that tumbled over large boulders. A perfectly manicured lawn fanned out in front of the house, with colorful flowers lining a walkway to the front porch.

"This place looks more like a bed and breakfast than a nightclub, or strip joint." Rhetta bounced out of the SUV and walked to the gate. Overhead she glimpsed a small camera that swept back and forth, aimed at anyone standing at the gate. A security system. The green light atop the camera indicated it was operating. Great. Now they'd be on Candid Camera at the Partridge.

A simple sign, no bigger than a turkey platter, was mounted on one of the rock wall pillars that supported an iron gate. In flowing script that required being within a foot to read it, the sign read, *The Pink Partridge Gentlemen's Club opens at 7:00* on the first line. The script was appropriately colored partridge pink.

And on the second line: *Mylene Allard, Proprietor.*

Rhetta returned to her car, giving the camera a jaunty salute as she went past. "I think we just found Mylene Allard's hideout."

CHAPTER 41

RHETTA DROPPED RICKY AT her home, making it back to the office just in time to meet LuEllen, who was in her car, getting ready to leave for the day. They waved as their cars passed each other.

Woody's Jeep was snugged up to the building. The lights inside the office were on, as were the computer monitors. Rhetta took a deep breath and strode in.

Woody merely nodded as she asked, "Hi, Woody, are you okay?"

"Why wouldn't I be?" He didn't turn around from studying his monitor.

"LuEllen said that you weren't feeling well this morning."

"That was this morning. I'm fine now."

He swiveled his chair to look at her, then leaned back so he could point to his monitor. "I see you took Paducah by storm today. Where are you going tomorrow? Things have been pretty quiet in St. Louis lately." The corners of his mouth twitched upward.

She felt relief wash over her. She hadn't realized how much she was worried about Woody until this very second. Woody wore a full out grin by the time she reached his desk and joined him in watching streaming video featuring herself and Ricky on *Live News at 5*. Woody, the newsaholic, had the local television station's news website up following the story.

Her cell phone barked Randolph's "Who Let the Dogs Out?" ring tone. She winced as she answered, knowing that he had probably just watched the same coverage on the television news.

"Hi, Sweets."

"Please don't tell me you got arrested in Paducah today. Where are you?"

"I didn't get arrested and I'm in my office. Didn't you get your voice mail? I didn't even get a ticket going through Illinois." Randolph groaned. She was glad they were having this conversation by phone.

"No, I didn't get any voice mail from you." He paused a moment. "I just looked and I'm sorry, there was a missed call and message from you. I guess I just didn't see it. The main reason I'm calling is that I don't have good news for you. Although, I'm just glad you don't have more bad news for me."

Maybe she should've waited until she got home to talk to him about the trip to Paducah. But then, it was Randolph who'd called her. He usually didn't break bad news on the phone. She hoped he hadn't run over one of the cats. Her heart leapt up her throat and stuck in her windpipe.

"Did you run over one of the cats?"

"What? No, why do you ask? The cats are fine."

She didn't realize she'd been holding her breath. She let it out in a long sigh.

"Then what's the bad news?"

Now it was Randolph's turn to sound uncomfortable. "The Alexander County State's Attorney just called."

Her stomach knotted.

"He said he'd see you in court next week."

Chapter 42

RHETTA'S STOMACH LURCHED. SHE didn't have the heart or guts or any other innards strong enough to tell Woody the bad news. She'd wait until morning, after she had a chance to talk it over with Randolph at home. See what their options were. Those being—according to Randolph—bad and worse.

She told Woody, "I've had a horrible day, and I'm sore all over. I'm heading home. I suggest you leave too. We're technically closed, and the phones are on auto answer now, anyway." The clock read 5:30. She gathered up her briefcase and purse.

"I'm waiting for the Greens to get here. They couldn't come until after they got off work at five, so they should be here any second."

Rhetta logged off and shut down her computer. "You have keys, right?"

"Yes." He answered abruptly as he always did when she mentioned keys. She asked him that regularly now whenever she left before he did. Ever since the time he had hauled several trash bags out and tossed his keys and cell phone into the Dumpster along with the trash. He claimed the keys and phone were in his hand one second and flying out the next, following the trash. He swore a poltergeist had snatched them. He had crawled up and over and into the bin to retrieve his phone and keys, but when he got in, he couldn't get out. After rooting through God-knows-what and finally finding the keys and phone, he'd been forced to call Jenn to come and get him. And, to bring a ladder. He had to take the Jeep to the car wash the next morning to hose the stench out of the interior.

The Greens, a pleasant-looking older couple arrived just as she was leaving. Rhetta asked Woody if he needed anything else, and when he said he didn't, she left. Just as she aimed the key fob at the door to unlock it, she remembered that her iPhone was on her desk. She returned to the office, muttering to herself about being so forgetful. She heard her generic ring tone as soon as she opened the door. She lurched across the office and snatched it up just in time. The next ring would've probably sent the call to voice mail.

"Why didn't you come on in?"

Rhetta instantly recognized the voice. "I, uh." Rhetta didn't know what to say. There were few times in her life that she'd ever been at a loss for words. Apparently, this would be one of them.

"I followed your adventure on the news this evening. My, my, you do get around."

"We went to Paducah to get Ricky's money back from a scammer," Rhetta finally said. Why did she feel like she had to justify why she was in Paducah to Mylene?

"You shouldn't be trying to find me. That could prove dangerous for you. Leave well enough alone, Rhetta McCarter. I had a soft spot for you when I heard about you finding my father's remains. I wanted to enlist your help to solve the riddle about my father. I bailed you out of the Cairo hellhole. I've changed my mind. Do yourself a favor, and don't come looking for me anymore, all right? Jeremy is dead. Don't you be next."

"What do you know about Jeremy? What—" Rhetta was talking to air. Mylene was gone. The call had been from a blocked number so she couldn't call her back.

Rhetta stared at the phone. *What did she mean, next? Next to die?*

CHAPTER 43

"I DON'T KNOW WHAT to make of it, Randolph. Was she threatening me? I want to let the Sheriff's office sort it out. I'm done with the whole mess. I never should have gotten myself involved." Rhetta played with her food, then set her fork down. Randolph had surprised her by preparing his trademark meal—home-cooked spaghetti. While she appreciated his kindness in fixing supper, she was too wound up to eat it. She pushed her meal aside. They had taken their plates out to the table on the back deck, and now found themselves surrounded by plaintive felines.

"You didn't eat much," Randolph commented as he eyed her nearly full plate.

"I'm not very hungry. I just can't get Mylene's phone call out of my mind. Maybe she killed Jeremy. She didn't seem very surprised or sorry about his death. In fact, she sounded like she didn't care much for him at all, calling him her bastard brother." Rhetta reached down to stroke a black and orange tabby that she named Pirate, because he always stole every other cat's toys and food. The fur encircling his right eye was black, and looked like a pirate's eye patch, giving further merit to his name.

Randolph cleared away the remnants of the meal, and returned with fresh glasses of iced tea. The sun had nearly set, casting crimson-tinged shadows along the horizon. Rhetta sat back, and Pirate jumped on her lap, curled into a fat orange and black ball of fur, and began purring.

Randolph handed her a beverage, then pulled a chair up alongside hers. "This business in Alexander County isn't going away, so let's deal with that first. Also, I want you to completely stay away from the Jeremy Spears and Malcom Griffith investigations. Hear?" He smiled.

"I hear." Although she knew Randolph was right about removing her sticky nose from the investigation, she felt she had to stand up for herself. "In my own defense, I didn't mean to get involved. We couldn't help it that we found Malcom Griffith's body. It's not like we set out to find him. As to Mylene Allard, I wouldn't have gotten involved with her, if she hadn't called me."

"Uh-huh, but speaking about Mylene Allard, let's get back to the Alexander County problem. I need to find a criminal lawyer for you."

Rhetta's heart sank. "And for Woody, too."

"Yes, Woody, too. Of course. I'm checking with some friends who practice civil law over there, so they can refer me to a good criminal defense lawyer."

She winced. Just hearing the words criminal defense lawyer in reference to herself made her stomach clench. She thought she wouldn't be able to eat again until this was resolved. The reality that she might go to prison made her sick. "Randolph, I'm sure Mylene will give them a statement that we had nothing to do with whatever was going on."

"What makes you think Mylene plans on doing anything to clear your names? She'll be looking out for herself, I'm sure." Greystone, a solid grey, formerly feral cat jumped into Randolph's lap. Rhetta had rescued Greystone when he was a tiny spitting and clawing kitten stuck in a downspout on her office building. He had managed to draw blood on Rhetta's hand as she worked to extricate him. Now, he was another fat McCarter feline. His contented purr could be heard over Pirate's.

Rhetta and Randolph sat a few more minutes in silence, petting the lap cats. The other two cats sat nearby, tails swishing, waiting for supper. Rhetta's mind spun with everything that had happened. Who had killed Malcom Griffith? Who killed Jeremy? Was it the same person? And why? As far as Rhetta was concerned, Mylene was the obvious suspect. Her thoughts churned up a scenario where Mylene could have also killed her father. She tried to let on to Rhetta that she loved her father, but that could've been all show. Mylene was, after all, in show business. Okay, not exactly show business, but body-showing business. Same difference.

What about the affair between Anjanette Spears and Malcom Griffith? Did Anjanette's husband know about it? Could he have killed Malcom Griffith? It would have taken someone strong to push the Z28 over the spot where Malcom was buried, unless someone used a truck or another car to push it. Did Mr. Spears really die from a stroke, and how much money did Anjanette or Jeremy come into? Was Jeremy cooking the books for the subdivision and did someone find out about it? Like one of the California investors? Could they be mobsters who decided to take care of Jeremy for skimming their money? But if they were mobsters, they probably would have shot him, and not conked him on the head with a metal detector that happened to be lying around. That made Rhetta think it might be a crime of anger and opportunity. Someone who knew him. Ricky? No, she shook that thought away. She circled back to Mylene. How did she fit into all of this?

Her head spun itself into a major headache. She set a protesting Pirate down and went to the master bedroom bath in search of Advil. When she returned, she spotted her phone on the counter in the kitchen. She carried it along with her iced tea refill to the table outside.

Just as she sat, and Pirate returned to her lap, the phone vibrated and she heard the metallic strains of the William Tell Overture, the former Lone Ranger television show theme music. She set it for Woody because he liked to call himself *The Loan Arranger*.

"Hey, Rhetta, I forgot to tell you that you need to go to the post office to pick up a certified letter. It came today, but required your signature. I thought you might want to get it before you come to the office tomorrow."

"Did you get one today, too?" Rhetta's heart thrummed thinking it was some sort of letter to notify her that she needed to be in court.

"No, why?'

"No reason, just wondering."

"Uh-huh. Something's up, and you're not telling me. See you in the morning," Woody said, and disconnected.

"What was all that about?" Randolph had emptied his lap of his feline, and was feeding all the cats their supper. Pirate reluctantly left Rhetta's lap to join the others.

"Woody forgot to tell me that I have a certified letter at the post office. Would the Alexander County court send me something certified?"

Randolph shook his head. "No, that's very doubtful."

Now, what?

CHAPTER 44

THE HEADACHE THAT BEGAN the night before ballooned into a full-blown migraine by morning. Rhetta pulled the covers over her head after Randolph got out of bed. When he peered in the doorway of the bedroom a few minutes later and asked if she was going to run with him, she groaned.

"I take that as a no." He tiptoed to the bed and patted her shoulder. "Can I get you anything?"

Her head hurt too badly to shake it, so she muttered, "No," and burrowed into the cocoon of sheets wrapped around her head.

Randolph went to the closet and rummaged through it, returning with a heating pad. He plugged it in and laid it across her neck. Relaxing tight neck muscles always seemed to help her whenever she came down with a skull-crusher. She hadn't suffered a killer headache in a long time.

"Thanks," was all she could manage and she was sure it wasn't much more than a mumble. Talking hurt her head. She lay on her stomach, heating pad across her neck and fell into a pain-induced stupor.

* * *

It was three hours later when Rhetta next opened her eyes. While the headache wasn't completely gone, she realized now that she might live. She listened to the quiet house. Rolling over, she peered at the clock. Nearly 9:00. She rolled to the edge of the bed and sat up. Her head didn't spin out of control like it had when she awoke earlier and the headache had swamped her. She slipped on her slippers and padded to the bathroom. Propped on the sink was a note in her husband's looping writing: *"I called Woody and told him you weren't well, and that you wouldn't be in. Go back to bed. XOXOXO"*

Rhetta hugged the note to her chest, and returned to the heating pad.

* * *

The next time Rhetta woke up, she did so with a start. Her head and neck were drenched in sweat. It took her a moment to realize it was from the heating pad. The clock read 11:30, and the house was still silent. If Randolph had gone running without her, he must've showered in the guest room.

The intense throbbing pain had dimmed to where her head felt reasonably normal, so she slid her feet into slippers again, donned a robe and swayed her way to the kitchen. She was still dizzy and felt like she was walking on a planet that was losing its gravitational pull.

After loading the coffee maker, she propped herself on a stool at the counter and reached for her cell phone, still plugged into the wall charger. Although she didn't think she could eat anything yet, the tantalizing coffee aroma wafting from the other end of the counter made her stomach growl. The phone's screen revealed a flurry of missed calls, mostly business. Not that business calls weren't important; right now she didn't feel like returning any of them. Two were from Ricky. She tapped the voice mail that had accompanied the last one.

"Hi, Rhetta. Just wanted to let you know I'm taking a few days off and going out camping near Billy Dan's place. He invited me to go fishing with him. I've got the dogs. See you Monday or Tuesday. I'll have my phone, if it'll work out in Bollinger County."

In spite of feeling less than human, she had to smile. Ricky sounded like she was getting back to her old self. Rhetta was pleased to hear her friend was going to spend some time with Billy Dan. She believed they'd struck up a friendship last spring. Then, Jeremy entered the picture and Ricky had stopped mentioning Billy Dan.

Never remarrying after a divorce many years earlier, Billy Dan had retired to a secluded wooded property west of Marble Hill, about thirty miles from Cape Girardeau. He had a large lake well stocked with fish, and claimed his retirement was dedicated to fishing.

Rhetta carried her coffee with her to the bathroom, turned on the shower, and breathed in the steam. The hot water sluicing over her tired body and aching head worked wonders. She decided she felt about as normal as she was going to, given all the excitement of the past couple of days and the raging headache she'd just battled.

After she dressed and had worked her hair into its spiky do, she decided to strip the bedclothes and throw them into the washer. She had sweated profusely for a few hours, and wanted a nice fresh bed tonight.

* * *

Woody had just returned from lunch when she turned into the parking lot. He stepped out of his Jeep and waited for her to catch up. "Randolph said you weren't feeling well. Are you better? Did you get your registered letter?"

Mental head slap. She had forgotten all about the letter. "Oh, crap, Woody. I'll go get it now. Be back in a few."

"The last time you said you were going to the post office you found a body. And look how that's worked out for you. Don't take any detours this time." He shook his head and went on in to the office.

She turned Streak around and headed downtown where she lucked into a parking spot close to the front door of the Frederick Street Main Post Office. She locked the car and slipped inside. The tiny lobby was crowded to capacity and she managed to wedge herself between a man carrying a box the size of Connecticut and a very large Southeast Missouri University student with biceps resembling footballs. Probably a member of the football team. When he turned around to make room for her, his T-shirt said, "Math majors salute Einstein." Go figure.

Fifteen minutes later, she'd finally inched her way to the counter and requested her letter. After duly signing the required forms, she glanced at the large manila envelope, but without her glasses, was unable to tell who it was from. She tucked it into her purse and edged toward the door. She hugged her purse securely to her chest, hoping she wouldn't injure anyone with it. Earlier, while she'd worn it slung over her shoulder, she'd turned abruptly when she thought she spotted Adele Griffith scooting out the front door. She had nearly wiped out an elderly man who'd been standing beside her. Luckily, she caught him before he went down. He mumbled something under his breath that sounded a lot like "crazy woman."

Outside and on the sidewalk, she peered around hoping to catch sight of the woman she thought was Adele Griffith. Unable to locate her, she gave up and climbed into Streak, rolled down the windows to let out the heat, and tossed her purse on the passenger seat. The envelope slid out and landed on the floorboard. She snatched up the pair of reading glasses she kept in the tray under the dash, then retrieved it. The return address leapt off the page at her: The National Personnel Records Center on Page Ave, St. Louis.

Her heart began to thump. Two months ago, she'd filled out a standard Form 180 Request Pertaining to Military Records on her father, Alexander Franklin Caldwell. It had taken her a while to find his social security number, but she finally managed to locate it in some of her mother's things. She had nearly forgotten about the request. Until now. She'd wait and open it at her office.

When her father had shown up last spring and handed her a locket containing a picture of her and her mother, Rhetta had been angry and wanted nothing to do with him. He'd walked out on her life when she was too young to remember him. Later, she thought a lot about what he'd told her—that he had been in the military and that her mother, Renate, had been the one to send him away. At first, hearing him say that made her want to run over him. Now, she just wanted to find out how much of what he'd said during that encounter had been the truth.

She switched on her left turn signal, and sized up her opportunities to leave the curb. As she waited, a high riding, four-wheel drive truck pulled out from two spaces behind her and rumbled past her. There in the driver's seat, her head barely clearing the top of the steering wheel, sat Adele Griffith.

CHAPTER 45

SURELY, THIS CAN'T BE the same frail woman that required a ride home from the sheriff's office? Nevertheless, here she was, short, grey-haired woman peeping up and over the steering wheel, deftly maneuvering an enormous Dodge four-by-four through Frederick Street traffic, then Broadway, and then south on Kingshighway. Rhetta caught the personalized license plate—ADELE. This must've been the truck Woody spotted while he was peeling his head at the car wash.

Rhetta quickly discovered how well the older woman could drive when she had trouble keeping up with the pickup. Rhetta tried staying about four car-lengths behind, hoping that Adele wouldn't recognize her in Streak. Then she nearly lost the truck at the Independence Street stoplight. Adele turned right while Rhetta was in the left lane. Rhetta managed to slide over and follow, but by the time she spotted the truck again, it had topped the hill and began dropping out of sight. Not spotting any police cars in the vicinity, Rhetta took a chance and floored it. When she topped the hill at the Mount Auburn Road intersection, she lost the truck, and this time for good. She sat at the stop sign, scanning up and down Mount Auburn. The driver behind her began honking. Rhetta turned right, drove down to Kingshighway, and back to the office.

She wasn't sure why she tailed the woman, except that she was so surprised at discovering Adele behind the wheel of the pickup that she had to positively identify the woman driving. And to figure out what she was up to. That Adele had lied to the deputy about not driving bothered Rhetta. Was she merely angling for sympathy? Or was there another reason?

***

"Woody, you were right about Adele Griffith driving a ginormous pickup." Rhetta plopped into her chair and adjusted it. She propped her purse and the registered letter on her desk and began searching for her phone. First, she needed her glasses, so she could identify the phone among the items in the bottom of her purse. She was getting tired of dumping the contents out every time she needed her phone. "Where are my glasses?" She scanned the desktop, and felt the tops of files and papers to determine if the glasses were underneath. She grid-searched the office, backtracking everywhere she'd been. "Have you seen my glasses?" she called out as she returned from the kitchen.

"Are you looking for different glasses other than the ones on your head?" Woody asked as she sailed past his desk.

She snatched them off her head.

"No. These are the only ones I was searching for." She glanced at Woody, who had swiveled back to his computer monitor but not fast enough to hide the smile wrinkling the corner of his mouth. Smile? It was more of a Woody smirk.

"I went to pick up the registered letter and spotted Adele Griffith at the post office. She was driving a four-by-four and I followed her as far as Mount Auburn Road, but then I lost her." Rhetta opened the top middle drawer of her desk and removed the dagger-style letter opener with the MCB logo on it. She didn't really remember exactly when she'd gotten it, but it always reminded her of a stiletto. She recalled that the bank had given them out as a promotional item at one time. Why would the bank have ever done that? She shrugged. She'd had it for several years. Back in the day, nobody worried that it could be a lethal weapon. She took a deep breath and slit the envelope open.

Emptying the contents on the desk, she reached first for the letter accompanying the few sheets of enclosed papers. Scanning quickly past the usual greeting from the records Center, her eyes locked on the second paragraph: *First Lieutenant Alexander Franklin Caldwell, U S Army, died from injuries sustained in service to his country on August 6, 1973.* She would've been six years old, nearly seven. Her heart thumped. Why hadn't her mother told her any of this?

Rhetta's arms and shoulders erupted in goose flesh. She stared at the enclosed Certificate of Death along with the plot number where her father was buried in Jefferson Barracks Cemetery.

According to the proof she held in her hands, her father had died during the Vietnam War. If that was true, then who was the imposter who tracked her down to give her a locket that had belonged to her mother? Something didn't jive. She was positive the man claiming to be her father was indeed her father. He had seemed familiar when she first saw him. Was her memory playing tricks on her? If he was her father, then what did the records center send her? The social security number matched the one she had found in her mother's things.

She returned the contents to the envelope, then slid the envelope into her desk drawer. She would have to think about this later. There was too much swirling around in her head to make any sense out of what she'd just seen.

She sat back, and began massaging her temples. The skull-crushing headache was working its way back. She had too much to think about. From the day she and Ricky found the remains of Malcom Griffith, too much had happened in too short a time.

Randolph made it clear that he didn't want her involved in any investigating, and wasn't too thrilled about her finding Mylene Allard. Yet, she couldn't help herself. After all, Sheriff Unreasonable had even hinted that she could be a suspect in Jeremy's death. Look what happened to Ricky. They arrested her.

A cold finger of fear inched up her spine. Could Ricky have killed Jeremy? She admitted that they'd quarreled. No. Definitely not. She shook her head to chase that notion away. Ricky? Never.

However, somebody killed him.

Was it Mylene? Did she kill the brother she hated? Is that why she warned Rhetta away? Then why had she called Rhetta to meet her at the barn? Thinking about that, Rhetta wondered if Mylene wanted to lure her to the barn to possibly frame her for the murder she was planning. Then there was Anjanette. Maybe she really was Jeremy's stepmother, not his real mother, and killed him over money? What Rhetta overheard from the closet didn't reassure her that Jeremy wasn't bilking Anjanette. There was no doubt in Rhetta's mind that Jeremy was pond scum.

"What was the letter about? Do you owe a million dollars in back taxes and the feds are going to come and get you?" Woody's question snapped Rhetta back to reality.

"No. Nothing like that. It's about my father. I sent for his military records. They really don't tell me much." She wasn't ready to discuss the conflicting information about Alexander Franklin Caldwell. She didn't really even want to think about her father. She'd harbored years of hatred for the man, so she wasn't going to let him intrude now.

She had a murder or two to solve. In spite of her husband's warnings.

CHAPTER 46

RHETTA JOLTED AWAKE WHEN the house phone on her nightstand shrilled at 5:30 in the morning about a foot from her head. No one ever called on the house phone. Especially at 5:30. Particularly on a Saturday morning.

The night had been a long one. After supper, Randolph had gone to his studio to work, and she'd gone to bed with a book. After finishing the mystery novel she'd started weeks ago, she had a terrible time falling asleep. Randolph had come to bed, had fallen instantly asleep and was snoring and she was still wide awake. When she finally did sleep, her slumber was invaded by a jumble of dreams. In one, her father was dangling a locket in front of her face. When she reached for it, he disappeared. Then she was driving Cami down a gravel road and was engulfed by a cloud of dust, which caused her to drive into a ditch. Then, quickly she was ten years old again and cruising with her mother in her mother's yellow '76 Camaro. Then she was fourteen and just received news that she'd lost a seventh grade spelling bee. She woke up confused, but conscious enough to realize these dreams all pointed to losing something precious. Her brain was trying to tell her something. She didn't have a clue as to what and rolled over in search of more sleep. The house was quiet except for the whoosh of the air conditioning system when she stole a one-eyed glance at the clock. It was 4:20. She didn't think she had fallen asleep until the house phone jangled her awake. Heart hammering, she snatched it to her ear.

The caller ID revealed it was Woody.

"What's wrong?" she whispered loudly, hoping to prevent Randolph from waking. Too late. He had already stirred and was sitting up, a puzzled look on his face as he squinted to read the clock display.

"I'm sorry to wake you up, but I got a call from Ricky just now. She and Billy Dan are at Merc's in Marble Hill. They want to wait for you guys to eat breakfast."

Wondering if she had forgotten a date made with Ricky, Rhetta shook her head, trying to clear out the sleep bunnies. She couldn't remember making a breakfast date with Ricky.

Woody went on. "She tried to call you on your cell, but you didn't answer. So she called me, and I told her I'd call you. Her cell phone battery is nearly dead."

Rhetta leaned over to study the clock. "It's five-thirty. I didn't answer the cell because I'm asleep. I don't have any appointment to meet Ricky, and by the way, is something wrong for you to be up already?"

"No. Jenn has to work this morning, and I was planning on going into the office."

Rhetta's lack of sleep overloaded her patience. She didn't want to hear about Woody's day. Her day's plans had included sleeping in. So much for her plans. "Why does Ricky need to talk to me at five-freaking-thirty on a Saturday morning?" She groaned and lay back against her pillow. Randolph had already gotten up, visited the bathroom, and was on his way to the kitchen. "Never mind, I'm sorry I'm grumpy. Not enough sleep. No problem. We're all up. Now."

Woody ignored her sarcasm. In fact, she thought he sounded worried. "She says she really needs to talk to you. Could you call her at Merc's right away?"

Rhetta swung her legs over the side of the bed, fully awake and alert. "Is something wrong?"

"She didn't tell me, only told me to have you call her."

Rhetta thanked Woody for delivering the message, then headed to the bathroom. She splashed water on her face, and brushed her teeth. She began to feel human. What would necessitate a call to Rhetta at an hour when even respectable chickens weren't up? If Ricky and Billy Dan were getting along well, she wouldn't be calling. If she and Billy Dan weren't getting along, she wouldn't be calling. So, why was she calling?

Rhetta padded to the kitchen, found her cell phone and a pair of glasses. She located Ricky's number in her favorites. As soon as it began ringing, she remembered Woody had said to call Ricky at Merc's. She was about to hang up, when Ricky answered.

"Rhetta, my battery is dying. Can you and Randolph meet us at Merc's? Billy Dan and I have something to show you. You're not go—" The phone went dead.

Randolph had already put on a pot of coffee and slipped out to the deck in search of the felines. She smiled as she saw the four cats curled together on a padded deck chair. They ignored him, obviously not ready to start their day. He poured out their food and returned to the kitchen.

"Do you feel like eating breakfast at Merc's in Marble Hill?" Rhetta asked, pouring herself a cup of coffee. She inhaled the rich aroma appreciatively. She followed that with sweetener and milk. Coffee was indeed the nectar of the gods. She couldn't consider herself functioning until she had her caffeine.

"Why not? It's a great day to go to Marble Hill." He kissed the top of her head and headed for the shower.

* * *

Rhetta was waiting, two full coffee travel mugs in hand, by the time Randolph drove the Artmobile around to the front door and picked her up. He'd already turned the air on, although they could have driven with just the windows down, except for the dusty county road. The morning hadn't yet blossomed into a sauna, although the weather girl had called for another hot, humid day. The sun rising in the east was a giant orange ball peering over the horizon.

"What's the rush about?" Randolph asked, as he donned sunglasses and guided the truck out on to Highway 34, then westward to Bollinger County.

"Not sure, Sweets. It's not like Ricky to disturb anybody, so for her to have called Woody so early to call me, it must have been something she couldn't wait to tell us." She sipped her coffee, allowing the events of the past week to tumble around her brain. She shook her head. "I can't imagine."

"By the way, I found you and Woody an excellent attorney for your Illinois court date on Thursday. I'll go over everything with you later. His name is Carlton Hightower, and he comes highly recommended. Seems like he has plenty of experience dealing with the regime in Alexander County."

"He'll represent us both?"

"Yes, unless something happens that indicates you need separate counsel, he's agreed to represent both of you." Randolph turned off the radio, which had been playing in the background. He normally listened to talk radio, but this morning she found the political bickering too banal to put up with. He must have agreed.

"What do you think is going to happen to Woody and me?" She had been so busy that she hadn't really given much thought about what the outcome of their court appearance would be. She hadn't thought about it, and was probably blocking it out. In truth, she feared the worst, that they'd be put back in jail for something they hadn't done. "We didn't do anything. We truly were at the wrong place at the wrong time. What will we have to do to convince the judge?"

"That's what we'll be discussing with Mr. Hightower. We're to meet with him on Monday. Need both of you to be there."

"Of course. Will you go with us?"

Randolph reached over and squeezed her hand. "What do you think?"

* * *

Merc's, a converted Tastee-Freez built alongside Crooked Creek in the 70s, was bustling with activity. Initially constructed as a small walk-up ice cream stand, Merc (short for Mercury) Leadbetter bought the business fifteen years earlier and added on a large dining room and full kitchen. He re-opened as a full service restaurant. Being situated practically on the creek bank, the cedar sided building had suffered through several floods. Each time high water had invaded his building, Merc rebuilt and his loyal customers always returned.

The regulars were already guzzling coffee and discussing serious issues, like the best ponds for catfish. Farmers and politicians alike mingled for breakfast at Merc's. This being an election year, Rhetta guessed there were way too many politicians to suit the farmers.

Ricky spotted Rhetta and Randolph as soon as they strolled into the smoking section of the dining room, and motioned them over to the booth she shared with Billy Dan.

Rhetta slid in next to Ricky, while Randolph shook hands with Billy Dan, then joined him on his side of the booth.

Krista, the waitress Billy Dan insisted on calling Kathy, immediately appeared at the table with two cups and a steaming pot of coffee. "Hi, Judge, Miss Rhetta. Goin' to have breakfast this morning?" She filled their cups, refilled Billy Dan's and Ricky's and found the stainless creamer pitcher, sliding it toward Randolph. She waited, pad and pencil ready, to take their order.

"Just coffee for me," Rhetta said.

Randolph said, "I'll have the bacon and egg biscuit. And a glass of orange juice." Billy Dan and Ricky ordered the same thing.

Krista nodded. "Be up in a sec." She disappeared around the corner to turn in the order.

Billy Dan's hand snaked to the pack of cigarettes in his shirt pocket. Ricky shook her head, and Billy Dan aborted the trip.

Rhetta knew instantly that Ricky was trying to keep her from experiencing a nicotine craving, but with so much smoke in the smoking section, there wasn't much chance that the effort would succeed. Rhetta already craved one. "All right, girlfriend, what on earth is so critical that you dragged me out of bed in the middle of the night?" She settled for drinking more coffee, hoping that would kill the urge.

Ricky glanced at her watch, then grinned. "Yeah. Sorry about that. I guess it was a little early. But wait 'til you hear this." She turned to Billy Dan.

"I think you might want to see a place out on Whispering Pines Lake," Billy Dan said, and reached again for his pack again. Whispering Pines Lake was a recreational area that boasted a fifty-acre lake that a local developer built about thirty years earlier. He'd planned to sell lakeside tracts for cabins, but only about half the lots ever sold, and only a few of them had cabins built.

Billy Dan patted out a cigarette and offered the pack around the table. Everyone declined. Rhetta ate one with her eyes, then drained her coffee. Billy Dan lit up, inhaled and blew the smoke upward, away from the table before he continued.

"About fifteen years ago, I wired up a cabin for Malcom and Adele Griffith. I guess, now that I talk it over with Ricky here, it was probably just before Mr. Griffith disappeared. Never thought too much about it, until we were talking about how you girls found his remains."

"Why exactly does that require me to sacrifice my sleep this morning?" Rhetta held her cup up at Krista as a signal she needed a refill. She'd need plenty of caffeine to fight the nicotine war.

Ricky leaned over and whispered loudly to Billy Dan, "I told you she'd be like a bear just out of hibernation if we called her too early."

Billy Dan flicked ash of the end of his cigarette and chuckled. "Not much, except that after I wired their cabin, Mrs. Griffith never came back up here except one time that I know of. Folks in the area say they never see her. She let that friend of Ricky's, Jeremy Spears, use it occasionally. Once in a while, I've seen a few other folks there over the years, mostly during hunting season. Anyhow, that weekend, Adele was here by herself, and called me to ask how to turn the power off when they weren't here. I drove over and showed her."

Krista appeared with both arms stacked with plates of breakfast. After placing everyone's food correctly on the first try, she snatched the coffee carafe and refilled everyone's cups. "Why do you think that's so interesting?" Randolph asked, closing his hand over the fresh steamy biscuit, which he guided to his mouth. Krista left to refill more cups around the room.

Billy Dan took another drag on his cigarette, blew a long trail of smoke toward the ceiling then stubbed it out and reached for his biscuit. After chewing a moment, he turned his gray eyes to Randolph. "Nothing all that interesting at the time, except she's not ever been back, and when she left that day, she had Jeremy Spears come and get her. He left the truck she drove out here parked in the garage and drove Adele home in his car. No one ever came back to pick up the truck."

Thinking that Ricky must've wanted Rhetta to invest in the antique truck, Rhetta piped up, "I'm not interested in restoring an antique truck." She glanced at Randolph. "What I really want is a Camaro. Preferably, Cami." She downed more coffee and glanced around for Krista. It was going to be a twenty-cup morning at this rate. She wasn't sure why she mentioned wanting Cami. She knew that could never be. The car had burned up, was totaled, and probably already crushed into scrap metal.

Ricky swallowed a mouthful of eggs. "We're working on getting that Z28 back, and finishing it up for you, but hey, this is different. I think we should go and see this truck," Ricky said, giving in and joining Billy Dan in a cigarette. She cut her eyes toward Randolph. He was busy spreading jelly on a biscuit.

"Randolph, would you mind to go and find Krista? I'd like to get the bill so we can leave." Rhetta could tell from Ricky's eye gesturing that she wanted to talk without Randolph hearing.

Randolph swallowed a drink of coffee, then stood and peered around the room for Krista. Not finding her, he headed to the kitchen. As soon as he was out of earshot, Ricky leaned in close to Rhetta and whispered, "We need to see this truck."

"It's in a large shed with a window in it, so it's not hard to get a good view of the front end of the truck," Billy Dan said, running his fingers through his thick, prematurely silver hair.

"Are we just going to barge in and peer into the garage? Won't anyone be there?"

"Like I said, no one ever comes down to the cabin anymore. My nephew mows the grass and takes care of the place in the summer." He tucked the package of cigarettes into his shirt pocket.

"All right, why do we want to see the truck so badly?" Rhetta felt herself growing mildly annoyed. She was beginning to crave a cigarette really badly. As grumpy as she felt, she was on the verge of snatching one away from Billy Dan. Instead, she closed her eyes and willed herself out of the temptation. The nicotine devil danced on her shoulder and poked her with his spear.

Ricky answered. "Because the front bumper is scuffed and dented in a way and with a color that I think exactly corresponds to the dents on the rear bumper cover and trunk panel of your Z28."

CHAPTER 47

Rhetta bolted upright, the caffeine working its magic and jolting her alert. Could her barnfind Z28 have dents put there by a truck now sitting in Adele Griffith's shed in Bollinger County? How could that be possible?

Ricky said, "I'm wondering if that truck may have been used by the killer to push the Z28 over the spot where he killed and buried Malcom." Rhetta was glad that Ricky spoke softly. She didn't want their conversation picked up by the locals, or Randolph, who was making his way back toward the table. "And that it might have been Jeremy who killed Malcom. He could've hidden the truck out here for nobody to ever find. He may have told Adele that he'd come back and get the truck later."

"Why would Adele have even called him out here to pick her up?"

"I haven't worked that part out yet. Unless...."

Randolph had been stopped by an old friend, and was busy standing and chatting.

Rhetta went on. "Do you think they could have been in on it together?" She leaned toward Ricky. "How could we prove that? That truck's been in that shed an awfully long time, and now the Cape County Keystone Kops have my Z28 and all the parts. So that theory isn't going to be easily verified."

Ricky set her plate with the remaining morsel of biscuit aside. "I doubt if Adele had anything to do with killing her husband, if for no other reason than she depended on him for income. She's been near poverty's doorstep ever since he disappeared. Well, poverty as compared to how large they lived before. She bought a duplex, and rents out one side and lives in the other. She bought that with the life insurance policy she got when Randolph declared him dead. Up to that time, she got by working as a bookkeeper for one of the real estate agencies here in town. Riverbluff Realty, I think."

Ricky slid her cup aside and shook her head, and held her hand over her cup to signal Krista she didn't need a refill. "Anyhow, knowing Jeremy, if he was the one who killed Griffith, he could've conjured a reason to come and get Adele so he could leave the truck there. Remember, the two families were pretty tight. If we can get to the truck, I'll scrape some of the paint from the front end and bumper. I can match it, unscientifically of course, to your car. I'll get Custom Fabio at the Custom Fab shop to scan the paint. He can tell me what type of paint, and what model car it comes from. The paint they used back in the day was much different than paint is today." Ricky began gathering up her cigarettes and phone and stuffing them into her tiny shoulder bag.

"Custom Fabio? That's his name? Is that a joke?" Rhetta stared at her friend's small purse. How could the woman possibly fit anything in there?

"Not at all." Ricky's ponytail bounced under her ball cap when she shook her head. "He calls himself Custom Fabio. Although he resembles Eddie Murphy more than he does that gorgeous model, Fabio. Custom Fabio wears his long hair in dreads and he has three gold teeth. I think his real name is Fablonzo."

"What's the plan?" Rhetta asked, fishing money out of her purse to leave a tip. Randolph had already picked up the tab for the breakfasts and was headed to the cashier. Luckily, he was out of earshot when Ricky laid out her theory.

Ricky leaned in close to Rhetta and whispered. "I've scoped it out. Billy Dan and I peered in the window. That's how I saw the scrapes and paint chips on that truck. They are a totally different color. I can crawl in through the window, snatch some paint scrapings and hoist myself back out. Thing is, what will Randolph say?" She jutted her chin toward Randolph, who'd paid the cashier and was heading back to the table.

Rhetta whispered, "We can't tell him. He'd never allow us to break and enter, especially after what happened out at Jeremy's barn." Ricky nodded her agreement.

Billy Dan groaned. "What will we do with Randolph?"

"I'll think of something by the time we get there." Rhetta joined Randolph who was waiting for them by the front door and slipped her arm into his. They led the way into the sparkling sunshine and nearly empty parking lot. She didn't have the vaguest idea how to get him to turn his eyes away while they broke into yet another building.

The four stood outside, next to three vehicles. Ricky and Billy Dan had driven separately, so they debated which vehicle to take to the cabin on the back country roads. Randolph suggested they all ride together in the Artmobile.

Ricky solved the problem. "Billy Dan, why don't you lead the way, and let Randolph follow you in his truck? I need to take my truck anyway. I have a few groceries in there and I need to get them into a cooler. I'll make a quick detour to my campsite." Billy Dan nodded, unlocked his Ford Ranger's door, and slid behind the wheel.

Ricky continued. "Rhetta why not ride with me? My campsite is close to where we're going. We'll meet the guys at the Griffith cabin. I know where it is."

Randolph's window glided down noiselessly. "That's fine, I'll follow Billy Dan, and that way no one will have to drive anyone back into town." He waited for Billy Dan to pull out on to Highway 34 before slipping in behind him.

Rhetta slid into the passenger seat of Ricky's two door Ford 150 work truck. There was no back seat, and no groceries on the front seat. She raised an eyebrow at Ricky.

Ricky grinned. "I had to think of something. Billy Dan whispered to me that he could take the long way to Whispering Pines Lake. We should get there ahead of them, and have time to nab the paint flakes off that truck and get out of the shed before they get there."

Rhetta high-fived Ricky. "That's what friends are for!"

CHAPTER 48

RICKY SLID BEHIND THE wheel of her little truck. Rhetta snapped her seat belt on, and they set out on Highway 34. By now, Rhetta couldn't spot either Billy Dan or Randolph.

Ricky must've noticed Rhetta peering around. "They've already pulled off on The Old Dump Road. That winds around and comes out at Whispering Pines Lake. But we're going to have to step on it, to get there before they do." With that, she veered on to a dusty, narrow gravel road.

Rhetta rolled up her passenger door window against the cloud of red gravel road dust, and turned on Ricky's air. "Spill it, sister. Why did Billy Dan take you out to Adele's cabin?"

"I told Billy Dan about finding the body. Billy Dan knew I'd been seeing Jeremy. He never asked anything about me and Jeremy, but I volunteered the details."

Rhetta said, "The details?"

"Some of the details. That's when he told me about wiring up Adele's cabin. We weren't far from it so we drove past it. We stopped and peeked into the shed." She glanced at Rhetta. "You know, Jeremy and I were breaking up. I discovered a lot about him that I had never suspected."

Rhetta nodded. "Such as?"

Ricky took another right turn on to an even narrower road, one that went partially through a creek bottom. She pointed to a cluster of trees inside a small area enclosed by an ancient wire fence. "There's a Union Soldier's grave over there. Billy Dan told me about it." She slowed the truck as they passed over a road filled with boulders the size of Kentucky.

Rhetta turned to Ricky. "You're stalling."

They angled up a creek bank and the road improved. Ricky continued. "The night of the pool party, I overheard Jeremy talking smack to Anjanette. He was overdrawn in his construction account, and dear mother didn't want to give him more money. He threatened her. I'm not sure what that was about, and I don't know with what. At the time, I didn't make much of it, except that I pegged him then and there for a first class loser. We fought when I caught him with his pants down. I split."

Ricky kept one hand on the wheel and rummaged through her purse with the other. "I wonder if he was blackmailing his own mother. Maybe Anjanette is the one responsible for killing Malcom, and somehow Jeremy knew that?" She found her cell phone. She glanced at it, and returned it to her bag. "No signal," she muttered.

"Or, what if Jeremy is the one who killed Malcom and Anjanette knew it, but never turned him in?" Rhetta glanced at her own cell phone. "No Service" displayed where bars and 3G should have been.

Ricky nodded slowly. "But who killed Jeremy?"

"My money is on Mylene Allard. She told me she hated Jeremy, and she called me to meet her at the barn that night. She might have been setting me up. Why, I don't know. If I ever see her again, I plan on asking her." Rhetta sat back against the seat and sighed. "I just don't know. It's too confusing. The two deaths are related. We need to figure out who hated both Malcom Griffith and Jeremy Spears."

Ricky held up her hand and began raising a finger at a time as she ticked off her list. "First, there's Anjanette. She probably hated Malcom for not leaving Adele when he found out she was pregnant with Jeremy." Another finger popped up. "Next we have Mylene Allard, Malcom's daughter, who hated Jeremy, and was probably really ticked with her own father. Maybe enough to get into an argument with him and kill him accidentally. Or on purpose. From what you've told me, she's a pretty rough character." A third finger. "There's Adele Griffith. She couldn't stomach Malcom fooling around with Anjanette, so she offed him."

"Offed him?" Rhetta asked. "You sound like you've been watching too many movies."

Ricky laughed, but without any trace of humor. "I didn't like Jeremy much either, but I sure didn't kill him. Even though Sheriff Reasoner hasn't cleared me."

Rhetta took up the list. "We have Anjanette, Mylene, Jeremy, and Adele. Who can we rule out?" Now it was her turn to tick off suspects. "I think we can rule out Anjanette because she loved Malcom. Also Adele. Even if she knew her husband was fooling around with Anjanette, she still loved him and needed his income. I think Jeremy makes a good suspect in Malcom's death. Maybe he'd been blackmailing Malcom and they got into a fight."

"Malcom owned that property back then. So it's possible Jeremy went over there." Ricky nodded. "That makes sense."

Rhetta turned to Ricky. "Who is the common denominator to both dead men?"

They replied in unison. "Mylene Allard."

CHAPTER 49

As Ricky topped a hill, the serene blue of Whispering Pines Lake sprawled over several acres in the valley below them. Ricky slowed at a gravel drive. Two square columns, built from cemented creek rocks much like the boulders they'd just driven over, stood like sentries, one on each side of the entrance. A wrought iron arch connected across the top of the two pillars. The name *Griffith* was welded into the crown of the arch, although the "h" in the sign had come loose from the welds and listed to the right. Definitely a rustic effect. The driveway looked in better shape than the gravel road they'd just traveled. Ricky had pointed out they had come in the back way. The road going away from the cabin was in much better shape. At least, the boulders were smaller.

Ricky turned and drove through the gateway and down the hill. As the driveway curled around a century old oak, a log cabin appeared. Ricky pulled up in front. There was no sign of Billy Dan or Randolph. The yard needed tending. What was left of a lawn was overgrown with dandelions and crabgrass at least a foot high. A wild climbing rose vine battled with morning glory and blackberry brambles for space on a tattered trellis leaning against the front of the cabin porch. A piece of plywood nailed over the glass in the front door displayed a "No Trespassing" sign. The oversize hasp and padlock would've stood little chance against a couple of hammer blows.

Ricky pulled a Baggie out of her purse and slid out of the truck.

"Come on. Let's do this before the guys get here." She began loping around back toward a metal shed that stood about thirty feet directly behind the cabin, hidden from the drive. Rhetta scrambled after her. Luckily she'd worn jeans and tennis shoes.

"Do you always keep empty Baggies in your purse?" Rhetta asked as she caught up with Ricky.

"What?" Ricky glanced at the Baggie. "Of course."

"Why?" By now they'd reached the side of the garage, and Ricky was evaluating the window.

"In case I have the dogs with me, and I have to walk them in town. You know, to pick up doggie stuff."

"Oh. Right." Cat owners never worried about outdoor droppings. Mainly because cats like to hide their messes.

Ricky had already hoisted herself up to the sill and was kneeling sideways on its narrow ledge, tugging at the window, trying to raise it. "I bet this crummy window hasn't been opened in years." The window held fast. She grunted and pushed up as hard as she could on the double hung window. Painting over the trim had probably sealed the window forever. It remained stubbornly unyielding.

Rhetta said, "Move over, I'll climb up there too and maybe we can open it together." Ricky reached down and clasped one of Rhetta's hands and pulled while Rhetta boosted herself up next to Ricky. The two of them squeezed together on the sill and tried pushing up on the window frame. It still didn't budge.

"I'm not sure how we're going to get this window open, short of breaking it." Rhetta said, her forehead sweating and her hands filthy from the window dirt. She wiped her hands across her thigh to remove the dirt. Then she wiped her face with the back of her hand.

"I guess that's why the term is called breaking and entering. Ya gotta break it before you can enter." Ricky giggled.

"We better not do that. Randolph will have a stroke. Let's get down and try the door. With any luck, it's unlocked." Rhetta began peering over her shoulder to see where she could drop without landing on the rocky gravel below.

"It's not. Billy Dan and I tried it the other day."

Before Rhetta could drop safely to the ground, a gunshot exploded, shattering the window, sending glass and wood shards in every direction. Ricky pitched forward and, with a loud thud, toppled through the window to the inside of the building. Rhetta screamed and fell backward to the gravel below.

CHAPTER 50

BEFORE THE ECHOING REVERBERATION of the first shot had died away, another shot rang out. Rhetta had the wind knocked out of her when she landed on her back, but the bullet whizzing past her head and slamming into the side of the garage fueled her adrenalin. She rolled over and scrabbled for cover.

Not daring to stand and run, besides being unable to, she scuttled on her hands and knees around to the edge of the garage. She propped her back against the building, gasping for air. Her heart slammed against her ribs and she felt like her lungs had seized. She panted, desperate to replenish her lungs and kick start them. Fear made it harder for her to gasp for air. Blackness accompanied by dancing points of light edged inward from her peripheral vision. She was on the verge of passing out. Her head spun and she slumped sideways, yielding to the nothingness. Then her lungs began working, the reflexive breathing pushing oxygen to her starved brain. The darkness around her eyes gave way to light again. She could breathe!

"Ricky," she whispered. "Can you hear me?" No answer.

Rhetta gulped a few more breaths and crawled around to the side of the shed opposite from where they had perched on the sill. No doors. She flopped over and continued until she came to the end of the garage where there was a single rollup door held in place by a locked padlock. She edged away from the garage and crouched behind a dense wild olive bush. There were no more shots. Instead, she heard the distinct crunch of gravel from footsteps as someone slowly walked around the building. She flattened herself to the ground and prayed that her raspy breathing wasn't so loud as to alert the intruder to her position. She dared a peek upward through the brush, but could only see a slim form in jeans and wearing boots, a black T-shirt and matching ball cap. Although his back was to her, she clearly saw the handgun he clutched, muzzle up, like they do in cop shows. When he reached the window, he was too short to see into the shed. After a couple of attempts to jump up and peer in, he gave up and moved on away. Rhetta failed to get a glimpse of his face.

He walked toward the cabin, his back to her the whole time. She lost sight of him as he rounded to the front of the cabin. A motor turned over followed by the crunch of gravel and squealing tires. Then, quiet.

With her breathing coming more regularly, Rhetta dared to stand. Her heart was still jackhammering in her chest, but she managed to sprint to the garage window and shout to Ricky. "Are you okay? Ricky, please answer me."

A muffled sound answered her from somewhere inside.

Rhetta shouted, "He's gone, Ricky. Are you hurt?"

Ricky answered a little louder this time. "I think I broke my arm."

"Hang on, I'll try to break the padlock and get you out."

"Go to the toolbox in the back of my truck. I have a big pair of cutters in there."

"I'm on my way. Don't go anywhere," and bolted for the bolt cutters.

She scrambled into the bed of the pickup and popped open the lid of the unlocked toolbox. She quickly spotted a pair of bolt cutters suitable for busting bolts on an elephant's leash. She picked them up and lugged them to the end of the truck, rolled over and let herself down and dragged them back to the padlocked door. It took all her strength to spread the cutter arms apart. Still weak and gasping for breath, she dropped the cutters. She made a second attempt, and this time, took a deep breath and pressed the two handles together. The padlock snapped and fell to the ground. Rhetta dropped the cutters, and pushed as hard as she could until the door finally managed to slide about two feet open. She squeezed through and into the dark interior.

Ricky was standing near a dusty seventies-model pickup truck. She supported one arm with her opposite hand, and called Rhetta over. "Come over here, and pull this Baggie out of my pocket." She twisted sideways to present her right pocket.

Rhetta removed the Baggie. "Are you okay?"

Ricky limped over to the front of the truck. "Like I said, I think I may have broken my arm when I fell." She hopped a few more steps. "I think I twisted my ankle, too." She stopped at the front end of the truck, which had been backed into the garage. Rhetta saw now how Ricky had been able to see the front of the truck from the window.

"Look right there," Ricky said, pointing to two unmistakable dents and paint scrapings. "See if you can gather those paint scrapings into the Baggie." Rhetta bent to examine the scrapings. Sure enough, they were definitely white, or off-white. They couldn't have been from the truck, which was the same shade of green as goose poo. The top of the old truck was covered in bird droppings and bits of nest material and feathers. Evidently, the starlings had no trouble finding a way in to the locked garage.

Using her fingernails, Rhetta scraped the bits of paint into the plastic bag and carefully folded the top. She turned to Ricky. "Can you walk enough to get out of here?" She stuffed the Baggie into her jeans pocket. "Here, lean on me." She slipped an arm around Ricky's waist.

Ricky accepted the help, then limped toward the door, shinnying through the small opening. Rhetta followed. Where they emerged they were met by a glowering Randolph, arms folded, looking like he was about to explode.

CHAPTER 51

"JUST WHAT WERE YOU two doing in there?" Randolph asked, his calm voice belying the thundercloud that darkened his deep blue eyes to nearly coal black.

"Oh, Randolph, I'm so glad you're here!" Rhetta rushed to her husband in relief.

From his surprised expression, that probably wasn't the reaction Randolph expected from her. "What's wrong?" he asked, concern seeming to replace any anger. After receiving her hug, he stood back and studied her.

She knew she probably had muddy streaks and bits of gravel, brush and dirt clinging to her hair and face. He reached up and brushed a twig out of her hair.

"I'll admit that we tried getting into the garage through the window," Rhetta said and pointed to the shattered window. "But before we could pry it open, someone began shooting at us, and blew out the window. Luckily for us they missed, but Ricky fell in, and I fell back. I think Ricky has a broken arm and a sprained ankle."

"Shot at you?" He turned to Ricky, who nodded. "Let's get you to the clinic in town. We need to call the sheriff, too."

Billy Dan put a protective arm around Ricky's shoulder. "I'll take her, Judge. You take care of Rhetta."

Billy Dan supported Ricky while propelling her to his Ranger. He stopped, opened and then held the door. Ricky winced, then climbed in gingerly. He dashed around to the driver's side, started the truck and sped away in a shower of gravel.

Randolph studied his cell phone and shook his head. "No signal." He stepped around Rhetta to study the ground under the window and then the gash where a bullet had punctured the metal side of the garage. "Why would anyone be shooting at you? And who could it have been?" He squatted and studied the hole. "Looks like someone used a hunting rifle. Maybe they were target shooting from farther up the ridge, and the bullets went astray. That happens out here in the country." He stood and then examined the window.

"After the shooting I saw someone walking around the building, gripping a hand gun. Looked like a .38. Then he walked around the garage, and left. I didn't see what he was driving." Rhetta joined Randolph in the examination. "He shot at us when we were on the window ledge first. It's a wonder we didn't get cut to pieces." With that, Rhetta found a stray piece of glass in her hair and plucked it out.

"Did you say you thought he had a .38?" Randolph stooped again to study the garage. He reached in his pocket for his pocketknife, then proceeded to dig out the spent bullet. "This isn't from a .38, Rhetta." He bounced the spent bullet in his hand. "This was shot from a hunting rifle, possibly a 30-06."

Rhetta shook her head. "I don't understand. The guy I saw definitely had a handgun. He held it in both hands like they do on those TV cop shows." Rhetta pointed to the marks in the dirt under the window ledge. "He also stood right here and tried to jump up to look into the window but was too short." They both studied the shoe prints in the dusty earth near the garage. Rhetta examined the bottom of her sneakers, then pointed to some patterns. "I think those are our footprints, mine and Ricky's where stood before we climbed in. But look here." She pointed to boot tracks that circled the garage. "See? That's where he walked around the garage. These have to be his boot tracks." They both examined the prints. They were made by a foot no larger than Rhetta's size 7, which she proved by standing alongside one of the impressions.

"Mighty small feet for a man," Randolph said.

"Then maybe it wasn't a man, but a woman!" Rhetta stood under the window. "Come here, Randolph and stand by me." He did.

"I'm pretty short so if I want to see in, I can barely get my chin up to the window sill. But you can look in. You're taller than me." She reached up and patted the window ledge. "Whoever stood here was jumping up to see who might be in the garage." She whirled around to face Randolph. "Whoever was here was as short as me. Whoever was here was a small woman with a handgun. Who was the shooter? What the heck's going on?"

Randolph checked his phone again. "Still nothing. I guess we're too far out for the tower. We'll call the sheriff and report this as soon as we get a signal. We may have to come back out here. I'll drive Ricky's truck, if you'll take the Artmobile. I'll follow you to her campsite."

"Why don't you drive her truck to Billy Dan's and I'll follow you. We can leave it there."

Rhetta climbed in behind the wheel of the Artmobile, and adjusted the seat, steering wheel and mirror. "I don't exactly know where her campsite is, since we didn't actually go by there on the way out here."

Randolph leaned in to the driver's side window. "Why am I not surprised?" He sighed, then ambled to Ricky's truck. As he rummaged around the front seat, probably looking for the keys, which Ricky always tucked behind the overhead visor, Rhetta spotted a flash of red farther down the road. Her curiosity aroused, she stood on the running board of the Artmobile and peered down the gravel road that led away from the cabin, and on into the valley below. From here she could see a long ways, perhaps a mile. A cloud of dust rose as the vehicle flew around a curve. As it came out of the cloud, Rhetta spotted a red sports car.

She shouted at Randolph. "Get in with me, and leave Ricky's truck. I think I just saw Mylene Allard's car!"

Randolph made it to the truck in three strides. Rhetta shot out of the driveway as soon as he had the door shut. He fumbled to fasten his seat belt as she careened down the driveway and took a hard right on to the gravel road. She accelerated as fast as she dared. Thankfully, this way wasn't as pothole-and boulder-strewn as the way she and Ricky had come. This gravel road was level and for now, at least, free of traffic.

"How do you know it's her?" Randolph managed to get the belt fastened. He held on to the assist grip over the door to keep from knocking his head against the glass as Rhetta caromed down the county road.

"I only know of one red sports car like it. I'm pretty sure it was a Viper."

CHAPTER 52

BY THE TIME RHETTA reached the highway, the red sports car had vanished. She stopped in a cloud of dust at the intersection of Highway 34 and the Old Dump Road, and pounded her palm on the steering wheel. "We lost her. She couldn't have made it here this quickly." Rhetta glanced up and down the only straight part of Highway 34. "I don't see her."

Randolph began dialing his cell phone, "I have three bars," he announced as he dialed directly to the sheriff's office. "I need Frizz, please," he said pleasantly when the dispatcher answered, "Bollinger County Sheriff's Department." No hint of urgency in his voice. Unlike Rhetta, his calm manner always prevailed under stress.

Everyone called Sheriff Dodson "Frizz," because of his unruly black curly hair that sprang out in all directions from his large square head. When Rhetta had once asked Randolph what the sheriff's real name was, he confessed he couldn't remember, and doubted if he'd ever known it. Frizz had been called Frizz since he was a kid growing up near Castor River. Randolph said his head was square back then, too.

After being on hold so long that Randolph had to check his phone to be sure the call was still connected, a frazzled-sounding Frizz picked up. Randolph switched on the speaker so Rhetta could hear the conversation.

"Dodson," he grunted.

"Frizz, this is Randolph McCarter, and I'd like to report a shooting at Whispering Pines Lake. One person—"

Before he could finish, Frizz interrupted him. "Damn. Who got shot?"

"No one got shot, but my wife and her friend, Ricky Lane, were shot *at.*" Randolph emphasized the word "*at.*"

"Is anybody hurt?"

"Not from a bullet. Miss Lane, ah...well, she stumbled and hurt her ankle. My wife saw the shooter and would like to make a report. It happened at the Griffith cabin."

"Griffith cabin, you say? Wasn't that the fella your wife and Miss Lane found in that barn? What were you folks doin' up to the cabin?"

When Randolph hesitated, Rhetta mouthed the words "real estate agent" at her husband.

"Miss Lane is a real estate agent in Cape County, and I believe she was looking to list the property."

Rhetta nodded enthusiastically and held up both thumbs.

"Well, that's pretty damn creepy, you ask me," Dodson said. "First, she finds the remains, then she wants to list the property. Them real-a-tors in Cape got no respect for the dead."

"I'm sorry, Frizz, but I'm not sure I make the connection. If you could come out to the property, you can see all of this for yourself, and we can get this report filed."

Dodson grumbled something incoherent, then added. "Meet me there in half an hour." Then he disconnected.

Rhetta leaned back against the leather seat. The air conditioning had finally gotten cool enough to suit her. She ran her fingers through her hair and found more debris. She examined a piece of twig, then tossed it out the window. "Guess we need to go back up to the cabin and get our story coordinated for the good sheriff."

"I've been thinking about that." Randolph said. "Please don't blurt out what brought us up here in the first place. Let's stick to the real estate story."

Rhetta nodded, put the Artmobile into reverse, and headed back to the cabin. Along the way she kept watching for the red sports car, sure that it couldn't have made it all the way to the highway and zoomed off that quickly. They reached the driveway to the Griffith cabin without further sighting it. It seemed Mylene Allard had evaporated into thin air.

CHAPTER 53

"I HOPE BILLY DAN takes Ricky to the clinic in town. I know how stubborn she can be, and probably won't want to admit her arm is broken, just so she won't have to wear a cast." Rhetta had climbed out of the Artmobile and was leaning against the front fender. She stuffed her hands into her pockets to prevent them from groping their way to the cigarettes in Ricky's truck.

In her lust for cigarettes, she'd forgotten about the Baggie with the paint chips. She pulled it out and held it to Randolph. "Our whole escapade wasn't in vain. Look at this."

He reached for the Baggie.

"Those are paint chips from the front of the truck inside the shed." Rhetta strolled over to the doorway they'd come out of, pocketed the padlock she'd cut and began closing the door. "I think this should be shut when the sheriff gets here." The door slid into place just as she spotted dust billowing on the gravel road. She hurried over to stand by Randolph. He handed her the Baggie and she slipped it back into her pocket just as the approaching vehicle skidded down the driveway.

When it stopped, Sheriff Frizz Dodson heaved himself out of the passenger side of a battered white Chevy Tahoe bearing foot high black lettering on each front door that said, *Bollinger County Sheriff*. The lawman was wedged into a tan uniform shirt that bore large half-moons of sweat under the arms. His radio crackled from his shoulder and he paused, slapping at the transmitter to reply.

Sweat drizzled down his face as he lumbered toward them. "Can you tell me what happened?" he asked, swiveling his big head, taking in the surroundings. He wiped an absurdly oversized handkerchief across his wide forehead before stuffing it into his back pocket.

Randolph signaled for Rhetta to begin.

"My friend Ricky asked me to accompany her here because she wanted to try and get the cabin listed for Mrs. Griffith," Rhetta said. She glanced at Randolph. His expression remained blank.

"Uh-huh," Dodson said. "Where is she now?"

"When she began running, she fell and twisted her ankle, so Billy Dan Kercheval took her into town to the clinic."

"Uh-huh," Dodson repeated. "Billy Dan, you say?'

"That's right. We said we'd stay here and notify you and report the shooting. We had to go down to the highway before we could get a signal. We drove back to meet you here."

"Do you want to see where the slug landed in the building?" Randolph asked and began leading Frizz to the shed.

Dodson gazed around and shrugged and then groaned with the effort of stooping to look at the hole where the bullet had been. He stood, removed his cowboy hat and wiped more sweat from his brow. "I don't see as how there's anything to report. Folks out here in the country shoot guns all the time. I expect somebody was target practicin' from over yonder, and the bullet strayed this way." He waved dismissively toward the trees.

Randolph stepped forward, and extended his hand. The sheriff glanced at it for a beat before he returned the handshake.

"I think you're probably right, Frizz. You know how city folks are. Hearing guns automatically makes us nervous," Randolph and smiled.

"Well, then, I'll be getting along." The sheriff screwed the hat on his sweaty head and touched the stained brim in a farewell gesture.

Rhetta frowned, but remained silent.

Frizz lumbered back to his Tahoe, and stuffed himself in behind the wheel. He powered down the window. "I came out here because it was you, Judge. I don't see anything to report, so that's it, then. Have a nice day." The window slid back up, the car started and Frizz sprayed gravel as he made a big show of leaving. Apparently, the sheriff wasn't interested. But he was obviously irritated.

"Hearing guns makes us nervous? Only when they're shooting at us," Rhetta said, spinning toward Randolph. "Why on earth did you say that?"

"To get him to leave. I decided we're better off figuring this out for ourselves. I don't think Frizz cares much for either one of us, so he's not going to bust his butt to help us in any way."

Rhetta nodded. Sheriff Frizz Dodson had made it clear that he was certain Randolph's drunk driving caused his accident earlier in the year and spread his misinformation all over the county. He had yet to apologize to Randolph. Rhetta had once pointedly reminded the sheriff of that. He'd only scowled and muttered.

Once Frizz left and the dust settled, Rhetta watched as Randolph squatted near the bullet hole in the shed, examining it again. Then he withdrew the spent bullet from his pocket, and studied it carefully, returning it to his pocket as he stood. He walked slowly around the shed one more time. "Looks like the shot came from above, angling downward. Whoever was shooting had a spot higher than the shed."

Rhetta turned to scope out the surroundings. Her eyes landed on the dormer window at the back of the cabin. The white lace curtain had been pushed aside and its ragged bottom edge fluttered out through the bottom, where the window was definitely opened a crack. Had that window always been open? Rhetta knew she hadn't really studied the cabin closely when she and Ricky had arrived. They were intent on the shed. Had someone watched them from up there? Was the window open enough to slide the barrel of a rifle through? Turning back to Randolph, she pointed upward to the window. "Maybe from there?"

"Let's check the doors," Randolph said. "Maybe someone broke in, and was using her cabin. Maybe they just fired a warning shot to scare you off."

"Mission accomplished," Rhetta said. "The scaring part, anyway. But then the cavalry arrived—you and Billy Dan—and we still didn't leave right away." She lowered her voice to a whisper. "Do you think someone could still be in there?"

They mounted the front steps, and tried the sturdy metal door handle. Locked. They rounded the small cabin, and rattled the back screen door. It was locked from the inside.

"If anyone's been in here, they left by the front door, and locked it behind them," Rhetta said, as they returned to the front of the cabin, and to their truck.

"Unless someone is still inside." Randolph glanced back at the cabin.

Gooseflesh erupted on Rhetta's arm at her husband's words. Could the shooter still be inside? If so, who was it?

"Let's get out of here. We need to get back to town anyway, so we can check on Ricky. Can you drive her truck? We'll leave it at Merc's." Randolph broke into her thoughts.

Rhetta nodded, and jogged to it. Beckoning to her from the seat was Ricky's opened pack of cigarettes. Rhetta thought Ricky wouldn't miss just one. The pack stayed on the seat only as long as it took for Rhetta to reach a spot in the road where Randolph couldn't see her.

She tossed them out the window.

CHAPTER 54

THE AFTERNOON SUN HAD warmed Ricky's truck to a toasty temperature. Rhetta blasted on the cold air, and, finally, the cab cooled down enough to allow her to gulp fresh air as she bumped along the county road in a dust cloud behind the Artmobile.

Randolph stopped at the stop sign at Highway 34 and waited for her to catch up. She pulled in behind him, glancing down at her cell phone to see if she had service. The screen displayed a message that she had two missed calls.

Randolph sauntered over to her window, and leaned in after she rolled it down. "Are you all right?"

"Sure. Why?"

He glanced around the cab. "I saw you throw something out."

Crap. Busted. "I did."

He arched his eyebrows.

"Her cigarettes. I didn't want to be tempted."

He leaned in and kissed her cheek, then returned to his truck.

He knows me so well. Rhetta shook her head and grinned. She was a lucky woman. Who else would put up with her? She thanked God every day for him, and for Rosswell Carew, another judge and mutual friend who had introduced them. She and Carew volunteered together on the fund raising committee for the local Humane Society. He'd insisted she and Randolph meet. He'd been sure they'd hit it off. He was right. They did.

She also prayed for Carew, whose descent into an alcohol-filled chasm had nearly caused his death from a violent crash into a tree. That happened a few months before Randolph had his accident. Randolph had then quit the bottle.

Rhetta glanced at her phone and remembered the two missed calls. They were both from Ricky's cell phone. Ricky's message sounded almost cheerful as she told Rhetta the good news that her arm wasn't broken, but the bad news that she'd sprained some "tendons or ligaments or something" and would have to wear a wrap and keep her arm in a sling. Billy Dan was taking her home, and would Rhetta mind dropping her truck off sometime in the next day or so?

That made Rhetta grin, since she doubted the sling would last very long if it got in the way of the sanding block. The wrap might not last either.

CHAPTER 55

RANDOLPH WAS UP AND about and had completed his morning ablutions by the time Rhetta's eyes sprang open the next morning. She'd wrestled the sheets through another fitful night, waking several times from bizarre dreams. She craved more sleep. Reluctantly, she threw her legs over the side of the bed, and felt around with her foot in search of her slippers. Finding only one, she climbed out, knelt on the floor and located the other far under the king-sized bed. She crawled all the way under to retrieve it. She never realized how many dust bunnies made their home under there. She came out sneezing, resolving to clean them out before bed tonight.

Classical Beethoven by the Boston Pops drifted from the living room stereo. Rhetta found her robe, and padded down the hall.

"How about brunch today at The Venue?" Randolph asked as he met her in the kitchen and poured coffee into her favorite glass mug.

"Sounds wonderful." She could almost taste their famous blueberry pancakes. She glanced at the large round kitchen clock and was shocked to see it was nearly nine.

"I didn't think I had slept much, but apparently I got more sleep than I realized." No wonder her stomach grumbled.

"Shall we go for a run this morning first? She realized he had on his running shorts, and was ready to go. No wonder she hadn't heard the shower. He hadn't been in there yet.

"Be ready in a few." She swallowed the last of the coffee and headed for the bedroom to change.

* * *

Rhetta was glad that Randolph had persuaded her to run. Although she initially wanted to give in and be lazy, she was exhilarated after four miles along the park trails.

She finished dressing, picking yellow Capris and a white embroidered tee, and fed the cats while waiting for Randolph to shower. He emerged from the bathroom wrapped in a bath towel, and headed into the dressing room. He came out wearing crisp chinos and a white golf shirt. He left his hair to air dry, and picked up his phone and keys.

"How about I drive Ricky's truck and you follow me to The Venue? That way, I can run it over to her on the way back, and you can follow me to her house," Rhetta said, swinging her purse over her shoulder and grabbing a pair of sunglasses on her way to the driveway. She chose a practical pair of white leather sandals since she'd be driving a stick shift, and didn't want her heels to get stuck on the floor mat.

"I need to swing by the gallery for a few hours today, so why don't I go there after brunch, then I'll pick you up later at Ricky's? You two ladies can gab for a bit, can't you?"

* * *

"Something's been bothering me about the shooting at the Griffith cabin," Rhetta said, returning to their table with plates from the food bar.

"You mean besides someone trying to take your life?" Randolph set his fork down, and reached for his coffee.

"That's just it, I'm trying to figure out who and why."

"Not sure about either, but perhaps Frizz was partially right in that it may have been someone local whose shot went wide." He resumed working on his pancakes.

"You think someone may have been upstairs in the cabin and just wanted to run us off? Wouldn't shouting 'get off my property' accomplish the same thing without the possibility of bloodshed?" She said that a bit too loudly. A young couple at the next table stopped eating and gawked at Rhetta. "No, I think whoever shot at us meant to hurt us. But I can't figure out who the person with the .38 was. The more I think about it, I think it was

Mylene Allard. After all, we did see her car. I think she's a killer out to get me." The young couple stood, looked around and then left.

Randolph chewed a large mouthful of pancakes and swallowed. Before he responded, he gulped down his coffee. "No. *You* saw a red car. I didn't see anything. I was too busy hanging on for my life when you took off." When she started to protest, he held up his hand, which clutched a fork dripping with pancake syrup. "You saw a red sports car, that's it. You also saw someone carrying a .38. We don't know if these two things are connected. It's a big leap to accuse Mylene Allard. Besides, why would she be skulking around the shed? And why was she carrying a .38 and what happened to the rifle?" He displayed two fingers. "I don't think Mylene Allard was the one who shot at you with a rifle. I think there were two people out there."

"Two? Who else could there be? That's the worst part. I can't rationalize any of this, or put any pieces together." Rhetta worked her brain, trying to complete the puzzle. There had to be some missing pieces. "Does this have anything to do with Jeremy's death or is it all a bad coincidence?"

Randolph dabbed at his mouth with a napkin. "When did you start believing in coincidences?"

"Exactly."

CHAPTER 56

RANDOLPH CLIMBED INTO THE Artmobile, which had the trailer hooked to it. Before he could leave the parking lot, a man approached him and he climbed out of the truck to chat. Rhetta waved at him as she steered Ricky's truck around them to the exit. Traffic was light on William Street, so she made it to Gordonville in less than ten minutes. She slowed diligently as she passed the firehouse, spotting the constable's car in the driveway. As she did, a red sports car rocketed past her. Rhetta cringed, knowing the constable would pull out and give chase.

That didn't happen. The constable must have taken the day off. The sports car continued racing through town. She realized with a jolt who went flying past. Mylene Allard. Again. This time, Rhetta wanted to make sure she wouldn't get away. Feeling safe from the cops, she floored Ricky's truck and fell in way behind the car.

As before, she chased the Viper, but again, with no luck. By the time Ricky's clunker truck made it to the top of the hill, there was no Viper to be seen anywhere. Rhetta couldn't spot any dust clouds on either of the two gravel roads. Mylene must've continued along the paved road, but was too far ahead to catch.

Crap. Rhetta thumped the steering wheel in frustration. Instead of chasing Mylene, she turned left down Ricky's gravel road. In a minute she pulled into the driveway.

Ricky was in the shop, so Rhetta parked the truck near the house and jogged over to see her. Sure enough, Ricky wasn't wearing a sling. She did, however, still have the arm wrapped.

Ricky limped toward Rhetta, holding up her injured arm. "Good thing it's not broken."

Rhetta frowned at Ricky and looked pointedly at the arm. "Shouldn't that be in a sling?'

"No, it's gonna be fine," Ricky said and wiggled the fingers on the injured arm. "See? No pain."

"Right. And how many painkillers did you take this morning?'

"None, I swear. Cross my heart." She followed that with a heart-crossing gesture that landed closer to her stomach than her heart.

"That's not your heart, but that's all right. I'm just glad you're doing good. What about the ankle?"

Ricky held out her bandaged ankle for Rhetta's inspection. "It's not even sprained. Just bruised." She glanced behind Rhetta. "Where's Randolph? Is he coming to get you? I'm not supposed to drive for a couple of days."

"He wanted to go by the gallery for a bit. He'll come by later and pick me up." Rhetta strolled around the bright red two-seater on the lift. She couldn't tell exactly what it was. She peered under it. "Did you find anything suspicious in this car?"

"No, thank God. Once in a lifetime is all anyone needs." Ricky joined Rhetta and they both inspected it. "This jewel belongs to a man in Jackson, by the name of P. Body Shuttleworth. He collects muscle cars, but doesn't show them. This one's a '69 Shelby Cobra 427. It's worth a ton of money. He wants me to make sure it's road sound. He just bought it at Mecum's Auction, and he actually wants to drive it. This is one hot little beast." They burst into a duet of *Hey Little Cobra* and soon both were doubled over laughing.

When Rhetta composed herself, she said, "Did you say Peabody Shuttleworth? That's his real name?" Rhetta dabbed her eyes, and began snickering again. His unusual name started another fit of giggles.

Ricky nodded, and wrestled a tissue around to wipe her eyes. "He spells it *P* period, *Body* then *Shuttleworth*."

"Whew, there's a man oughta hate his momma." They laughed again. When their snickering finally subsided, Rhetta asked, "Speaking about mothers, that reminds me. Have you heard any news from Anjanette Spears about the funeral service for Jeremy?"

Ricky went from laughter to anger. "No, I haven't heard a word from her. I read his obituary in the paper. It said visitation will be tomorrow, and the funeral will be Tuesday at the First Christian Church on Broadway." Ricky held her chin up, and took a deep breath. "I'm not going."

Rhetta patted Ricky's good hand. "I totally understand, and I don't blame you. I'm definitely not going either."

Rhetta could sense that Ricky was beginning to fade. "Hey, girlfriend, how about let's take Monster for a ride? I'm missing Cami so much. I need to feel the wind in my hair in a real muscle car."

Ricky brightened. "Sure, but you have to drive. I have an injured wing, so I won't be able to shift very well."

Rhetta rubbed her hands together gleefully. "Woo-hoo, let's go!"

Ricky led Rhetta around her shop to the side garage where she kept her Trans Am, instead of cutting through the third bay area.

"How come we have to go the long way around?" Rhetta grumbled, as she stopped to wipe dust off her sandals. Somehow, a smudge of something dark found its way to her pant leg. She fervently hoped it wasn't grease. She swiped at it with her hand and was relieved to see that it brushed it off so she smiled and followed Ricky. *It wasn't grease.*

"Come on Rhetta. Monster is waiting," Ricky said and laughed as Rhetta worked on getting rid of whatever was on her pant leg. "You're just too dressy for a garage. You need to wear coveralls if you're going to hang around here very much."

"I still have the ones you gave me when we were working on Cami a few years ago," Rhetta said. "I don't wear them for anything, so they're almost new." She wrinkled her nose. "They aren't exactly a fashion statement. Besides, it's Sunday, and Randolph and I had brunch at The Venue before I came over here." She slapped at another spot on her thigh.

"That may be so, but overalls sure save wear and tear on decent clothes."

"I wouldn't need them if we'd have just cut across that bay," Rhetta said, pointing toward a bay containing a car concealed under a car cover.

Rhetta stopped, remembering what Woody had told her about a Camaro being in Ricky's shop. She couldn't be sure what this car was under the tarp. She began to veer off toward the bay. Was this the mystery Camaro that Woody saw? Maybe she'd peek under the cover.

The familiar roar of the LS1 engine in Monster called to her. Ricky had continued ahead of her and fired up the Trans Am. The throaty rumble settled in the pit of her stomach. She couldn't conceal her excitement. She left the hidden car for another time.

Ricky was standing by the overhead door while Monster throbbed in the garage. "I'll close the door," Ricky said. "You get in and back her out."

Rhetta slid behind the wheel and grasped the T-shaped shifter. It vibrated gently, previewing the power about to unleash when Monster slid into gear. Rhetta grinned in satisfaction. She loved these cars. It made her miss Cami even more. Her Camaro had the same LS1 and four speed transmission as Monster, although Ricky had tinkered with her own car to deliver a few more horsepower than Cami. Rhetta decided she wanted her Z28 to feel like this. Gas prices be damned.

Rhetta guided the glossy black car out of the garage and waited as Ricky locked up the shop. Rhetta caressed the top of the dash. Surely Ricky didn't really want to sell this beauty? Maybe she should try to buy it instead of waiting on the Z28 that she might never get back from the sheriff's department. However, she didn't like black cars, and the interior, although of a beautiful tan leather, wasn't her taste, either. This was tomboy Ricky's car, through and through. She decided she'd wait for her Z28.

"All right, sister, let's hit it," Ricky proclaimed as she buckled into the passenger seat. "Let's see if you remember how to drive a real car!"

Rhetta gave her two thumbs up, then eased the shifter into first and spit gravel against the metal shed as she roared away.

The T-tops were still on, so Rhetta reached for the controls to turn on the air.

"Sorry, no A/C today," Ricky said. "Remember? I took it all out, so the car would run better. Ditched all that anti-pollution junk, too, so the car can breathe and run faster." Ricky reached to the console and pressed the switch to slide down the electric windows. "Let's do the 270 air thing today. Two windows down and seventy miles an hour." She grinned at Rhetta.

When Ricky said it, Rhetta remembered. Neither speed, efficiency nor the promise of better gas mileage would convince her not to have AC in her Z28. No negotiating there.

"Let's go into town and get an Andy's frozen custard," Ricky suggested when they stopped at the four way stop sign where Ricky's county road met the highway. "My treat." A right turn and they'd be on their way to town. Rhetta turned left.

"No ice cream?" Ricky asked, sounding a little disappointed.

"Can we do that on the way home?" Rhetta shifted effortlessly. Monster responded obediently as Rhetta aimed it down the highway away from town, and toward Whispering Oaks.

And the barn from hell.

CHAPTER 57

"WHERE ARE WE GOING? Like I don't know," Ricky lamented, answering herself. "Are you a glutton for punishment? Why on earth are we going to the damned barn?" Ricky folded her arms across her chest and shook her head. "This day started out to be fun. Please, Rhetta. Turn around."

"I'll turn around if this upsets you." Rhetta eased off on to the shoulder of County Road 811. Monster rumbled, but the silence inside the cab was louder than the car. Eventually, Ricky said, "You go to that barn again, Randolph will divorce you and then shoot you on the way out of court, just for good measure."

Rhetta ignored her protests. "Earlier, when I was on my way to your place with your truck, I spotted a red Viper heading this way. I tried, but I couldn't keep up, and lost sight of the car. Your old truck doesn't get up much thrust. Not like this baby." She patted the dash. "Or like Cami. Anyhow, I wondered if it was Mylene and why she'd be going to the barn. I just wanted to drive by, that's all. If we see her car there, we'll call the cops, okay?"

"Mylene? Why didn't you say so? We're wasting time sitting on the side of the road!" Ricky leaned forward. "How long ago did you say it was that you saw her? Do you have your .38?"

"No, I don't have the gun, but I wouldn't dare try to do anything anyway. We'll drive by, that's all." Rhetta held up her palm in emphasis. "We need to let the cops know if we see her car. Even if she sees this car, she won't know who it is. I saw her zoom past me in Gordonville before I got to your place, so she may not be anywhere around. But if she's there, we'll call the cops."

"Let's go, then," Ricky said, and re-buckled her seat belt. She'd unfastened it when they'd stopped.

Rhetta arrowed toward Whispering Oaks.

"Do you think Mylene is the murderer?" Ricky asked, as Rhetta made the transition from smooth blacktop road to gravel county road. A plume of grey dust rose skyward like a heavy rooster tail behind them as they raced along the chat road.

"I don't see who else it could be. I can think of all kinds of reasons she wanted both of them dead. But why does she keep coming back over here? What's she looking for? That's what I can't figure out."

Rhetta slowed, then stopped alongside the entryway. She spotted two vehicles parked near the barn—a brilliant red Viper and a pickup truck. Rhetta squinted at the truck, and called out the letters on the license plate. "A-D-E-L-E."

"Holy Smokes," Ricky shouted, leaning forward, peering through the windshield. "That's Adele Griffith's truck. That means she's in there with Mylene. Adele could be in danger, even if Mylene is her daughter. What do you suppose they're doing there?"

Rhetta maneuvered off the road and onto the shoulder across from the driveway. She fumbled in her purse until she found her cell phone. She punched 9-1-1. Nothing. She glanced at the phone—one bar of service and the word "searching" scrolling across the top of the screen. "Crap. No service here. What about your phone? Can you get any service?"

"I didn't bring my purse, or my phone," Ricky said. "I only have my keys. I locked my purse inside the garage," Ricky jangled her keys at Rhetta. "I didn't think I'd need anything. All I have is some money in my pocket. What should we do?"

Rhetta dropped her forehead on to the steering wheel. "Let me think. I just don't know." She popped back up. "Wait, maybe we can drive to someone's house and call from there?" She swiveled her head around in search. There were no houses as far as she could see. She didn't remember seeing any for a couple of miles back as they drove in. This part of the county was sparsely populated. Most of the area was devoted to corn and cattle.

Rhetta slid the shifter into reverse, backed quickly, and then turned into the driveway.

"Are we going up there?" Ricky's eyes widened.

"If anything bad is happening, just hearing us pull up might stop things from getting worse." That sounded pretty lame, even to Rhetta.

"Things like what?" Ricky didn't sound as though she really wanted to know what things.

Within seconds, the Trans Am rumbled to a stop several yards from the barn. Both women listened for sounds from the barn. They heard nothing but the steady rumble from the Monster.

"I'm going to go around to the side and try to look in," Rhetta whispered.

"Why are we whispering?"

Rhetta rolled her eyes and put her index fingers to her lips in a quieting motion. "We should be as quiet as we can. No telling what's going on there."

"Like they couldn't hear this Trans Am as it snuck in? Right," Ricky whispered. "Oh, God, unless they're both dead!" Ricky seemed to realize what she said and stuffed her fist into her mouth. "This is the barn of death. Let's get out of here. You said we'd call the cops and I think that's what we need to do." Her voice began rising.

"Calm down. You're going to alert them we're here. Shhh." Rhetta had started out of the car, but turned back to Ricky. "Do you think you can drive enough to get out of here? That way if they see the car leave, they'll just think someone was turning around. I'm going to stay here and see if I can stop Mylene from hurting her mother. I'll tell her the deputies are on their way. Now, go call the cops!"

Ricky nodded. "I can do that. Let me have your phone and as soon as I get a signal I'll call them." Rhetta tossed Ricky her cell phone. Rhetta scrambled out and Ricky limped to the driver's side, and slid in. Rhetta ran to the barn and flattened herself against the side as Ricky quickly turned the car around and roared down the lane.

The dust began settling and still there was no sound, nor any movement from within the barn. Rhetta's heart hammered against her rib cage. Why the heck hadn't she gone with Ricky? She reminded herself it was because she needed to talk Mylene out of hurting anyone else. She sucked in a deep breath. *I don't want to do this. I need to leave. Or at least hide. What in God's name was I thinking? This is a job for cops, not a banker. If I live through this, Ricky's right. Randolph will kill me when he finds out.*

Her hands began shaking and sweat poured off her forehead. She searched for an opening as she inched her way sideways down the length of the barn. She paused, took two deep breaths and centered herself as she focused on Adele instead of the giant fear ball that had invaded her stomach.

The barn's sliding door that had been padlocked now stood open a foot. She stopped, back to the wall, listening. Not a sound emerged from inside the barn. If anyone was in there, they were so quiet, they may not have been breathing. *Oh, God, I don't want to find any more bodies.* That thought made the ball rise to her throat. She swallowed and made a face. She didn't want to spit out the bile it left for fear of being heard.

The dead can't hear. Thinking that anybody else may be dead inside the barn made her stomach flip again. *Turn around and leave and wait for Ricky to bring the cavalry. Before you throw up.*

Too late. Rhetta's stomach began heaving. She sucked in deep breaths, and gradually, the urge subsided. Her forehead flashed over with sweat as she inched along again. She found the door and slipped through it.

Inside the barn was dim, with the only light coming from what little sunlight filtered in through the slats of the wood boards. It wasn't cool in here, like the first time she'd explored the barn. The air was close and smelled of chemicals. Probably from the forensic crew. Dust motes pirouetted in the sun's rays.

Rhetta crouched behind a half wall that had once held a feed crib for cattle. She paused, listened, heard nothing. She maneuvered around the wall until she reached the back wall and, still crouching, followed it into the corner, where another half wall, with the crib intact, jutted perpendicularly. She glanced around and recognized the hand-made ladder that led upward to a three foot square cut into the loft. She sucked in a breath and scrambled into the loft. She toppled on to her back, panting.

That's when she heard the voices.

CHAPTER 58

RHETTA LISTENED AS TWO women spoke calmly. She swore she heard a reference to the weather. *What the heck? Mylene and Adele are here in the barn of death talking about the freakin' weather? Wouldn't it have been easier to meet at Starbucks? At least Starbucks has great coffee.*

She flipped over onto her stomach, snatched bits of hay from her hair, spit out what she hoped wasn't a spider web. She leaned and peered through the opening she'd just crawled through. She couldn't see anyone. She stood, but immediately squatted when she spied three other similar square holes, fearing she might be seen by the women below. The openings were set above where each set of cribs were located. That was for hay tossed down during feeding time. Rhetta dropped to hands and knees and crawled slowly to the next opening. As she did, decades of accumulated dust swirled around her face. She gazed down. No one below. When a sneeze threatened, she buried her face in the crook of her arm and stifled it as best she could. Another one followed. *Crap. Now isn't the time for my allergies to flare up and give me away.* When she felt the sneezing urge had subsided, she crawled to another opening.

When she craned forward this time, she drew back, sucking in a breath. Light glinted off the business end of a rifle.

Mylene is holding Adele at gunpoint! Then why were they talking in such calm voices? Rhetta strained to hear more. This time, she heard Adele laugh. *What th—?*

Rhetta didn't complete her thought before Mylene's voice rose clearly. "You're a crazy old woman."

What Rhetta heard didn't compute. Just who was the crazy one in the barn? She answered herself. *That would be me, for being here.* She prayed Ricky had called the cops and that they were on their way.

The rifle barrel moved. Rhetta craned a bit more over the edge for a better view, but feared being seen from below. She couldn't pinpoint either woman, only the rifle.

"I'm not your mother," Adele said.

Rhetta rocked back. *What?*

A noise croaked upward from Adele, something between a laugh and a cry. "One night, way after midnight, your father, the bastard, brought you, his little baby bastard, home to me, swaddled up in a bundle of blankets. Said you survived but the mother didn't. At first I didn't understand. I wanted to call the police if there was an accident somewhere. He looked me straight in the eye. 'No accident,' he says. Seems his whore, your real mother, had given birth to you at her home, and she died in delivery. He did what he always did. He disappeared with the evidence—you. I was forced to become your mother so Malcom could keep you. No wonder you were daddy's pet." Adele's mirthless laugh pierced the dust motes and sent them scattering.

Rhetta's heart thumped against her rib cage. Until now, she'd hoped that Mylene couldn't shoot her mother. This revelation changed everything. Mylene now had a green light. Rhetta had to do something. But what?

She listened intently, praying to hear sirens. Nothing.

Adele's life was in danger, and Rhetta felt helpless. She glanced around the loft for something to use as a weapon. Nothing but dust bunnies and dried bits of hay. She dared another look over the edge of the opening. Lying on the floor against the outside wall, she made out the handle of a pitchfork protruding from a small pile of old hay. She strained to see if the fork part was still attached. Even if it wasn't, she could use the handle as a bat to knock the rifle out of Mylene's hands. That is if she could get to it and sneak up on Mylene. She prayed for the cops to hurry.

She reversed and scrabbled across the loft to where she'd climbed up. By her calculation, it was on the opposite side of the barn from where the standoff was occurring.

Facing the loft with her back to the barn, she set a foot down on the top rung of the ladder. Moving slowly, making sure she didn't slip and fall and create a disturbance, she descended another rung. It was harder going down than the climb up had been. She couldn't see where to put her feet. Her hands shook as she gripped the side of the ladder. As she finally slid to the bottom step, she snagged a splinter in the palm of her hand. She closed her eyes and winced, holding her breath until the initial stab of pain dwindled to a throb. She checked her hand and the angry two-inch sliver. After making sure both feet were on the ground, she grasped the splinter in her teeth and pulled it out. A trickle of blood followed. She sucked in a breath. The throbbing continued.

She crept as quietly as she could, praying that Mylene couldn't hear her heart pounding. Every time her heart pounded, her palm throbbed. She reached into her pants pocket, found a tissue and pressed it into her wounded hand, hoping it would catch any droplets of blood.

She tried to keep her eye on the prize, the pitchfork, but she'd momentarily lost sight of it. She felt panic rise, until she neared the wall, and spied the fork. It looked different on the ground, smaller somehow. Two of the tines had rusted off, but the rest of it looked intact.

She inched along the wall, and using both hands, eased the pitchfork out from under the hay. It freed effortlessly. She glanced at her hand and was relieved that her wound was no longer bleeding.

With her weapon gripped in both hands, she shuffled, back pressed to the wall, dragging each foot sideways down the wall toward the women. They were still exchanging barbs, but at least no gunfire, yet. At the end of the perpendicular wall that separated her from the two women, Rhetta sucked in a deep breath. She peered through the slats, and again spied the barrel of the weapon. It bobbed as the women raised their voices. She didn't have time to form a thorough plan. Her best offense was surprise. She decided to scream, jump out and slam the pitchfork into the barrel of the gun, and hopefully, when it dropped, be able to grab it away before Mylene could. If she failed, she knew she and Adele were goners.

She hefted her weapon, and implored a quick prayer. *God help us, please.*

She leapt from her hiding place, swinging the pitchfork as hard as she could, like she would a baseball bat trying to hit a home run. It connected with the gun barrel and sent it skittering to the floor. She forgot to scream. She threw herself after the weapon and landed on it, chest first. The air whooshed out of her lungs followed by a hot stab of pain in her side. She realized instantly that she probably broke a rib.

She moaned, and tried to turn over. As she did, she heard a woman's voice. "Oh, my God. You just saved my life. That crazy woman tried to kill me."

The pain made Rhetta dizzy, but she clearly heard the rumble of a vehicle driving off. *Crap, Mylene was getting away.* She shook her head in frustration. A hand reached down to help her. When she gazed up at her rescuer, a shaken Rhetta recognized Mylene.

CHAPTER 59

FEAR SQUEEZED RHETTA'S HEART when Mylene gripped her hand. Rhetta waited for her life to flash like a color movie before her eyes, as she'd always heard happened when death was imminent. Nothing flashed, not even a quick silent movie. Mylene gripped Rhetta's hand until she managed to pull her to her feet.

Rhetta jerked loose from her captor and threw herself down again. She'd intended to grab the rifle, roll over and aim it at Mylene, like she'd seen done in countless movies. However, searing pain shooting from her side stopped her cold.

"What are you doing?" Mylene asked, as Rhetta yelped from facedown in the dirt.

Mylene calmly reached for the weapon, then ejected the shells. She set the rifle against the wall, then reached for Rhetta. "Don't throw yourself to the ground again. That had to hurt. Adele took off. I expect we can at least get the cops to find her." Once again, she tugged Rhetta to her feet.

This time, Rhetta stayed put, moaning and holding her side, unable to speak for a moment.

Mylene brushed at Rhetta's back, knocking off some twigs and a few globs of mud. "You certainly came out of nowhere. I'm very glad that you did." Mylene hefted the rifle easily. "Or else that crazy Adele would have killed me, too."

"Adele?" Rhetta was confused. She shook her head, and swiped at the dirt covering her Capris, decided cleaning them off was useless, and gave up. The motion caused another shooting pain through her rib cage. She panted. "Adele killed her husband? And Jeremy? Ow," she added as she took a deep breath. "I think I broke a rib."

Mylene clicked her tongue in sympathy. "That hurts like the devil. Do you want me to take you to a hospital?"

"No, no, it's not that bad." Rhetta wasn't about to miss out on any of the action.

Mylene continued, "Adele admitted murdering my father when she found out that Jeremy was his son with Anjanette Spears. I bet she got white-hot crazy angry. I think she must've lured him out here, and killed him. Jeremy figured it out after you found the body. He called me and told me his suspicions. He also remembered the old truck that's been out at the cabin for years. Instead of going to the police, Jeremy figured he'd blackmail Adele. He was always looking for an easy buck, the good-for-nothing."

Rhetta began to feel clammy from the pain. She sank to the floor. "Why didn't you just go to the police?" She wanted to tell Mylene that she agreed with her assessment of Jeremy, but her mother had always told her not to speak ill of the dead.

Mylene scoffed. "Are you kidding? I didn't have any proof. Jeremy said he'd deny knowing anything. All I had was suspicions, and besides, the cops and I don't exactly have a great track record together." Mylene began pacing. "I called you and wanted to meet you at the barn to find out if that old car you bought had been moved over the body. I suspected that Adele used one of the company trucks to push the car over where she had buried the body."

She leaned over Rhetta. "I think I should take you to a clinic, or something."

Rhetta stood. She took a few deep breaths and found the pain had lessened. "No, actually, I'm feeling better." She steered the conversation back to the events. "What kind of proof do we have that Adele really killed Jeremy?" Rhetta asked.

"Other than she confessed to me, nothing at all."

"And the only proof that she killed Malcom is that truck, whose paint scrapings and dents we think correspond to the bumper on my Z28," Rhetta said. "That is, if we can get the cops to go to Bollinger County and impound that truck."

"Come with me. I'll take you to get looked at. I think you're in a lot of pain." Mylene said. "We can call the sheriff and tell him about what we suspect."

Rhetta shook her head. "Can't go just yet. Ricky left here to call the cops. They should be arriving any time. We can tell them in person."

Mylene nodded, a brief smile twitching her lips. "I thought I heard someone pull in and then leave. So that was Ricky, your friend? She left, but you stayed." Mylene nodded her understanding. "No wonder I didn't know where you popped in from." It was Mylene's turn to shake her head at that discovery. "Foolish Rhetta. But very brave, too. I'm grateful for your courage." She steered Rhetta outside to the shiny Viper, opened the passenger door, and eased her into the seat. "I can run the air conditioner until the cops get here. That is, if they don't take all day. I only have a half tank of gas." She smiled.

Rhetta moaned when she saw the white leather interior that reminded her of Cami's. She gazed down at her dirt and blood covered, formerly white Capris. She sank into the seat, letting the cool air carry her away.

* * *

Wailing sirens jarred Rhetta awake. Lying back against the Viper's cool interior, she'd closed her eyes, hoping to stay quiet and ease the pain in her side. She lurched for the door handle, pushed open the passenger door and was immediately smothered by a blast of summer heat.

Mylene was leaning against the front fender, smoking a cigarette. Rhetta nearly begged her for one, but stopped herself when she spotted a black Trans Am following the squad car into the driveway. She knew she didn't have time to smoke it.

After Rhetta clambered out of the car, Mylene opened the driver's door and turned off the ignition. She stepped back, ground out her cigarette with the heel of her shoe, then joined Rhetta on the passenger side of the Viper. Mylene's hair was damp with perspiration, her lips set in a grim line. She propped herself against her car, and crossed her arms across her chest. It was clear from her body language she didn't want anything to do with the deputies.

Beads of sweat danced across Rhetta's forehead and threatened to trickle down her nose. She swiped the back of her hand across her brow.

Wiping her hands on her pants leg, she turned and examined the car seat she'd just vacated. An outline of dirt revealed where she'd been sitting.

A Cape County Sheriff's patrol car with swirling red and blue flashing lights emerged from a giant dust cloud and skidded to a stop alongside the Viper. In synchronized movement, two deputies left their car and approached them. Each man rested a hand on the butt of a holstered service weapon. Ricky slammed her driver's door and hobbled toward Rhetta and Mylene. If she was surprised to see Mylene standing next to Rhetta, she didn't say.

Everyone converged on the Viper.

CHAPTER 60

A LANKY DEPUTY WEARING a perfectly pressed uniform and sporting a pencil-thin dark mustache held up a hand and signaled for silence. "Good grief, can someone take a breath here and tell me what's going on?" He studied the three women, and from the expression on his face, Rhetta felt it was with strong disapproval. She swore she saw his lip curl.

Properly chastised, everyone stopped talking and nobody spoke.

He walked around each of them. "Alrighty, then." He rubbed his hands together. "Can someone tell me why we got a call to come out here?" he said, removing his flat brimmed hat and slapping dust off the outer brim. He returned it carefully to his head, reached into his breast pocket for a notebook, flipped it open and waited. "You can all start by giving me your names."

Mylene, arms still crossed, silently shook her head, glanced sidelong at Rhetta. Then she leaned over and whispered, "We need to go after Adele. I bet anything she's going out to Bollinger County to destroy the truck. That's the only evidence that she killed my father. That is, besides the fact that she admitted it to me."

Rhetta nodded.

Ricky said, "I don't know anything. I just called 9-1-1, is all." She whispered to Rhetta. "So, Mylene's not the killer?" Ricky leaned against the Viper, stretching her injured foot out ahead of her, but not before she caressed the shiny hood.

"Nope," Rhetta said.

The deputy, apparently noticing everyone deferring to Rhetta, ambled over to stand in front of her, pencil poised. The second deputy stayed back, hand on his weapon while his head swiveled, as though scoping out the area.

"Care to tell me what happened here?" He gestured to the barn. He turned to the other deputy, a short wall of a man in a tight uniform. "This barn and development has just been a regular hubbub of activity lately."

Mylene slid her hand alongside her mouth and whispered to Rhetta, "Did he just say hubbub?" They choked back a snicker.

One by one, the three of them identified themselves. Then, Rhetta related what happened, ending with, "We believe Adele Griffith is on her way to her cabin in Bollinger County to destroy evidence. You need to notify the Bollinger County Sheriff's office right away."

"Right. You're saying Adele Griffith admitted to killing her husband and Jeremy Spears? And did both of them in at this old barn?" He looked over at his partner, who shrugged.

"Guess it has sentimental value for her," Mylene muttered.

"Can't you please call the Bollinger County Sheriff and have him go to the cabin to arrest Adele Griffith?" Rhetta asked.

After the deputy took his time in scrutinizing the three women, he shook his head in obvious disapproval. "I don't see where any crime has been committed here." Then he ambled over to Ricky. "Ms. Lane, I suggest you stay away from this barn. As I recall, you're a suspect in Mr. Spears' death."

Ricky visibly paled and shrank against the car. Rhetta stepped between them.

"Officer, Ms. Lane is not under arrest. None of us is. I suggest that you are threatening Ms. Lane, and maybe you ought to stop. Go after the real killer, Adele Griffith." She ran her hands through her hair in frustration. She could imagine how she must look—filthy with bits and pieces of dried hay sticking out from her hair.

The deputy shook his head. "Arrest Mrs. Griffith? That's a leap. I don't have a warrant for her. All I have is the word of three, shall I say, highly emotional women."

Rhetta said, "I'm reporting your attitude to your boss."

Ricky said nothing.

"Oinker," Mylene said.

With that, the deputy glared at them, snapped his notepad closed, tucked it into his shirt pocket. He nodded toward his partner in a signal to leave. They touched the brim of their hats as a goodbye gesture and ambled to their patrol car.

As soon as they both reached their car, Rhetta asked Ricky, "Can I have my phone back?" Ricky reached into her jeans pocket and handed it over. Almost no battery power remained. A few more minutes of a phone call and a red line would replace the green and she would be out of power. Her charger was still at home in her Trailblazer.

"Ricky, please go home and call Randolph. Tell him what's going on." Ricky nodded and hopped over to her car. The Trans Am rumbled to life. Ricky punched the accelerator. She shifted, then zigzagged down the driveway as the muscle car sought purchase on the gravel. The throaty LT1 resonated as Ricky defied the speed limit down the county road.

Rhetta turned to Mylene, patting the Viper's hood. "How fast can this baby get us to Bollinger County?"

CHAPTER 61

RHETTA COLLAPSED INTO THE passenger seat as Mylene ran to the driver's side and slid behind the wheel, and was still buckling in when Mylene took off. A quick glance assured her that Mylene had fastened her seat belt. Another glance, this time at her cell phone confirmed that her battery was dead.

"Do you have a cell phone?" she asked Mylene.

Mylene shook her head. "I lost it sometime today, probably at the barn."

"Then I sure hope Ricky called Randolph, or we may be out there by ourselves." At Mylene's questioning look, Rhetta explained. "Randolph is my husband, and if Ricky called him, he'll be burning rubber to get here, and will call the sheriff." Rhetta massaged her side, grateful that the pain was subsiding. Maybe she didn't break a rib after all.

Mylene turned to Rhetta when then hit the highway and the Viper was throttling toward Bollinger County. "What does your husband think of you chasing all over creation after bad guys?"

Rhetta waited to answer until Mylene stopped skidding along the gravel. She didn't want to be the reason Mylene would slide off the road. She needn't have worried. Mylene handled the Viper perfectly. "Let's just say that if Adele doesn't kill me, Randolph might."

Mylene shot her a sideways glance. "I owe you for what you did back there at the barn. I truly thought Adele would shoot me. She's hated me all my life, as she hated Jeremy. Actually, as it turned out, she hated Malcom, too." Mylene downshifted as she came to the four-way at Highways 51 and

34 in Marble Hill, rolled through the stop and zoomed left in front of a log truck lumbering across the intersection. Then she scorched rubber and headed west. Rhetta squeezed her eyes closed and prayed. By the time she opened them, Mylene was sailing past Merc's and across the bridge out of town.

Mylene went on with the conversation as though she hadn't just nearly killed them both. "She's always been nuts. She'd go berserk if I did the least little thing and would take a rubber hose and beat me. She'd get a crazy look in her eye and tell me she'd kill me if I told my father. Then she'd laugh and beat me some more." She floored the Viper out of town toward the cabin.

"I loved my father, even though the world saw him as a scoundrel," Mylene said. "I was his pal and his daughter. He taught me to smoke and drink at a very early age. He never was allowed to be a father to Jeremy, and frankly, didn't like him all that well, even though he was in love with his mother." Mylene laughed. "We should plaster all our pictures in the dictionary under the word 'dysfunctional.'"

"I already have Anjanette Spears there in my dictionary, so I could make room for the rest of you." Rhetta made the mistake of pulling the visor down to shield her eyes from the afternoon sun and ended up catching her reflection in the visor mirror. She'd seen a horror movie with a zombie that looked better than she did. "Adele sure had everyone fooled," Rhetta said, tucking the visor back up. She couldn't stand looking at herself. "I thought she was this frail old lady. She's about as frail as a rattlesnake and twice as deadly." Rhetta felt a deep sadness for Mylene not experiencing the love from a mother to a daughter and knowing Adele passed Mylene off as her natural child. Rhetta shook her head. Tears welled for a moment as she remembered her own mother. She knew absolutely that her mother had loved her beyond anything else in the world. A hollow ache caught her heart as she remembered her mother's painful death.

"Dang allergies," She muttered a she swiped the back of her hand across her cheek.

Mylene swerved left again and barreled up a familiar gravel road. Rhetta sat up and peered ahead through the cloud of gravel dust, searching for Adele's truck. At the top of the hill they would make a right turn into the cabin's driveway and be a big red target for Adele's high-powered rifle

"Let's stop here and walk the rest of the way," Rhetta suggested. "We don't want Adele shooting at us."

Mylene veered over into a turnout from a private drive and killed the engine. "You're right, of course," she said, shrugging out of her seat belt and shoulder strap. "You should wait here, Rhetta." She reached across Rhetta to the glove box and withdrew a .38 pistol. That was indeed the gun Rhetta had seen her carry when she was out here before.

"Not on your life, sister. I didn't ride along just to keep you company. Let's go." Rhetta pushed open the door and hoped that Mylene didn't see her wince. She realized that she felt a lot better. Probably from adrenaline kicking in. Her heart began hammering the instant she slammed the door. Her in-her-head voice asked her if she was crazy. *Yes.* To Mylene, she said, "I sure don't see any law here." They picked their way slowly toward the cabin's driveway. The roadside was uneven, the loose gravel making Rhetta's sandals worthless as protection. She stubbed her toe on a rock the size of a cantaloupe. "Ow." Mylene ignored her discomfort.

"I think she'll head for the shed and that truck right away," Mylene said, checking her weapon.

"If she's here, where's her ride?" Rhetta asked, taking in the empty yard and driveway.

"Last time she parked at the neighbor's empty place just behind here. She only has to walk about thirty yards to get to the shed." Mylene indicated the shed where Rhetta and Ricky had been shot at. "Or, if she's really sneaky, she's upstairs and going to shoot at us through the window. Also like she did last time."

"So that was you I saw walking around the shed carrying a .38? I knew it wasn't a man by the size of the footprints." She leaned placed one of her feet against the side of Mylene's foot. "Your feet aren't any bigger than mine."

Mylene nodded. "Adele was upstairs when she shot at the two of you. When I heard the shot I followed her. I figured there was something out here that she wanted to get rid of. It has to be the truck."

Rhetta shuddered. "Randolph said he thought the shot came from above our heads and he was right. Lucky for us, she missed."

"Probably because she's losing some of her eyesight and is too proud to wear glasses, the old witch." Reaching one of the rock pillars at the entrance, Mylene crouched low, and motioned for Rhetta to do the same.

"Let's try to get to the garage and wait there," Mylene said. "She'll come, because she has to destroy the truck. It's evidence." Crouching, Mylene scrabbled her way to the shed. Rhetta followed. At the shed, Rhetta was breathing hard. She paused, forcing herself to take deep breaths. She wasn't out of shape, so the hard breathing had to be due to pure, unadulterated fear.

Mylene stood against the windowless end of the shed and motioned Rhetta to stay behind her. They eased along the wall, rounded the corner and saw the big sliding door. The door stood open a couple of feet. Rhetta was sure they had closed it up when they'd left. Her heart pounded. "I think she's here," she whispered. Before Mylene could answer, the smell of gasoline filled Rhetta's nostrils. Mylene must have noticed it, too. She bolted forward, shouting, "That bitch!" And disappeared inside the barn. Seconds later, an explosion slammed Rhetta to the ground. Flames burst through the door.

Momentarily dazed, Rhetta slowly pulled herself up. When she realized what happened, she forced herself to sprint toward the door, shouting Mylene's name. As she reached it, a small figure emerged, screaming for help. Rhetta grabbed her, and pulled her to the ground where she rolled her in the dirt. She recognized who she'd grasped. Adele had scorched her shirt and singed her hair and eyebrows, but seemed otherwise unhurt. Rhetta pulled the old woman to her feet and screamed. "Where's Mylene?' She shook the old lady when she didn't answer. Sobbing hysterically, the woman pointed to the barn. Rhetta had no sympathy for the murderous old bat. She shoved her aside roughly, took a deep breath, and ran inside the burning shed.

Where was Mylene?

CHAPTER 62

A PUTRID BLACK SMOKE filled the metal building, blinding Rhetta, and making her choke. Each cough produced a spasm of pain from her side, but she pushed forward, searching for Mylene. The old truck they needed for evidence was nothing but a charred hulk, and several fires burned the stacks of parts and rags scattered throughout the shed. Adele had set the truck on fire. The fumes and gasoline in containers in the shed had exploded, sending fuel and debris flying.

"Mylene," Rhetta gasped. "Where are you?" She choked and coughed again. She tried covering her mouth with her hands, but it wasn't enough to keep the smoke from her nostrils. She fought for breath. Her head began to spin and she went down on her knees. She knew she was running out of oxygen. She'd have to leave or die inside with Mylene. When she crouched closer to the floor, she found a small pocket of less smoky air. Her eyes stung, sending tears cascading down her face. She sucked air and inched toward the sliver of light she prayed was the door.

Her head began clearing, so she stood. Desperately scanning around the shed one more time, she spotted Mylene, crumpled on the floor near the front of the truck, about ten feet farther in. Rhetta dropped to her knees again, then to the floor where she rolled over and over toward Mylene. When she was next to her, she pulled herself to her knees and knelt over her, shouting at her. "Mylene, wake up! Mylene, we have to get out!" She shook her, but still Mylene didn't respond. Rhetta put her ear to her chest. Mylene breathed shallowly. Rhetta pulled her up to a sitting position, then faced her, and placed her unmoving arms over her own shoulders. With all the strength she had left, Rhetta grasped Mylene under her armpits and heaved her to her feet. When she did, Mylene moaned. *She's still alive. I've got to get us out.* "Come on, Mylene, help me," Rhetta urged as she dragged her toward the door. Rhetta coughed and gasped for a breath. Her head spun again. Mylene was too heavy. She was afraid she couldn't carry her all the way. Rhetta stopped, her heart pounding wildly, her head wringing wet with sweat and her eyes full of smoke and tears. She willed herself to keep dragging Mylene toward the door, toward the air, toward life.

Ten more feet to the door, then eight, then five. Then she was at the door. She propped Mylene against the wall and shoved the sliding door as hard as she could. Fresh air from outside rushed in. Gulping air into her scorched lungs, Rhetta grabbed her and toppled outside on to the ground. She lay gasping, sucking as much of the fresh air that she could. Gradually her head cleared. She leaned over and raised Mylene's head and ordered her to breathe. "Breathe, Mylene. You need oxygen. Breathe!" Mylene's chest heaved and she took a tiny breath. She followed it with a few more shallow breaths until her eyes fluttered open. Then they closed again, but she kept breathing.

The shed was in blazes, orange and yellow spires jutting through the tin roof. Heat rolled out through the door along with more flames. "We've got to get away from the shed. It may explode," Rhetta said, still panting. She struggled first to her knees, then finally stood and pulled Mylene to her feet. Grasping Mylene around her waist, she tugged until she managed to drag a stumbling Mylene away from the burning shed. Straining to fill their lungs with air, they collapsed on the grass thirty feet from the inferno.

"We're safe, now." Rhetta said, and lay back against a hard maple.

"Are you sure about that?" It was Adele. Rhetta stared up at the business end of a rifle for the second time that day.

CHAPTER 63

ALTHOUGH RHETTA KNEW IT was Adele, the woman could have been mistaken for the other zombie in the movie Rhetta had seen. Rhetta's initial appraisal of the woman's injuries was way off the mark. Adele's face was blackened with soot, her shirt was covered with scorch marks and burn holes ringed in black. Her arms were red and oozing from the burns. What was left of her grey hair was singed and stuck out at every imaginable angle from a tiny head, and her eyebrows were completely gone.

Yet she stood defiantly in front of them, waving the rifle, as though in no pain at all. A wicked grin split her blackened lips.

That must hurt. Rhetta wondered how this old lady could have such a high pain threshold. Mylene ignored the woman and lay on her back, still breathing in shallow gasps. Rhetta leaned against the tree and held her hands up, palms out. "Adele, you're finished. The sheriff's department is on its way here with the fire department." *God, I hope that's true!* "Unless you get out of here this instant, they're going to catch you and arrest you."

"I'm going to tell them you two were trespassing and set my shed on fire, and I caught you red-handed. You tried to run away, so I shot you. That's what I'm going to tell them." Adele's voice was high pitched and her head bobbed furiously as though convincing herself.

"Should we stand up and start running so you can take us down, to make your story work?" Rhetta heaved to her feet. "Otherwise, how are you going to explain shooting us under the tree, here?" Rhetta turned toward the tree, and Mylene, still on the ground. "Or do you plan on dragging our bodies and positioning them. You could always hook up a chain to your truck and drag us. Honestly, Adele, don't you think the cops would figure that out? And really, you don't have time for all of that." She turned back and threw her hands up. "So, if you don't mind, I'm going to find a more comfortable spot and try to get my breath. I suggest you hit the road while you still can." Rhetta turned, pretending to search for a spot to lie down.

Her stomach spasmed. She was going to puke. She never thought about how people's knees could knock together before now, but she was learning firsthand how that phenomenon feels. Her heart was running the Kentucky Derby. Absurdly, she realized her side didn't hurt any more.

In spite of her quaking, she formed a plan. While talking to Adele, she'd spotted a fallen limb roughly the diameter of a ball bat, about four feet in length. It nearly touched her foot. If she could distract Adele even for an instant, she'd grab the stick and try to smack her head. She only had one chance. If she missed, Adele would shoot. Adele meant to shoot anyway, so anything was worth a try.

Rhetta calculated that Adele was at least six feet away, which meant that she'd have to grab the stick and lunge forward in order to connect with her. Precious seconds could be lost. Enough time for Adele to turn the gun and fire. Rhetta swallowed down the bile, praying she wouldn't throw up.

She leaned over Mylene and inventoried her condition. She'd need to get her to a hospital soon. Her breathing was still shallow, her responses nil.

Rhetta straightened and glanced toward the road. Did she see a cloud of dust? Maybe two or three? Was help coming? Would they get there on time?

"Too late, Adele," Rhetta pointed to the road and the dust clouds. "The cops are on their way."

With a stricken look, Adele turned sideways. That was the distraction Rhetta had prayed for. She snatched the deadfall limb and surged toward Adele, screaming at the top of her scorched lungs, "You miserable hag!" She swung at her head as hard as Babe Ruth had ever swung a bat. She miscalculated and connected with Adele's upper arm, instead—her scorched upper arm. Adele howled in pain and grabbed her arm, dropping the rifle. Rhetta pounced on it and swung the business end around towards Adele. "Enough of this, you old bat. Get over there and sit down and shut up!" She ordered Adele to the driveway and forced her to sit on the hard gravel. "There, that ought to suit you."

Three clouds of dust materialized in the driveway and morphed into a sheriff's car, a fire truck and Randolph's truck. The fire truck roared past them and on down to the burning shed. The sheriff's deputy stopped short of running over Adele. Rhetta had no idea who'd called the cops, but she was overwhelmingly grateful that they, and her husband, had arrived in time.

Randolph's truck squealed to a stop behind the patrol car. He threw his door open and rushed to his wife.

Rhetta collapsed in his arms.

CHAPTER 64
Four Weeks Later

"ARE YOU SURE MYLENE is coming from Paducah for this shindig?" Randolph asked as he padded into the kitchen. He poured them each a cup of coffee and joined his wife on the newly cleaned and spruced-up patio. They'd both enjoyed an exhilarating morning run, followed by a spoil-your-wife breakfast that Randolph had prepared. She'd snarfed down the blueberry pancakes without a single thought about any calorie budget.

Rhetta's birthday had fallen on Columbus Day—a bank holiday and a Monday this year. Randolph wanted to throw a party. He'd promised to get everything ready, but she decided to help him. She wanted to have the yard and flower beds looking their best.

She took a day's vacation on the Friday before, and spent the entire day mowing and trimming. The weather had co-operated with plenty of brilliant blue sky and warm breezes. She strung white lights around the patio and onto the potted trees she bought on clearance to decorate. She'd lucked into end-of-the-season cushions for the wicker furniture at Trees n Trends and Randolph had splurged on a new gas grill.

They left early Saturday morning for Bollinger County. After a country breakfast at Merc's in Marble Hill, they stopped at Green's Grocery for the world's best fried bologna sandwiches. They tucked them into a picnic basket and spent the day at Billy Dan's fishing with Ricky and Billy Dan. They'd caught a mess of catfish, and stayed late cooking them and enjoying a fish fry with Billy Dan as chef.

Early Sunday morning, Rhetta left Randolph sleeping soundly and, instead of running, she drove into town to the Lutheran church and sat in the back pew for early Sunday service. She scooted out just as it ended, and was home before Randolph had awakened. She had plenty to be thankful for these days, and was exploring a reunion with her former church. She'd talk to Randolph about it and maybe he'd accompany her next Sunday. They spent the rest of the day shopping for food for Monday's party, and relaxing.

Now, hours before the party, Rhetta relieved Randolph's concerns. "I talked to Mylene this morning and she said wild jackasses couldn't keep her away." She sipped her coffee and grinned. "She really is a great gal, and although we met under peculiar circumstances, I'm glad we've become friends." Rhetta stroked Greystone, who had commandeered her lap. The other cats purred lazily.

Randolph raised an eyebrow. "Peculiar circumstances? You have a way with words, Rhetta."

Rhetta ignored the comment. "She must've threatened the Alexander County muckety-mucks. Or, she may have had video of the cops and the prosecutor relaxing at her establishment."

"Stop." Randolph coughed, nearly spitting out his coffee. "I don't even want to know how she got the charges dropped." He put his hands up in a surrendering gesture. "I never thought my wife would be best buds with a pole dancer."

"Former pole dancer," Rhetta corrected. "Business woman, now."

"Right. Whatever you say." He tried another sip of coffee.

"I know she's one tough cookie," Rhetta said, emptying her cup. "She only spent one night in the hospital after the fire. I was scared for her. For a while out there I thought she was a goner."

Randolph stood, collected her empty coffee cup and kissed her cheek. "For that matter, I thought you might have been a goner, too."

She hugged his neck in return. Then she stood back and straightened his collar. "Lucky for me the neighbor across the road heard the explosion and ran to see what happened."

"And that Ricky called me as soon as she got a signal, to tell me she thought you might head out to the cabin. She was right." Randolph kissed the top of her head. "As I told you before, I hope this teaches you a lesson about not getting involved in police work." Randolph carried the two cups.

Rhetta followed him into the kitchen. "I wouldn't have gotten involved, if the police had actually done their work." When he shot her The

Look, she added, "What's going to happen to Adele? Will she go to the pen?"

"I doubt if the State of Missouri will show much mercy for a cold-blooded killer, no matter what her age. She pled guilty to second-degree murder in the deaths of her husband and Jeremy Spears, so she saved the State from trying her. However, she still has to stand trial for the attempted murder of you and Mylene. Either way, she'll be off to the Big House to enjoy her retirement."

"How exactly did she kill her husband? Did she say?" She stroked an appreciative Greystone, whose purring motor revved on high.

"According to her confession, she asked him to go to the barn and look at the Z28. She said she was thinking about buying it for Mylene. When he got there, he was leaning in, checking out the motor. She came prepared with a wrench, and smashed it over his head. He must've lost his wallet in the struggle, and then she lost the wrench after she walloped him. Just as you had figured out, she dug a hollow grave, pushed him in it, then went to their construction site and got a truck to push the Z28 over his grave. He stayed undiscovered all these years."

Randolph slid the door aside and slipped into the kitchen. The cats meowed, expecting food, no doubt. When Rhetta set Greystone down, he signaled his disapproval by swishing his tail and yowling.

She followed Randolph into the house and tapped on his shoulder as he stood at the sink rinsing out their cups. "You said you were getting me something special for my birthday. I'm ready now." She grinned and folded her arms.

"Not yet. I plan on giving it to you when everyone gets here."

Rhetta feigned annoyance. "You know Ricky will be late. You're going to make me wait until she gets here?"

Randolph smirked. "Yep."

Rhetta pretended to be miffed. "If that's the deal, then I'll go clean up."

Rhetta headed for the shower, and Randolph followed her. They had a couple of hours before their guests would arrive.

* * *

Woody and Jenn got there first. Jenn strode through the kitchen and set a large bag bearing the logo for Primo Vino! on the island counter top. "Happy Birthday, Rhetta," Woody said, and Jenn hugged her, joining in, singing, "Happy Birthday to you!" Rhetta hugged them back.

When the doorbell next chimed, Rhetta spotted Mrs. Koblyk peering in through the glass in the front door. Mr. Koblyk stood by her side, smiling. Rhetta opened the door wide. "Hello, Missus," her neighbor said, handing her a large pan containing a spectacularly sinful dessert. "This is for having birthday. Much chocolate. Special occasion." She beamed at Rhetta.

Mr. Koblyk grinned broadly and bobbed his head in agreement. "Very special day, you wait and see," he said. They trooped in and joined the others in the kitchen.

Mylene's red Viper slithered up the driveway and stopped behind the Koblyk's car.

"My, my, such a red car," Mrs. Koblyk said. Rhetta waved to Mylene.

By two o'clock, the party was in full swing and everyone had arrived but Ricky and Billy Dan. Randolph had donned a white apron and chef's hat and commanded the grill like a captain at sea. Steak and chops sizzled, and the mouth-watering aroma wafted across the yard. The cats were languishing expectantly at the base of the grill. The guests sipped wine and milled around the patio.

"Who's bringing the birthday cake?" Mylene asked, swirling a light wine in her tall glass.

"Ricky," Randolph answered. "She called and was running a bit late. She said the bakery at Schnuck's was ten deep with people waiting for their cakes."

"Must be a popular day for birthdays," Rhetta said and giggled.

Ricky came bursting through the front door loaded down with a gigantic sheet cake. She rushed it to the kitchen, set it on the island countertop and sighed. "Whew, glad I made it here without spilling it all over the white upholstery."

Rhetta said, "What white upholstery? Your car has tan upholstery. And your truck is, well, dirty. What did you drive?" She started toward the door to peer outside at her ride, but was interrupted by Billy Dan who'd followed Ricky into the kitchen.

"Happy Birthday, Rhetta!" he said, and picked her up and swung her around. She began laughing.

Randolph appeared waving a red bandana. "It's time for your birthday present, but I have to blindfold you first and spin you around."

"Are we playing *Pin the Tail on the Donkey?*" Rhetta asked as she allowed Randolph to snug the scarf and block the light.

Placing his hands on her shoulders, he spun her around until she was properly disoriented. It didn't take much, since she'd had two glasses of wine. Cupping her elbow, he steered her around the house, dodging furniture and doorways until he stood at the garage door. He held his finger to his lips to caution everyone to be quiet, then silently opened the door, and guided her through. She sniffed. "Are we in the garage?" she said and extended her arms as though to feel her way. Randolph took both her hands and walked backward, leading her. He nodded at Ricky to remove the blindfold, which she did with a flourish.

"Happy birthday, darling." Randolph sidestepped so she could enjoy the full impact of her gift.

There, in her regular spot, gleaming and shiny, sat Cami. Impossible as it seemed, her '79 Camaro had been returned to her.

"But how...I thought...Is it really Cami?" She ventured to the car and caressed the hood. Tears runneled down her cheeks. She opened the driver's door and eased into the luxurious white interior. She closed her eyes and inhaled the sweet fragrance of new.

Her baby was truly home.

* * *

It was nearly ten o'clock when everyone finally left. Rhetta and Randolph picked up the remnants of the evening's fun, put the dirty dishes into the dishwasher, then sat exhausted, but happy, at the kitchen table. She reached over and grasped both his hands in hers. "I still can't believe that I really have Cami home again. I can't wait to drive her. I'm taking her to work tomorrow. She's beautiful and I love you."

Randolph kissed the back of her hands. "I was lucky to get her bought from the insurance company after they totaled her, but the real miracle was what Ricky did with her. Ricky certainly had her work cut out. The hardest part was keeping it a secret. Woody nearly found her when he was out there, as did you one time. Ricky said you are just too snoopy for your own good." He angled over to gaze straight at her. "And I agree. You've got to stay out of trouble for a while."

Rhetta smiled, and tears leaked again.

Randolph pulled her to her feet and hugged her. "Your birthday isn't over yet, my girl. I have one more gift for you." He reached into his pocket and removed a small blue velvet pouch with a corded drawstring. He opened her hand and placed it in her palm.

She turned it over and looked at him, puzzled. "Sweets, you more than made my birthday the best ever. What is this?"

"Open it." He stood back and smiled as she studied the pouch, turning it over in her hand.

Carefully, she unfolded the velvet cloth. Nestled inside on the end of a gleaming liquid gold chain, lay her mother's locket—the one she believed lost forever with Cami. Today had to be a dream. If it was, she never wanted to wake from it. She threw her arms around Randolph's neck and hugged her amazing husband. She was the luckiest woman in the world.

"How in the world did this survive?" Rhetta said, caressing the locket. "It looks perfect."

"The chain had melted, but the locket had slipped down under your leather calendar book, and was protected from the heat. Mr. Koblyk spent many hours restoring it." Randolph flicked his thumb across the tears streaming down her cheeks. He pulled out his handkerchief and handed it to her.

"I'm going to go over there tomorrow and give him the biggest hug," Rhetta said.

The house phone interrupted them, and Rhetta, still sniffling and mopping her tears, strode across the kitchen to answer it.

"I wanted to wish you Happy Birthday, Rhetta." The man began coughing deeply and was unable to go on for a few seconds. He wheezed when he spoke next. "You see, I never forgot."

Before she could ask who it was, she heard a click and the hum of a dial tone. At first, she couldn't place the raspy voice. Then it came to her. She stared at the receiver.

Her father had just called her.

THE END

SHARON WOODS HOPKINS

K*ILLERFIND*, SECOND BOOK IN the mystery series featuring mortgage banker Rhetta McCarter hits close to home. Sharon is a branch manager for a mortgage office of a Missouri bank. She also owns the original Cami, the car featured in the book.

Besides writing, Sharon's hobbies include painting, fishing, photography, flower gardening, and restoring muscle cars with her son, Jeff.

She is a member of the Mystery Writers of America, Sisters in Crime, the Southeast Missouri Writers' Guild, and the Missouri Writers' Guild. Her short story, DEATH BEE HUMBLE, will appear in the SEMO Writer's Guild Anthology for 2012. Her first Rhetta McCarter book, *KILLERWATT*, was nominated for a 2011 Lovey award for Best First Novel.

Sharon has been a regular contributor to www.wheel-emag.com and was a regular contributor to the Appaloosa Journal. She spent 30 years as an Appaloosa Horse Club judge, where she was privileged to judge all over the US, Canada, Mexico and Europe.

She also spent time in the air as a flight attendant for American Airlines, fifteen years as a real estate broker, and ten years in retail management.

Sharon lives on the family compound near Marble Hill, Missouri, with her husband, Bill, next door to her son, Jeff, his wife, Wendy, and her grandson, Dylan, plus two dogs, one cat, and assorted second generation Camaros.

Watch for Rhetta McCarter and the third book in the series, *KILLERTRUST*, coming soon.